HEROES AND VILLAINS

BOOKS BY JERRY BUMPUS

HEROES AND VILLAINS

stories

Jerry Bumpus

Fiction Collective
New York

First Edition

Library of Congress Cataloging in Publication Data
Bumpus, Jerry.
    Heroes and villains.

    Contents: Shame—The outdoorsman — K (etc.)
        I. Title.
PS3552.U464H4   1986   813'.54   84-25945
ISBN 0-914590-92-8
ISBN 0-914590-93-6 (pbk.)

Grateful acknowledgment is made to the following magazines in which these stories first appeared: *Epoch* for "Shame," "Heroes and Villains" and "Fable"; *Parisan Review* for "The Outdoorsman" and "Chums"; *Crazy Horse* for "K"; *The Paris Review* for "The Attack on San Clemente"; *Kansas Quarterly* for "Popinjay's African Notes"; and *Shenandoah* for "Plenty of Time."

Published by the Fiction Collective with assistance from the National Endowment for the Arts and the New York State Council on the Arts, and with cooperation of Brooklyn College, Illinois State University and Teachers & Writers Collaborative.

In addition, this publication is made possible, in part, with public funds, from the Greater New York Arts Development Fund, a project of the New York City Department of Cultural Affairs, as administered in Kings County by the Brooklyn Arts and Cultural Association, Inc. (BACA).

Typeset by The Print Center, a non-profit facility for the production of literary and arts-related publications, funded by the New York State Council on the Arts and the National Endowment for the Arts.

Manufactured in the United States of America.

Text design: Robin Tewes
Cover and Jacket design: Roy Colmer
Author photograph: Bettie Bumpus

For Bettie and Margot

CONTENTS

SHAME

They made it clear they despised roommates who want to sit in the kitchen and talk all night. But before they went to bed they had a couple of beers and talked about their jobs and other offices where they had worked. The conversation carefully strayed off to men: they both had been married, once, just after high school. After the second night of this, Marie yawned and was about to say she was going to bed, when Stephanie peeled apart a match down to its red little head, stood it in the ashtray, and said she wanted to get down to the shameful stuff.

Marie laughed. "Certain things . . . ." She didn't finish *should remain unsaid,* for something clicked softly but firmly inside her and she realized she, too, was ready for the shameful stuff. They talked till past three.

The alarm rang. They waited till the last minute before leaping up, dressing, and dashing out of the apartment without speaking or even glancing at each other. At the office Marie paused from her work, shuddering as she heard again something from last night. She wouldn't let herself get lured into that again. A little honesty, if you could call it that, goes a long way. Maybe Stephanie wouldn't come back to the apartment . . . . But that was ridiculous. Of course she would come back.

On Marie's coffee break the girls had a good laugh at the latest on the office simp, Teri O'Connell, alias St. Teresa.

Then they discussed Sheila Poska. That morning, while
Poska's back was turned, someone cut her artificial daisies
into pieces. Andrea had overheard Poska telling Mr.
Wilson she couldn't leave her desk a minute without something
happening, but this time she knew which of the bums had
done it. "How do you like that?" Andrea asked the girls.
"Now we're a bunch of bums." Mr. Wilson was going to
handle it this afternoon. There would be a big scene, accusations, some shouting. They compared notes on retaliation.

Marie stopped listening. From the ceiling, she looked
down at Stephanie and herself in their little yellow kitchen.
The kitchen got smaller and more intensely yellow as they
talked . . . . "What's wrong with you?"

Marie looked up. The girls were staring at her. "Oh . . . ."
She shrugged.

"Don't tell me you're pregnant again." That was Jennifer
and it came out wrong. Jennifer was new, she didn't know
how to play rough. It appeared she might never learn. Which
meant, especially if she took many shots like that, she had
better watch out.

Speaking across the table to Andrea, Marie said, "I'm
just tired, I guess. My new roommate and I stayed up late last
night."

Andrea nudged Naomi and they went into their winking
and snickering routine, which they were very good at. Marie
said it wasn't the way it sounded. "My roommate's a girl."

"A girl?" Andrea said. "Hey, that's even better, I mean
worse. I don't suppose you'd want to tell us all about it."

Marie blushed and they laughed. A truly great blusher
when she felt like it, she could do it in varying shades to fit
the occasion. But this time while she did her blush she was
thinking of a little something Stephanie told her last night
about what some women did to a lesbian Stephanie used to
know. The girls certainly wouldn't think *that* was funny.

Instead of telling that, Marie laid out Stephanie's big
problem. Stephanie was the supervisor where she worked,

which was the same job Mr. Wilson had here, and her boss
was trying to drive her out so he could move his buddy into
her job. God, was he making life miserable for her! He and
his buddy watched every move Stephanie made, and jumped
on her for every little mistake, and accused her of messing up
even though she was doing her job perfectly. And there was
no one to stand beside her, all the other women were jealous
of her and though they watched everything with great
interest, they didn't really care what happened . . . .

Andrea broke in—"Sounds like your roommate's got real
problems. But," she turned to the rest of the girls, "you
know what I'm going go do if they accuse me of cutting up
those flowers? I'm going to tell Mr. Wilson I went to the
john and caught Poska and Saint Teresa jacking off."

They had a good laugh, even Marie.

When she got home that evening not only was Stephanie
there, she had cleaned the apartment and put t.v. dinners in
the oven. And after supper she stuffed a bag with her and
Marie's dirty clothes and said she was off to the laundry.
Marie wanted to help, but Stephanie insisted on doing it
alone. Marie took a shower, rolled her hair, and was looking
at a magazine when Stephanie returned. "Hi," she said,
"What's new in the laundry room?"

Stephanie slung the bag in a corner. "Schmucks." She
went into the bathroom and slammed the door. Marie stood
with her hand on the knob. "Stephanie . . .?" The shower
started and Marie hesitated before turning away to sort the
clothes.

Stephanie came out in red silk pajamas, with her short
black hair shiny and slicked down. Marie waited, thinking
Stephanie might tell what happened downstairs, but when it
became clear she had nothing to say, Marie asked if she
would like a beer. Stephanie shrugged, said okay, and they
did it again.

Stephanie was still going strong at three a.m. God, was she hyped up! She could have talked nonstop for days. But not to Marie. Standing up, Marie yawned mightily. She thanked God it was Friday and announced plans to sleep all weekend.

Stephanie watched her clear the table and brush the corpses of split matches off into her hand. Then something strange happened. Stephanie said out loud exactly what Marie was thinking. She said they both probably suspected the other of making up all this.

The coincidence, if that's what it was, stunned Marie. That, and something else, a question and its immediate answer which slid down to the center of Marie as if she had swallowed an ice cube and then another—*Is this what comes next?* And—*Yes.* Giving away your worst secrets leaves you wide open. For the person you tell can reach right in any time she wants.

The way Stephanie was watching her . . . Marie almost said, *Are you really a woman?* She wondered where that came from! But Marie had never seen Stephanie naked, so how could she know for sure? Maybe Stephanie was a pale little man. Or a teenage boy pulling a very complicated trick on everyone, especially Marie.

"Nothing I've told you is made up," Stephanie said. "Who would make up such things?" Tilting a corner of her mouth sadly and slyly, exactly like a world-weary teenage boy, she started talking about her mother.

Marie didn't listen. One thing at a time. She had to decide . . .

Stephanie's face was pale and narrow. She was pretty in a way. Very thin, and very determined, and quick—jerkily, nervously quick. Her hands were short and wide, with blunt fingers and short unpolished fingernails. Those on the first two fingers of her right hand were chewed into the quick.

That night Marie dreamed about children. She herself

wasn't one of them, and she didn't recognize anyone from her childhood. They were all strangers, skinny gray kids running through chutes into big wooden boxes.

She hadn't come out with the whole thing yet, but now Marie knew Stephanie's mother had done something really terrible to her, something irreparable, the kind of thing that is just unimaginable and that the average person can never get adequately braced for. God, how Marie dreaded finding out what it was! But there was no way of avoiding it. It was on its way. One of these nights between 10 p.m. and 2 a.m. it would arrive, a gigantic leather bird-thing that would squeeze through the front door, and, hearing Stephanie and Marie talking, cram itself into the hall and start wriggling toward the kitchen. Incredibly, Marie and Stephanie wouldn't hear it coming. Marie would turn just as the thing stuck its long beak around the corner, and Stephanie would look up and say, "Well, look who's here!"

Meanwhile, there was all the rest.

Such as the fight to the death with di Angelo, her boss, and Fabrizzi, the buddy di Angelo intended to put in Stephanie's job after they broke her back. "I don't know why I even want to keep the lousy job," Stephanie said. "But I'll be damned if I'll give in."

"I can't believe *everyone* in the office is against you."

"Against me? That doesn't quite get it. I could cope with them being against me. But they're all schizoidal."

Her eyes gleamed. "That's right." This time she resonantly nasaled it—"Schiz*oidal*." That often happened—what she heard herself saying clearly delighted the hell out of her. That, and seeing the way it bowled Marie over.

"That's schizoidal wacko, just short of nuthouse crazy. They've all got this thing for fighting, this *mania*. What's that called? There must be a name for it . . . . Anyway, the only reason they get up in the morning and come to work is so they can fight. That's right. It's what they live for. When they're not fighting with me, they're fighting with each other. And I don't mean they sit around and take witty little insulting potshots at each other. I mean they slug it out. "See, they're really serious about it, you might even say they're aficionerdos.

They've scouted around, they've worked at this place"—holding her hands in front of her and ticking them back and forth as if going into a little dance—"and they've worked at that place, and they've come to the conclusion that this office is the best place for fights in the whole goddamn city. And it's just my luck that that's where I work.

"Marie, they are what used to be called lunatics, every one of them. Fifty-eight lunatics in the same office. And they're goosers. You know, *goosers*. When they aren't fighting, they sneak around goosing each other. It's the God's truth."

With such people you always have something hanging over your head. Yesterday Rose Gonzalez, sensitive about a remark Stephanie made about her knockers, swore she would get her. Stephanie is worried how Gonzalez will get her, and to what degree. "How was I to know she's so touchy? After all, when you've got a set like hers, you should be prepared for a comment now and then. I mean, people are going to notice, right?"

"You should get a different job."

"And give di Angelo and Fabrizzi the pleasure of thinking I cracked? Not on your life. Anyway, if I quit and got another job the rest of them would keep in touch. There's no getting away from them, I've tried. You don't believe me? Ten of them worked at the last place where I was. I quit, so they quit too and followed me."

"Oh, I don't believe that."

"Don't believe me! Why should I lie?"

Stephanie analyzes at length the methods by which she is screwed, by which she means cheated. She is screwed continuously. And that's no exaggeration, she has proof. She shows Marie her paycheck statements. In six months she has never been paid the same amount. Long ago she stopped going in to hassle with the payroll office—the more she fought with them the worse they screwed her.

She also gets screwed buying clothes. She pays ninety bucks for a pair of really nice boots and the heels come off the first time she wears them. She shells out sixty bucks for a black polyester crepe blouse and one of the sleeves fall off. And last week she bought a skirt and when she put it on Marie spotted a big wad stuck to the back of the skirt, bubble gum, though it was black and hard, maybe it was tar. Then Stephanie discovered that the jerk at the store gave her the wrong receipt. Stephanie took back the skirt anyway. She returned a couple hours later, threw the skirt on the floor in the closet, and refused to discuss the fight at the store.

For the last two weeks when Stephanie bought the groceries and added up the itemized receipt, the total was as much as three bucks less than she had paid. Though of course she never discovered this until she got back to the apartment. So she took her little Zigatron 100. But the Zigatron 100 came up with $58.65 for one bag of groceries! After she got home and took everything out of the sack, item by item, checking each thing off the list and adding it up again, the total came out $1.62 less than she had paid. Marie suggested that maybe the taxes were added on separately.

"Taxes schmackses. It's another screwing." She looked around the room, at the walls, the ceiling, as if screwings were lined up everywhere waiting for her. "When I'm gone . . . . Just wait and see, when I'm gone Moluska'll lower the rent again." She shook her head and held up her hand against what Marie tried to say. (Marie wasn't going to argue the point. Mr. Moluska had raised the rent when Stephanie moved in because he didn't like her looks, or so Stephanie said. She had fought with the old creep for three hours. As for Mr. Moluska lowering the rent spontaneously, he just might. "Who knows? But that wasn't what Marie was going to ask Stephanie about. She wanted to ask what Stephanie meant by "when I'm gone.")

Marie started doing all the grocery shopping. She wasn't screwed once.

Stephanie shook her head with disgust after going over the latest receipt. "You know, that's very cruel."

"I'm cruel?" Marie said.

"Not you. Yes, you—it—everything. I mean if you got screwed, you wouldn't even notice. Right?" Marie agreed. "And if you got screwed, you wouldn't really *mind,* would you?" Marie shrugged. "I hate it," Stephanie said flatly. "God, how I hate it."

Stephanie's skin is drying out. She folds back the sleeves of her kimono and shows her arms. She shows her throat. She bares her breasts and shows the dry skin on her hard little nipples. Marie has to agree, here is a case of dry skin. "However," Marie says, "it's not actually what I'd call problem skin."

"Ah, but it's getting worse," Stephanie says. "It's worse now than it was last week. Anyway"—she quickly lights a cigarette—"that's not the point. The point is I've got dry skin but I don't care."

"Oh." The way Stephanie is staring at her, Marie knows more is expected. "Well, it's good that you don't worry."

"No," Stephanie says, squint-frowning as if she is going to shoot a headache at Marie. She explains that she worries more about not caring than she worries about her skin. "The hell with the skin," Stephanie says." "Let it go ahead and dry out. The hell with it, you know? I mean a person can only deal with so much. So I just don't care any more. But when you don't care, what then?"

Marie goes to the bathroom and brings back an arm-load of lotions and creams. Marie says she swears by this stuff and if it works for her it'll work for anyone, Stephanie included.

Stephanie refuses, staring off, ignoring the jars Marie unscrews and holds up to Stephanie's nose for a sniff. Stephanie jerks her arm away when Marie tries to dab some cream on her.

Stephanie begins speaking, cutting Marie off. At first Marie thinks she is smiling, then she realizes Stephanie's face is locked in the rigid expression she uses when she is coming to the worst and most important parts, or when she is about to work in one of her pet words such as corksocker. With her head tilted to one side, her eyes open wide, shining, almost perfectly round, she speaks from a straight-line puppet mouth, enunciating with prissy precision. "Dry skin, you see, does not matter a crap's worth. Do you want to know what *does* matter? Do you truly want to know?"

Marie did truly want to know. But Stephanie looked away and while Marie put the lids back on the jars, Stephanie's eyes dulled, her face went blank, and in a lower tone, played out, she went into a McIntyre story.

McIntyre's boss, Beck of Becky's Oh My Donuts, juggled McIntyre's hours so his days were nights and vice versa, and he never knew from one day or night to the next, or even from one hour to the next, how long he would be working or where, for Beck owned half a dozen Becky's Oh My Donuts shops, and twenty-four hours a day their neon signs showed a little Dutch girl in a blue bonnet and wooden shoes, no doubt Becky herself, stiffly putting something brown to her mouth and stiffly taking it away, back and forth, again and again. (A donut, sure, but Stephanie claims it's a cigar, so now that's what Marie sees every time she passes one of the shops.) Behind Becky a windmill, with windows like intense square eyes, and three big arms, tilts over to clobber the kid.

McIntyre called Stephanie at work to tell her he would be off from 4:15 to 5:30 a.m. tomorrow, so maybe they could meet and grab a bowl of chili and a hot dog . . .? He called

back and told her he was getting off from 6:00 to 7:30 a.m.,
so maybe Stephanie could leave early for work and come by
McIntyre's place and, you know, they'd heat up a can of
soup and look at some t.v., and, you know, talk and relax . . .?
Then he showed up at her office in the middle of the afternoon, ran in huffing and puffing with his sleeves rolled all the
way up to his shoulders, which made his arms look ten feet
long, and he told Stephanie his hours were changed again
but Beck had given him thirty minutes for breakfast, and he
asked Stephanie if she could take a break. He held up for her
and everyone in the office to see, as if they hadn't seen it
the instant he stepped through the door, a big blue paper bag
from Becky's Oh My Donuts, stamped with the kid smoking
her cigar under the windmill. McIntyre opened the bag and
offered a donut to none other than Rose Gonzales who
happened to be cruising by. Gonzales gave McIntyre a once-
over while McIntyre stared at her knockers . . . .
    "Well?" Marie said.
    "Well what?"
    "Did you take a break and go with him?"
    She would never know. Stephanie had her far-away
look. Anyway, whether Stephanie took a donut break with
McIntyre wasn't the point. Marie was beginning to understand that the point will never come when you expect it. She
also understood that Stephanie talked about McIntyre when
she was nearly warmed up for her mother.
    "Mother," Stephanie said, shaking her head and making
a loud klok with her tongue. Immediately Stephanie's mother
appears, tagged together with the few details of physical
description Stephanie has mentioned—thin, a 50-year-old
boyish teenager with stringy gray hair, she is wearing a yellow
dress which she tears off in a story Stephanie has run by
several times, one of Marie's favorite. As Marie watches,
Stephanie's mother turns away and looks over her shoulder,
which she has also done often before. "She never listened
to me," Stephanie says. "Like this"—Stephanie slings a glance

over her shoulder. "If she was sitting where you are she'd keep looking over there." Stephanie peels open a match and lines it up with the others. "'Who the hell you looking for?' I'd ask her. 'You expecting company? Somebody coming out of the refrigerator to pay us a visit?'"

Believe it or not, her mother was pretty, sometimes actually beautiful. Marie sees Stephanie's face on the vague thin woman. It's that beauty which is hand in glove with a completely opposite quality, a smallness and simplicity of line and feature which, when Stephanie's face isn't alive with what she's saying, is not only blank but flat, as if she can will her face to go away. But then it comes back. At least once a night Stephanie stops in the middle of what she's saying and her face takes on a cockily quizzical expression which ascends to something more acute that strikes Marie, who falls for it every time, as very intriguing, mysterious, out and out Egyptian—and then comes the tight, strained fart, brrrap, for which Marie has been spellbound into silence to fully appreciate.

One night, hypnotized and farted at, Marie was further stunned when Stephanie said how disgusted she had been by something her mother said about a dog. "What was it?" Marie said, holding her breath.

"It was a dog," Stephanie said.

"I mean what did your mother say about it?"

Stephanie shook her head. "Uh uh."

Oh, Marie *wanted* her to tell. She couldn't stand not hearing what Stephanie's mother said. She asked Stephanie again, she actually begged, which Marie really hated to do.

"No way," Stephanie said. "It's much too disgusting."

But she did say that, at a restaurant, her mother got a glass of water with a baby's thumb in an ice cube. A couple of nights later she told the same story, only then it was Stephanie, not her mother, who got the thumb in the ice cube. "What did you do?" Marie asked.

"I kept it a while, then I lost it."

"You lost it? How could you lose something like that?"
Stephanie shrugged. "I misplaced it."

Stephanie argues with Marie until Marie gives in. No more
make-up. Though without it Marie looks dull. But Stephanie
says no, she looks 100% better. "Anyone with a brain in her
head would realize how stupid you look when you put all
that stuff on your face."
Stephanie is so thin, so pale. By now Marie knows
Stephanie's incredible paleness is an act of defiance—against
the sun, the outdoors, the regular world and all of us regulars
walking around in it. And especially in defiance of all klutzes
who wear make-up. Her cheekbones are high, her chin small,
her eyes large and black, unbelieving, as if she is both baffled
and tickled by what she hears herself saying. As a kid she was
constantly overwhelmed, a very private child, one of those
kids who walks around in a daze, doing a lot inside her head.
How could her mother have done awful things to such a
child? Her nose is thin, delicate, a nose that must never, no
matter what, be struck. Though one night, talking about a
fight at the office, she described someone by mashing her
nose with her thumb—and in that moment it seemed to Marie
that Stephanie by accident suddenly freed herself—she became
a completely different person!
"One little thing changes everything," Marie said, feeling
the floating away, mildly sexual sensation she experiences
when she gets philosophical.
Of course Stephanie didn't let her get away with that.
"What the hell are you talking about?"
Marie explained. One little detail can make so much difference that it causes a woman, no matter how beautiful she
is, to hate her own face, her hair, everything, because she
must remain that one person, and never be all the different
women she might be if her nose were just a little shorter, or
if her mouth weren't so wide . . . .

"I don't quite know how to tell you this," Stephanie
said, "but, Marie honey, you're really stupid. Let me put it
this way. If you keep thinking that way about beauty and
being different women, there won't be any room left in your
head for anything else. That's right. And you'll forget what
little I've been able to teach you about what really matters.
You've got to stop thinking of yourself as a face in a mirror.
When you look in a mirror you know what you should see?"
Marie confessed she didn't know what she should see. "You
should see all the people standing behind you who have
made you the mess you are today."

Marie didn't let herself reply to that. She wanted to tell
Stephanie that, first, maybe some people would *prefer* to
forget what some people have taught them, one way or
another. And second, what's wrong with starting over each
day from zero? And third, what's so wrong with one face
per mirror?

Knowing Stephanie's mother begins with appreciating
how she loved to get right in to you. She had a genuine
talent. Devastating. She especially loved doing a whole room-
ful of people with one shot, with one smooth move or a
single word—she was that good. Stephanie, growing cagey,
kept people out of the house. (She had to come up with all
her own ideas, because her father checked out when she was
just a little kid.) When Stephanie's friends in high school (believe it or not she was pretty popular in high school) drove by
to pick her up, Stephanie would dash out before they could
even stop the car, she would jump in, and they would roar
off before her mother could come out front and perform a
stunt. (Stephanie stays vague on the stunts. But Marie has a
sneaking suspicion that one afternoon Stephanie's mother
came out onto the front porch, hiked up her yellow dress,
and did number two for the neighbors.) But by accident
people found their way into the house, and though Stephanie

would grab them and try to rush them out, Stephanie's mom would nail them before they reached the door. She would ask a very pointed question or two, or give some hair-raising advice, or shoot in with a daring offer such as one which knocked cold a boy who had fallen for Stephanie in algebra.

"'I'm a very loving person who lives in a bowl with a cold fish,'" Stephanie quotes her mother. Stephanie has to admit she was half-right. At least about Stephanie. "I'm cold," she says. "You don't have to know me forever to know that. But I had to be, after . . . you know."

Marie knows. The ultimate thing Stephanie's mother did to her.

"Stephanie," Marie says softly, thinking maybe tonight will be the night the great leather bird-monster will come and get them, "what did she do?"

But Stephanie shakes her head. She is maybe smiling, maybe that is what it is, a tight little smile. "Uh-uh. That stuff's not for you. What you need is sweetheart stuff. Right? Wouldn't you really rather have something nice and easy?"

Easy.
Easy Marie.
Sometimes she thinks there's a sign across her butt.

Here's Easy Marie!
Welcome to It!!!

Being easy has got Marie all the love a girl could want. *More* than a girl could want. Except it isn't exactly love.

In other words (Here it comes. The Great Secret.) Marie and Stephanie agree, without actually counting up, that Marie has had more men than Stephanie could ever have if she lives to be 80 or 90.

Not that Stephanie would ever want that many men. Not that Marie wanted that many men. No one wants that many men. But Marie has had men and more men. She knows everything there is to know about men, inside and out. The inside is no better than the outside.

So after Stephanie has laid it all out, for one night, and it's Marie's turn, she brings on the men.

(Marie's mother was okay. Loud, a religious nut, *very* stingy, but basically okay.)

Marie's men were as different as cars on the road and almost as numerous. "Men and cars." She sighs. "They may look alike but they're all different under the hood. And they can be dangerous if you get in their way. And who needs them, anyway?"

"It's safer to walk?" Stephanie says, and Marie agrees— "*Much* safer."

Marie has undergone abortions. Six. Probably not a world record, but Marie hopes it's *her* record. She tells of fumbling to get one of those rubber things on a guy and not being able to. For some reason that haunts her. At the oddest times she stops and thinks about trying to get the rubber thing on that guy. It happened a year ago—no, two years ago, when Marie had a roommate named Gladys.

Stephanie listens to the story of Marie fumbling with the rubber thing. She hasn't yet offered up anything even remotely comparable in the sex department, though Marie knows that Stephanie knows that Marie is waiting. It will come one of these days.

Though Stephanie has touched not one of them (or so she claims, and Marie believes her, at least for now), Stephanie's men are McIntyre, and of course di Angelo and Fabrizzi at the office.

And there are other men in the office . . . . Marie sees a huge ice rink with women sitting at desks while men zoom by shooting little wads at them—that's wit, nuance, innuendo—

and jerking little hand signals at them, twitchy man-woman
sign language. When they've worked their nerve up, they
close in for some physical contact with the goalie, a back-
hand stroke or two, some forehand tweeks and slammies,
maybe even some slapshot crammies . . . .
    Stephanie mentions Adelle, a former roommate. Adelle
practiced coldness. It was her specialty. She sank deeper into
Stephanie than all the gouges and scars that Stephanie uncovered and showed her. Stephanie smiles calmly. "Adelle
put a cage inside me. We were lovers." The cage would protect Stephanie from all the shit, the biting comments, the
paranoid viciousness which like a wolf in sheep's clothing
slips in and passes right along with the everyday blah blah
blah . . . .
    They sat in silence in the kitchen, not looking at each
other.
    Did she say lover?

    Di Angelo moved his desk in front of Stephanie's, right
up against it. Eight hours a day they sit facing each other.
And Fabrizzi's desk is beside di Angelo's. They criticize every
move she makes. They talk about her as if she can't hear
every word they say. And none of the others in the office
will speak to her. On coffee break they get up and move if
she sits at their table.
    She laughs silently, shakes her head. "God, how they
hate me! And why? What have I done to them? I guess that's
what makes it so effective, if you know what I mean. But
they can't get me. You know why?"
    "The cage?" Marie said.
    Stephanie nodded. "The cage. You ought to try it."
    Maybe she would. But so far Marie has never tried putting
anything inside herself that might do her some good. She
laughs and says someone should have put a diaphragm in her.
    Her family denounced her after abortion number two.

She has been on her own ever since. What would she do if she got pregnant again? She will never find out, for she has solved the problem, the Final Solution, as they used to say, and it is simple. To get pregnant, a girl must let a guy stick a thing into her called his wiener. Which goes under different names and disguises but which is the same thing ultimately. Marie has made a secret and holy vow that the next time she sees a wiener she will go as fast as possible in the opposite direction. She is talking about will power. In *some* situations it means will power. In *most* situations it means simply doing what you want to do anyway. 90% of Marie's shameful stuff concerns wieners. She calls them wieners because in her opinion that's exactly what they look like.

When Marie talks about the wiener problem Stephanie stops smoking and sits perfectly motionless, as if these are the first reports on wieners she has ever heard and she mustn't miss a word.

Stephanie wants to borrow Marie's girdles.

"Why do you want my girdles?"

"I'm going to wear them tomorrow."

"You want to wear one of my girdles," Marie says, nodding as if now she understands. "Okay, but I don't think it'll fit, Stephanie. I'm a large and you're probably a small, aren't you?"

Stephanie is shaking her head. "I want to borrow all of your girdles because I want to wear all of them at the same time. And it doesn't matter if they fit or not. That's not why I want to borrow them."

"Why do you want to borrow them?"

She wants to borrow them because it is open season on her.

They are goosing her. Always before, she was above all

that because she was the supervisor. But since di Angelo and Fabrizzi publicly declared that Stephanie is incompetent and that no one is to pay any attention to anything she says, it is open season on her.

"I really hate it," Stephanie says. "Have you ever been goosed?"

Yes, in her time Marie has been goosed, but not really a lot, and not recently, not since she was a kid.

"When you're a kid it's different," Stephanie says. "This is . . . ."

Marie looks away. If Stephanie cries it will be the first time ever.

She doesn't cry. "Well, it just isn't very nice," she says. "You know what I mean?"

Marie knows what she means.

At least Stephanie doesn't let them walk up and do it any old time they want to. It takes three to goose her, sometimes four. Two or three to hold her, another to goose. Marie gives her the girdles and she puts them on immediately. They're loose and bag down, but that's just fine, that's just the way Stephanie wants them.

When she came home Marie asked if the girdles worked. "I don't want to talk about it. I'm not going to waste the weekend thinking about it." She stood with her hands on her hips and looked around. "Do you know what?"

"What?"

"We're going to redecorate this place."

Saturday they painted the apartment from one end to the other. White enamel. The place *gleamed*. They lugged furniture around, put things here, then tried them there. Stephanie decided to get rid of all the old stuff.

"Don't worry!" she said, holding up her hand to stop Marie's protests which weren't forthcoming. "I'm buying!"

She rushed Marie to the nearest furniture store and

bought two large chairs, black canvas with chrome frames. $300 each! And two huge straw cockatoos from Haiti to hang on the wall, though she said she didn't like them but she saw Marie looking at them so she bought them for her. $120 for the birds. And a new lamp to match the chairs. And just because she was walking past it, a big ceramic pot—"We'll save pennies in it. We'll be rich!"

Standing with her hands on her hips, Stephanie told the clerk that unless all this stuff could be delivered this afternoon, it was no deal.

They rushed back to the apartment and moved all the old furniture down to the basement. Stephanie paced up and down until the new things came. Now the apartment was the way they wanted it. Simple. Most people would call it bare. Marie was one of those people. But if Stephanie liked it, Marie liked it.

They would spend all their weekends here, Stephanie explained, bringing Marie a beer and lighting her cigarette as Marie tried one of the new chairs. They wouldn't waste their time going out. They had everything here they needed, right? It was a beautiful apartment. Simple.

"Sunday is my favorite day," Stephanie confided to Marie the next morning. "You didn't know that, did you?" Marie admitted she didn't, and said she liked Sundays, too. Stephanie turned on the radio and found some music and they read the newspaper and sat in the new chairs. Now and then they traded. After lunch they set up the cardtable and played gin. Late in the afternoon Stephanie switched on the light and the tall narrow windows reflected the two of them, framed by the gleaming white walls, staring out.

Stephanie jerked the curtains closed. "Go take a bath. This whole goddamn room stinks. Give yourself a douche, for Chrissake." She walked down the hall to the bedroom and slammed the door.

Marie took a douche and showered. She put on double deodorant and, after she had cooled from the shower, her best perfume.

The bedroom door was still shut. She tiptoed to the kitchen and, careful not to bang the skillet or let the refrigerator door thunk, started supper.

She ate alone and watched television for a couple of hours. She went down the hall and slipped into bed. She knew Stephanie was awake, her mind zigzagging in the dark, slicing the silence into strips and wires. Marie couldn't take it. She turned on the bathroom light and left the door cracked so a gray fan spread across her half of the ceiling.

Monday night Stephanie came home with a paper sack over her right hand. When she took her hand out of the sack, it was in a big bloody wad of Kleenex. She unwrapped it and showed Marie. Someone had bitten her.

"Maybe it had rabies," Marie said. "You should get shots for rabies."

"I didn't say a dog bit me. A person bit me. A *man* bit me."

"On the bus?"

"Did I say on the bus? It happened at the office. Where else do people bite people?"

"But why would somebody bite you?"

Stephanie spoke. But Marie didn't hear what she said. Stephanie turned and went into the bedroom and shut the door. Then Marie realized she had, in fact, heard what Stephanie said. Stephanie had called Marie an asshole and asked if she had understood anything at all of what had been happening for the last five weeks for Chrissake.

Stephanie was stomping around in the bedroom. Drawers slammed. Marie heard her mumbling, cursing. The door flew open and Stephanie came out and kicked one of the new chairs in the back. It ripped. She gasped. "Would you look at that! My God, I don't believe it! I just give it a little shove and the goddamn thing falls apart."

Marie went into the kitchen and stayed there. She was eating a sandwich when she heard Stephanie dialing. She stopped chewing and listened.

"I'd like to speak with Adelle. . . . She and I used to. . . . No, I don't, I . . . . But why don't you let me tell you. . . . But . . . . Fuck you!" She slammed down the phone and it answered back with a little jingle.

Then she called long distance person to person to Adelle's brother. She started off apologizing about the last time she called. "I've got to know where she is."—"Right. Yes. But you've got to understand something. I . . . . Will you wait a minute? I just want to know where she *is*. I want to *talk* to her."—"You've got me all wrong. I had absolutely nothing to do with . . . . No way. Adelle and I are *friends*. We are the best of friends, the closest of friends. You've got to understand that." There was a long pause. "Aw, come on, will you cut out that shit? I want to know where she *is*. Now is that too much to ask?"—"Let me write that down. Evergreen. . . ." She started writing, stopped, then wrote it down. Very softly she said, "You're shitting me, aren't you?"—"Yes, I will go and see for myself, you can bet your ass I will go and see for myself . . . ." She sank back in the chair. "You mean that all this time, oh why didn't you tell me . . . why didn't you *tell* me?"

She moaned, long and low. She laid the phone in her lap and with her eyes closed rolled her head from side to side on the back of the chair. "Oh shit, Marie, she's dead. She's dead she's dead . . . ."

Marie was talking but she didn't know what she was saying as she stood beside Stephanie's chair and put her arm around her and hugged her and patted her shoulder, and Stephanie kept saying She's dead over and over.

Then Stephanie sat up straight and looked up at Marie. "She killed herself."

Marie didn't know what to say.

"It's no surprise," Stephanie said. She laughed silently

as if she were panting. "She said she would."

Marie helped her into the bedroom. They lay on Stephanie's bed with their arms around each other, their mouths touching in something like a kiss, while Stephanie talked on and on, telling how one night Adelle vowed she would do it, and Stephanie made her take it back by promising she would always take care of her. The bedroom became airy blue with dawn, then gray, and Marie and Stephanie were still holding each other and kissing when the alarm clock rang.

They slowly got up. Stephanie made the bed and when Marie came out of the bathroom Stephanie was fixing breakfast. "I'll finish," Marie said.

"No."

"Sure. You get dressed."

"I'm not getting dressed."

"You're not? Well, why not?"

"Because I'm not going back there. I'm done."

"Oh." Marie sat at the table and Stephanie finished breakfast, two eggs and toast for Marie but nothing for herself. She went into the living room and was smoking a cigarette and staring at the white wall when Marie came in.

"Listen, Stephanie, try not to take it too hard about Adelle."

Stephanie shook her head. "I knew it was coming. It's the rest of it. Everything. The whole endless bullshit. Those jerks at the office and everything else." She shook her head. "I'm not going back. Never."

When Marie came home after work the apartment was dark. Marie fixed supper and tried to get Stephanie to come and eat but she wouldn't. She wouldn't even answer her. But as Marie was doing the dishes, Stephanie called her.

In the dim light Stephanie's eyes were shining. Marie lay down beside her and for a long time they just lay there holding hands and looking at the ceiling. Marie turned and carefully put her arms around her. She kissed her and Stephanie started crying. Marie slept and woke holding her, her face wet with tears and kissing, and Stephanie was whispering. When the doctors were looking the other way the nurses ringed Adelle's arms and legs with rope burns and twisted her fingers and toes until they were crooked. They worked her over in teams. They knocked her out with paraldehyde and while she was unconscious they soaked her in a vat of maroon dye. A woman performed a special operation, what they call a hog-knob job, that took care of any plans Adelle might have had for being like other women. Then one night they strapped her down and stuffed her full of plastic tubes and pumped her up with ice water. When they finished with her they gave her a pus card and lined her up with an office job.

When Marie came home from work Stephanie had cleaned the apartment, the whole place was shining. Stephanie was wearing a black turtleneck and black slacks, and she whisked Marie out to dinner at Kung Food, Marie's favorite place.

She was excited. Almost happy. Marie was waiting for her to announce she had a new job. But when they finished eating, Stephanie said tomorrow she was going back to the office. "I refuse to let those vultures take possession of all my things. But this time I'll be prepared."

"For what?"

"For what they'll try when I walk in. Certain people you can depend on, but this time I'll be prepared." She opened her purse and took out two ice picks.

The kitchen clinched down to Stephanie's black eyes. Marie tried to convince her that carrying ice picks in your purse is crazy. But Marie couldn't convince her because she wasn't convinced herself. In fact it seemed pretty crazy *not* to carry an ice pick or two in your purse. "But at least don't go looking for fights."

"Who's looking for fights? I just want my stuff out of my desk and I want my last paycheck, and I know what they'll do when I show up."

Marie would go with her.

"Uh uh." Stephanie shook her head, her eyes shut tight. "No way. I'm doing this all by myself. Thanks anyway." She lit a cigarette and opened both hands wide. "Don't you see? I'm ready for this. I feel wonderful. Up until now I've been . . . Christ, I've been a *shrimp*. From now on no more of that shrimp shit for me. I'm going in there by myself."

They went to bed and lay kissing awhile, then Stephanie slept, or at least Marie thought she was asleep, hoped she was. Marie went to the bathroom and when she shut the door she heard something rattle under Stephanie's kimono hanging on the door. In the mirror she saw the point of an ice pick. Two ice picks were tied to a string that ran down to both sleeves. Three more were in the medicine cabinet. In the living room Marie found two Scotch-taped inside the chrome legs of the new chairs. And there were little lumps along the edge of the rug.

When the alarm went off Stephanie jumped out and had put on the black turtleneck and slacks before Marie could even sit up on the side of the bed. Stephanie went out to the kitchen, turned on the radio, and banged the skillet onto the stove. She sang along with the radio while Marie stood in the shower wondering how she would get through this day.

Marie waited around the corner, then followed Stephanie when she came out of the building. Stephanie had her purse and she was wearing her black raincoat, though it was a sunny day, a terrible, bright, glaring sunny day.

Marie stayed well back, but she didn't need to worry, she could have walked right beside her and Stephanie wouldn't have noticed—she walked fast, determinedly, not looking up when she crossed the street to the bus stop. Six or seven people were waiting at the stop. Good.

A bus came, Stephanie got on. After the others, Marie
got on. But when the bus started up, Marie glanced out a
window and saw Stephanie down on the sidewalk looking up
at her just like a detective movie. Except Stephanie wasn't
slyly smiling as they do in detective movies. She stared blankly
up at Marie. Marie stared back in exactly the same way.

Before going up on the elevator she phoned Mr. Wilson
and said she had to be a couple hours late. And how do you
like this?—Four years Marie had worked in that crummy
office, and Mr. Wilson informs her she is jeopardizing her em-
ployment. Was she aware that a lot of women were looking
for jobs? She meekly said she was indeed aware of that, and
she would never be late ever again, but she had to be late this
time because of an emergency. Which Mr. Wilson would
probably take to mean she was pregnant again and which he
would immediately spread from one end of the office to the
other. As she pleaded and cajoled, shifting from one foot to
the other in the phone booth, she pictured Stephanie sitting
across the kitchen table smiling crookedly at her. Stephanie
was right. She was right about everything. For fifty cents
Marie would go over to her own office and dump everything
out of her desk and tell Mr. Wilson to cram his stinking job
and tamp it. But she didn't.

Stephanie's office was about what Marie expected. Let's
face it, they're all alike. Marie wouldn't have been surprised
to see herself, Easy Marie, sitting down at the end of one of
the long rows of desks. She tried to spot the jerks Stephanie
had told her about, especially di Angelo and Fabrizzi, and she
looked for Rose Gonzales' famous knockers. But she recognized no one. But that meant nothing. Everyone, especially
the jerks, practices the sneaky art of ordinariness.
      She asked a woman where she could find Mr. di Angelo
and was directed to the far end of the office.

A hundred feet away sat a square glassed-in office. His desk was the only one in there. Maybe he had moved back into his cubicle after Stephanie knuckled under. But where was Fabrizzi? Di Angelo was the only man in the entire office. Looking down at something on his desk, di Angelo didn't see her coming. He was bald and wore a white short-sleeved shirt and a luminous chartreuse tie, one of the most sickening ties Marie had ever seen. There were half a dozen ballpoint pens on his desk and he was taking them apart.

Marie told him Stephanie was on her way to pick up her check and get her things, and Marie said she was worried abut her.

Di Angelo was shaking his head no before she finished. "She doesn't work here."

"I know that," Marie said. "That's what I'm talking about. She's coming to get her stuff, the things in her desk."

He was shaking his head again and he wasn't looking at her but at the ballpoint pens. He took the little copper tube and spring out of one and tried putting them in another. "You can tell her we don't have her stuff here."

Then Marie surprised herself. She felt herself leaning forward, toward di Angelo's bald head and his eyebrows and face. Maybe she was going to spit on his head. But her mouth was dry. When he looked up their faces were very close. Now what? She heard herself say, "You tell her, Fuck Face."

His forehead bunched together in the middle, his eyes tightened. The thought of fucking his face made Marie dizzy. She walked out of his cubicle and straight up the long aisle and out of the office.

She stood in the lobby for thirty minutes but had to give up. She couldn't afford to wait any longer, she had probably already lost her own job. But maybe Stephanie, on her way here, had said to hell with it, turned around, and gone home. Maybe at the bus stop she had turned around and gone back to the apartment.

Marie got a good chewing out from Mr. Wilson, but that she expected, she didn't really mind, and in fact it was all she could do, when Mr. Wilson finished with her, to keep from giving him a nice smile and saying, "Thanks a lot, Fuck Face." She phoned the apartment but got no answer. She tried on the lunch hour and again on her coffee break.

When she got home she went straight to the phone and called the numbers pinned to the little bulletin board which Marie hadn't let Stephanie throw away when they redecorated the apartment. Marie was surprised not to find McIntyre's name and number on the board. But he was never at one place long enough to be reached. She called some of Stephanie's numbers and most of them had been changed. Those that hadn't, the people weren't exactly enthusiastic about talking about Stephanie. They were quick to tell Marie they had no idea where she was.

There was nothing to do but wait. Stephanie would come home. Everything might be all right. In the meantime Marie went around the front room and gathered the ice picks from under the edge of the rug and from behind the cockatoos from Haiti. Three ice picks were floating in the toilet tank, and four were tucked in the folds of towels in the cabinet, and one was in the refrigerator, up with the ice. In the bedroom she noticed her bed was crooked. Stephanie was on the floor wedged between the bed and the wall.

Marie tried pulling her up but couldn't, and she couldn't move the bed because the rug was bunched up under it. She didn't know what to do. She went out and started supper. She came to the bedroom door a couple of times and talked to the bed and the dark wedge beyond it.

Marie ate in the kitchen, talking in to the bedroom. She went in with her coffee and sat on the bed and talked softly to her.

She took a shower and tried to watch television but gave up. She lay on her back staring at the gray light on the ceiling. Then she lay on her side at the edge of the bed. Stephanie wasn't breathing.

"Stephanie," Marie whispered. "Stephanie . . .?" She reached down . . . and jerked back her hand.

Was she dead?

Marie lay a long time staring down into the darkness. She made herself reach down again and find one of Stephanie's arms, the wrist, and she kept trying until she found Stephanie's pulse. She was alive!

Marie sighed. Tomorrow Stephanie would come out of it. Marie would fix breakfast and turn on the radio, and after a few minutes she would hear the shower, then the shower door would slam, and in a little while Stephanie would come into the kitchen.

Marie woke in the night and couldn't see Stephanie when she looked over the side of the bed. She turned on the light, and Stephanie was still there. The next time she woke she didn't turn on the light because the bedroom looked incredibly strange, as if this wasn't their room but a room in another apartment. She reached carefully over the side of the bed and touched Stephanie.

In the morning the black turtleneck and the black slacks were laid out full length between the bed and the wall.

She wasn't in the front room or the bathroom or the kitchen. Marie even looked in the cabinet under the kitchen sink. Then she saw spots on the carpet, trails of little black spots going up the hall and crisscrossing the living room. She pictured Stephanie, naked and pale and skinny, wandering around in the gray light of dawn.

From work she phoned the apartment several times, there was no answer, she knew there wouldn't be. When she got home there was no sign that Stephanie had been there. Marie's cereal bowl and coffee cup were exactly where she had left them, with the little black pool of cold coffee in the bottom of the cup.

Trish, her new roommate, liked the apartment, and Mr. Moluska liked Trish's looks—Who wouldn't?—so he lowered the rent.

Marie and Trish had to decide what to do with Stephanie's clothes and other things. There wasn't a lot, three suitcases and a cardboard box, so they put them in the back closet. Two days later Trish asked Mr. Moluska if he had room down in the basement and they took the things down there, carefully labeled with Stephanie's name.

Trish wasn't as young as she seemed at first glance or as young as she tried to act. She said she had never been married, though Saturday night, after she and Marie had been out with a couple of guys, she told Marie she had been married but it hadn't lasted long. She said she wasn't ashamed. That wasn't why she hadn't mentioned it before. She just didn't think people needed to go into every intimate detail.

The next morning they took their coffee in the front room. Opening the curtains, they sat in the sun streaming through the narrow high windows. Trish had some ideas about fixing up the apartment, that is, if Marie agreed. Marie liked Trish's ideas, especially one about doing the sunny part of the living room floor in bright Spanish tile, yellow and red and green. Trish and her ex-husband's breakfast nook had been in tile. It was beautiful. Trish looked around, and Marie looked, too, already seeing, almost, the tile shining in the morning sun.

THE OUTDOORSMAN

Because Bogsedge was rather oozy even on the brightest days, Mrs. Clarinda Sheehan had a table and chairs brought out onto the terrace; there she remained fidgeting and looking down the lawn to the brush creek and the heath beyond.

As the clock chimed four, Mrs. Sheehan heard the canine grunting and loud panting that always preceded her neighbor on the lane, Ursula Dolmon. Around the corner she came in her dogcart pulled by two tawny beasts straining for all they were worth. Short of the terrace steps the dogs collapsed, their tongues lolling, their eyes rolling back in their heads.

At that moment the French doors opened and Tina Buell, Mrs. Sheehan's niece, appeared. "Wonderful!" the young lady trilled and ran down the steps to assist Ursula Dolmon who was tilting the dogcart in her struggle to climb out.

Though Tina Buell was a neat little beauty with a perfect oval face, large and lucid eyes, and lips as purely shaped as the dreams of innocence, she lacquered her face to an otherworldly gleam, glued black sprigs to her eyes so when she blinked it appeared chorus lines of spiders were kicking up, and with a metallic unction she greased her lips to the obdurate sheen of aluminum. Tina's hair, today a golden green called Singapore Fudge, was knotted into a "beehive," and she wore a pink, dollish dress identical to one a movie starlet wore once—and alas forever in the pulpy catacombs of one of Tina's movie mags, as said starlet goes forth to dubious doings with her escorts, a sixty-year-old latex magnate and a celebrated young rake-hell with the flared nostrils and bulging eyes of a stallion. Tina wore green hose which with the fulsome glint of the South American anaconda succeeded in transforming the slender delicacy of her calves and thighs to a rippling muscularity.

Tina ran down the steps—breathtaking feat in itself, considering her shoes, plastic "platforms" seven inches high clamped to Tina's feet with wide brass bands—and reached Ursula Dolmon just as the dogcart was about to flip over on top of the large lady.

"Oh Ur, how wonderful of you to come!" Tina said. "You will get to meet my husband!"

"There, child," Ursula said, tapping Tina's cheek with a bending her like a twig as they climbed to the terrace where Mrs. Sheehan called, "Bless you for coming," and went back to her nervous waiting: now she stared at the wooden bridge up the way.

"Well," Ursula said. "So it's tea on the terrace, is it? All this for him, eh?" Not waiting for a reply from Mrs. Sheehan, Ursula called loudly, "My chair!" and two servants rushed out with an oak bench.

"Isn't it exciting, Ur?" Tina said. "My husband is an outdoorsman!"

"There child," Ursula said, tapping Tina's cheek with a thick finger.

"What really is an outdoorsman, Ur?" Tina said, kneeling at her feet.

Ursula called over her shoulder, "Haven't you told her anything?" In reply there was an incomprehensible twittering. "My child," Ursula said to Tina, "an outdoorsman is one who has such a tremendous urge to shoot, that he tromps through one jungle after another, traverses miles and miles of desert, tops all mountain peaks time allows, and returns home with a hundred stuffed heads. The outdoorsman then writes a book about the tribes he has outraged, and gives lectures on the numerous sheiks with whom he has palavered."

"Sheiks! How utterly grand! And will he take me with him on his desert treeks?"

"Treks, my dear. Only if you insist."

"Oh I shall! How grand it shall be! Won't it, Ur?"

Ursula Dolmon shook a packet of smokes from her big sleeve, lit up, and said, "Frankly, my dear, no. Wind, shifting sand, wild men . . . . I'll not likely forget sinking knee-deep in sand at the funeral of your dear mother. God rest her soul."

Tina bowed her beehive and her aluminum lips tapped out a quick prayer. Then she looked up and brightly said, "Was her death just awful?"

"Primitive rituals are always the worst. But I've told you all that a thousand times and I don't feel like mulling over it again." Ursula raised her voice and called, "I say, when is this person scheduled to get here?"

Mrs. Sheehan glanced at the little watch pinned to her dress and said, "Any minute. Oh my."

"I can hardly wait!" Tina said. She breathed rapidly and her face attempted to exude a childlike eagerness from beneath its lacquer. Her eyes grew huge and achieved a glazed dazzlement, as if some minute, delicate part—her tummy, heart, or liver—were about to pop.

She sprang up and like a marvelous tin puppet suddenly finding itself alive with everyone watching, exclaimed: "He's coming!" Clasping her hands and pressing them to her cheek, she whispered, "The man I love is on the way." Louder: "Great outdoorsman and chum of sheiks! Hurrying to me, Tina Buell! Oh, what a marvelous moment, is it not?"

"Oh gracious," Mrs. Sheehan said.

"Tina!" Ursula Dolmon banged on the table with her fist. "Restraint!"

But Tina's emotions whirred on. She panted and throbbed, her eyes burning like warning lights on a dynamo whining higher and higher into the red zone.

Still louder Ursula bellowed: "Your exercise! At once!"

Tina stumbled to a chair, tightly crossed her legs, and digging her elbows into her hips, took a deep breath. Her eyeballs pulsed with each thump of her heart, and Mrs. Sheehan and Ursula Dolmon listened to the clickety buzz as Tina whispered backward from one hundred. This took a while: Tina faltered often, lost her place, and had to be prompted by the ladies. She gasped through the sixties, toiled down the forties, but was rather herself when she at last sank to the bottom of the numbers, with Mrs. Sheehan and Ursula Dolmon nodding on each stroke and chanting ". . . five, four, three, two—one!"

Tina saw me the instant I stepped from the creek but she didn't flinch: perhaps I was emerging from a little dream spun by her dizziness. She blinked—and I was still there. She spoke, and Mrs. Sheehan and Ursula Dolmon turned.

I waved my big hat and started up the lawn, passing the cart and the unconscious dogs. At the steps, I bowed.

Mrs. Sheehan's lips twitched and flittered, balancing an expression between alarm and delight. Ursula Dolmon grunted uncertainly, but her suspicions quickly rallied and I heard quite clearly their brassy little voices yelling *Beware! Beware!* Ursula Dolmon's brows tightened, her eyes grayed, and it was evident her choice of weapons was meat axes: "Well. A fop. What do you want?"

Tina and Mrs. Sheehan were stunned by this rudeness.

But they were even more startled when I dashed up the steps, seized Tina's hand, and put my mouth on it.

On their own, the servants, who it seemed had earlier come to the windows to study Miss Tina's fit and had stayed on for my entrance, at that moment trotted out the tea things, and Mrs. Sheehan, Ursula Dolmon, and Tina Buell burst into speech, each on a different track: Ursula Dolmon reiterating her challenge, though somewhat less staunchly than before; Mrs. Sheehan expressing hopes that I hadn't dif-

ficulty finding Bogsedge, isolated as it happened to be; and
dear little Tina. . . .
    Fine and excessive though my earlier description is, still
it fails to convey Tina's beauty and its slick skin. As I held her
hand, breathing her perfume—Civet Murmur, or was it Primal
Repast?—I saw cumulus clouds rolling in great bawdy tussles
down the sky; I heard the dulcet slap of cards in the long
game of solitaire Goodness plays with Evil; and as a simper
glimmered on the lips of the Angel of Death, with a gold
tooth smack in the middle, I smelled her breath, warm fruit
and fish, as Tina smiled at me and said, "You're pretty."
    "Child!" Mrs. Sheehan exclaimed. Then to me, "You
must forgive her. She . . . ."
    "Sir," Ursula Dolmon said so loudly the teacups tottered
in their saucers. "Are you prepared to present Tina Buell a
decent prospect?"
    "Gracious!" Mrs. Sheehan said. "We're so clumsy. For-
give us, dear sir. And especially forgive poor Ursula's blunt-
ness. I hope you shan't. . . ."
    "Shan't us no shan'ts, Clarinda Sheehan," Ursula Dolmon
said. "I'll speak for myself and I'll speak uninterrupted."
Ursula glared at her until Mrs. Sheehan bowed her head.
"Now. Sir, let's hear your prospects."
    I slipped into a chair beside Tina's facing the ladies, and
took out my cigar case. "With your permission." I snipped
the end of a cheroot and lit it. Ursula Dolmon eyed every
move with the avidity of a great mongoose. Mrs. Sheehan
peeked up with an unctuous smile that urged me to feel right
at home. And Tina! Pearls of spittle glistened in the corners
of her mouth, stretched wide in a smile both enraptured and
entrancing.
    I uttered first a ring of smoke and the three of them
watched it shakily rise, open, and become nothing; and then:
"Hark! I believe I hear someone coming." They lifted their
heads in that inevitable and instinctual way. "Do I hear a
carriage rumbling across a wooden bridge . . .?"

But silence lay on the afternoon like a cow.

"My mistake," I said. "Perhaps he's here already."

Mrs. Sheehan peeped, "Oh my," and began blinking her eyes so rapidly surely all the difficulty, and everything else as well, took wings and flapped off. Ursula Dolmon's face thickened and clenched to the sourest of frowns. She nodded slowly and, leaning forward, closed in for the kill. And Tina gave a little gasp, for she and I saw what the ladies couldn't.

Behind them there appeared in the trees along the creek a dwarf—though thicker. Rather, a fellow squashed into himself, with the excesses bulging out everywhere, a very heavy dwarf, actually. But no—he seemed a dwarf merely because he stood in the shadows of the trees. As he came to the edge of the shade, Tina saw he was a regular-sized fellow. No again! He was a *large* fellow! And wearing a tweed suit and cap, with yellow gloves, and swinging a big shiny walking stick!

"But sir," Mrs. Sheehan said to me, "no one is coming. I mean . . . . *You* are. I mean . . . ."

"Fah!" Ursula Dolmon shook with wrath. "He's an imposter, Clarinda. A fop interloper! A snake in the grass!" She glared at me. "Tell us, my fine young fop, who are you if you're not who you're supposed to be."

"I don't understand that," I said quietly. "Who am I supposed to be?"

"Why, who you are, of course," Mrs. Sheehan said.

"Oh. You know who I am?"

"We thought we did," Mrs. Sheehan said, while Ursula Dolmon grumbled, "Fah! Oh Bloody fah!"

"And who might that be?" I said.

Mrs. Sheehan tried to speak but all her breath was gone. She sat with her eyes closed and her mouth open.

And it was left to Ursula Dolmon to say: "Hugh Venolio."

It undulated across the terrace and rippled down the lawn, echoing within itself as it does even when it is whispered, causing those who hear, no matter how often they

have heard it before, to repeat it to themselves, as in fact the four of us were doing at that moment, murmuring *Venolio, Venolio* . . . .
Though Tina uttered it louder than the rest of us. And with great urgency as her eyes went like darts to the face of the figure who upon hearing the purple smoke of that name stepped into the sunlight. Tina's next sound, another little gasp, had less delight than her first. And that was followed by as sincere a groan as ever was heard. Suddenly banging both plastic "platforms" on the terrace and leaning forward, rattling her beehive, Tina shot forth a piping, inchoate utterance, pathetic, desperate, and fierce. The ladies, densely preoccupied with their own matters, were oblivious to this display. But I recognized in Tina's outcry a word which Venolio himself no doubt could distinguish, but which the ladies mistook for "Noes," that is, Tina's naive disapproval of the ladies' confronting me in this way, expressed in term of not just one "no," but many of them!

And as that shriek pierced the afternoon, the figure spun about as if suddenly remembering something he left among the trees, or as if he hoped to undo this, to turn back and, reentering, slip under the skin of the moment: miraculously remaining unnoticed, he would again come up the lawn, perhaps this time walking sideways, it might help, cross the terrace, and sit at the table. He would even light one of my cigars. Then, leaning forward, he would say in the suavest tone imaginable, "Venolio at your service."

Of course all was forgiven when I confessed not to being Venolio and apologized for the confusion I had inadvertently created by seeming to be what I wasn't, and I moreover was asked to dinner when I let it slip that I had once heard a certain Venolio mentioned, though I was regrettably foggy as to when, where, and the circumstances. I was, however, positive that those circumstances were special, if not indeed peculiar. Needless to say, these circumstances were of colossal significance to Mrs. Sheehan and Ursula Dolmon who immediately set forth the premise that while sojourning in foreign lands I had actually encountered Venolio face to face, quite without knowing it was he—"Stranger things have happened," Mrs. Sheehan was quick to point out—and, furthermore, perhaps the right remark or odd nuance would whisk the fog from my memory. I conceded this wasn't an altogether ironclad impossibility, and I thrilled the ladies by agreeing I just might even recognize this Venolio were I to lay eyes on him again . . . .

At that, Mrs. Sheehan sent a servant galloping from the room. He returned with a folder of material Mrs. Sheehan had collected in her correspondence with Venolio's agent, one Cooper Goggins. "Perhaps you know him . . .?" Mrs. Sheehan ventured, but Ursula Dolmon cut her off—"Ridiculous! That's too much to hope for." Mrs. Sheehan opened the folder and carefully laid before me a snapshot.

Hugh Venolio in safari costume kneels beside an elephant. One looks first into the eyes of the beast, vapid in death, then at the rifle across the hunter's knee and pointed by cruel coincidence at one of those eyes. Then one looks at the hunter himself. But his face is turned away as he leans toward the beast as if he is about to touch one of its vast ears. But one hardly minds not seeing the man's face; one's eyes are drawn again to the elephant's face and on second glance the eyes seem less dead. Could it be the elephant isn't dead but in a swoon? Venolio, strolling a forest path, has come upon an elephant lying in the dust. And he kneels to slip into its ear the lilting echo which will surprise and please the beast, curiously encourage it, and send it on its way. But not yet: in our moment the elephant gazes abjectly down the length of its famous but melancholy proboscis sprawling before Venolio.

In another snap Venolio faces the camera! However, all but his eyes are covered by a parka's mask, for here the outdoorsman floats on the severe and dimensionless white of the Arctic, one arm around the neck of a propped-up walrus who stares bluntly into the camera, conveying an uncommon levelness about things, including death, and a candor certainly exceeding our own as we pry the coarse canvas of Venolio's parka, searching for some hint of the hidden face.

"Just these two?" I said.

As Mrs. Sheehan slid them back into the folder, Ursula Dolmon answered: "She asked for more, but these are all Goggins would send."

"And he stopped answering my letters," Mrs. Sheehan said.

"But you persisted?" I said.

She sighed. "It's like writing to the moon."

"Then what led you to believe Hugh Venolio would come to present himself today?"

Ursula Dolmon unrolled a scroll of thick yellow paper; hiding within the filigrees and flourishes of a grandiose hand was an epistle agreeing to terms set forth in Mrs. Sheehan's of Five October, and guaranteeing that "Mr. V." would appear for tea at Bogsedge on One April for further negotiations, contractualizations and finalizings with Tina Buell.

"So you see why the child's heart is broken," Mrs. Sheehan said. "Her day has come and gone." Tina had been carried upstairs, quaking and hacking, after the episode on the terrace. When Mrs. Sheehan last peeked in at her, Tina was whining in her sleep, poor thing, and thrashing her legs as if she were riding a bicycle across the ceiling.

"It is my judgment," I said, returning the letter to Mrs. Sheehan, "that this matter requires the greatest caution."

"Oh my," she whispered. She looked at her friend and said, "Caution, Ursula."

"I adivse you to prepare your defenses," I said, "while at the same time keeping open your ports."

Ursula frowned. "That seems to proceed on the assumption that Venolio still might come."

I said in the driest, most measured of tones, "It is of course merely a theory based on the impression we can piece together of your Venolio's modus operandi. Above all, he is unpredictable. One might go so far as to say he strives to be unknowable. But I have a hunch he'll come. It's a long shot"—I leaned forward, winked, and whispered, "but I'd bet my skin on it."

"Then you must stay!" Ursula said.

"Yes! You must!" Mrs. Sheehan said.

"Venolio has his Cooper Goggins," Ursula said.

"And we need one too," Mrs. Sheehan said. "Oh, *do* stay. I'll pay you handsomely."

I leaned back, my hand to my chin. "Frankly, I had other plans." Their faces crumbled. "I was on holiday, you know. Hiking the heath. However . . . ." Their eyes brightened. "Your situation is intriguing. You might say it has me trapped." I laughed ironically. "All right. I agree to serve as your adviser."

"Hurrah!"

"On one condition."

"Anything!"

"Tina Buell's welfare must be placed entirely in my hands."

Without hesitating they agreed; after all, this was what they were asking for, wasn't it?

We shook on it and, with toddies, toasted Tina's future. Then with that crafty bravado for which counselors and ministers of war are famous, I lifted my goblet to the window and the night beyond: "To Venolio!" They stiffened, but then drank, peering intently at me over the rims of their cups.

"Do tell me again about Tibet!" Tina said.

"There, child," Ursula Dolmon said, dozing by the fire. Mrs. Sheehan looked up from her sewing. "You mustn't tire Mr. Green. You've been at him all day."

"I'm not tiring him," Tina said. "Am I, Vance?"

I smiled into her waxed face, squarely framed with bangs and straight black hair: she had been Asiatic this evening.

"Always gets her way," Ursula sighed. Mrs. Sheehan returned to her stitches.

"Oh please," Tina said. "Travel widens, you know."

I obliged by repeating what Tina and the ladies had already heard several times that day: A Season on Top of the World, beginning with an account of simple pleasures of the mountain village: riding the yak, eating the Sherpas' famous brown cheese pie, and a reminiscence of the yogi who stopped his heart each afternoon from three to three-fifteen; and featuring An Assault on K2: bizarre misadventures; hallucinations unique to the Himalayas; intimations on the pathos of reversion; and mysticism, the rustic's mainstay.

As Ursula Dolmon and Mrs. Sheehan sank away, Tina tiptoed to the sofa and sat beside me. Her expression inscrutable, she whispered, "Tell me about the chicks."

I smiled.

"Are they cute?"

"Moderately."

"Are they fat or skinny?"

"They're so bundled up, it's hard to actually see them. But as a rule they're nicely plump."

"Oh, 'nicely.' So you like that, do you?"

"Do *I*? Yes, in a way."

She squinted for greater inscrutability and said, "And in what way do you like them which aren't plump?"

"Anyone you have in mind particularly?"

"Me, dummy!"

"Oh. Well, yes, I'd say you're a rather nice little thing."

"*Little* thing!" she squealed most scrutably, and woke the ladies.

"But of course if you give the yak its head, it will go right to the edge, for they love to look out into the sky. One wonders what they're thinking . . . ." Ursula Dolmon and Mrs.

Sheehan settled back.

"All right, you," Tina whispered, scooting closer. "What kind of 'little thing' am I?"

"Well . . . a peach. A ripe peach."

She closed her eyes. "Umm. I like that. Yes, I like that a lot. And am I sweet or tart?"

I sneaked a yawn. "Both at once."

"And do you nibble me or fill your mouth all at once and gobble me up?"

"Nibbles first, then to gobbling."

"Oh yes," and she opened her eyes—and looked not at me but over my shoulder, her eyes widening.

As I turned, a blur slid across the window, leaving after it the moon-gray night on the lawn.

"That was nothing," I said. "Your imagination. Or perhaps a very large owl."

"It was him," she whispered and an amazing thing then happened: her expression fell vacant, completely, and showing through her Asian mask I saw the structure of her skull and, hovering therein, her redoubtable ancestry, as dour and undeniable as stones and ancient trees. Astounding! Though Tina Buell had absolutely no awareness of it, this gel which she considered her "face," no matter whose it was from one day to the next, was fixed to a frame of hard old wood.

"You promised me he would never come back," Tina said—for earlier I had told her, whispering behind the ladies' backs, that I had seen the distressing person who had appeared from the creek yesterday, and told him to go away forever, and that he had forthwith gone away. "You lied to me!"—and she socked me in the jaw!

I jumped to my feet with a yelp which woke the ladies. Seeing me standing, they struggled to their feet. "Bedtime," Ursula said and yawned like a lion.

"Come along, Tina," Mrs. Sheehan said. "Tell Mr. Green good night. There'll be more lectures tomorrow."

As they ushered her out, she didn't say good night but

looked back with the same plain, wonderfully artless face which stared at me all night from the reflection on the window, drawing me into that blackness, deeper and deeper, until by dawn when I saw through again to the gray world and the heath, I was exhausted, weak with love and the foolishness of need. Lying on the bottom step, I convinced myself that in a few hours she would clomp down the stairs, little Heidi the milkmaid. Or fanfared by imaginary clarions she would come down in the sweeping gown and modest bonnet of Maid Marian. Or best of all she would be bound in the impenetrable black of Sister Mary Theresa, her face trussed and tiny as a daisy screwed into a rock.

"Hi, buster."

I lifted my head and, looking up a hundred miles to where she stood at the head of the stairs, I groaned. Her mouth glistened like a wound, as incredibly red as her hair, and she wore a silver dress so tight that as she came down the stairs every line of her body, every muscle, gleamed like salamanders swimming in mercury. "Hows about a picnic, big boy?"

And she was serious about the picnic, though Mrs. Sheehan showed her the sky, which had turned grayish green, and tried to convince her it would rain at any moment. But our pixie Rita Hayworth prevailed, and while the ladies sat on the terrace in caps and slickers with umbrellas at the ready, I spread a blanket on the lawn. Tina ate a deviled egg and smoked a cigarette. "Move."

She nodded to the side. "There." I sat between her and the terrace. "Now." Widely and redly she smiled from the 1940s, a smile of lilting sorrow which back then had something to do with the war but which now poured cruelty and courage into the same cup, inviting all comers while at the same time denying any chance of love. "You're going to tell me everything."

"Everything?"

"You know what I mean."

I took one of her cigarettes, lit it, and with my hand shaking, though I don't think she noticed, I said as suavely as I could, sounding I daresay quite a lot like Charles Boyer, "Maabe I do, on maabe I don't."

"Okay. I'll level." She leaned forward and put her hand on my knee. "I know why you're here."

"Ah." I smiled drolly. "On do you plan to . . . ." I nodded toward the terrace, "tell them?"

She opened her mouth as wide as she could and laughed. She turned, her hand still on my knee but not visible from the terrace, and raising her voice to bright girlishness, she called, "We're having such fun!"

"That's nice, dear," Ursula Dolmon called.

She turned back to me. "Don't worry, honey. If I told on you, what good would it do me? It would be a Phallic victory."

"Pyrrhic victory."

She lit another cigarette. "At first I thought you were just after money . . . ."

"Ah. Le spondulicks . . . ."

"But it's bigger than that, isn't it?"

I couldn't play back to this. I felt everything going out of me.

"And it's *worse* than that." She laughed silently. "Isn't it?"

I forced a dry chuckle. But there was no Boyer left. There was nothing left. Somehow she *knew*.

"So," she said smugly. "You can tell me."

"But I thought you knew," I said quickly, grasping at straws.

"I do. But not the full particulars, silly boy. You can go ahead and tell me, I'll not stop what you're up to. For you see"—she worked the cigarette into her lips without opening them. She inhaled deeply and, flaring her nostrils, breathed out the smoke—"I'm all for it."

I looked away. "You weren't last night."

She laughed. "That doesn't count. That wasn't *me.*"

"Too bad. I rather . . . ." My voice failed. I whispered. "I rather liked her."

"*You* would," she said.

I groaned.

"See!" She laughed in my face. "I understand!"

At that moment the sky broke and rain poured down. Tina jumped to her feet, hiked up her dress, and ran for the house. "What has he told you?" I called. I ran after her. "What has he told you about me?" She laughed over her shoulder, though I couldn't hear her voice for the rain, the wind, the thunder lumbering across the heath and up the lawn.

Ursula Dolmon held the door open for us and for that slithering rustle which follows people in from the rain. Ursula lit a lamp, but Tina, who had run upstairs and returned with her hair gray and pinned tightly to her head, and wearing one of Mrs. Sheehan's dresses, long-sleeved, dull purplish-brown like wood, the proper dress for sitting through dark afternoons, went straight over and turned out the lamp.

"But my dear . . . ." Mrs. Sheehan started.

"No." In the overprecise manner of the maiden lady who must through the brambles each moment presents somehow pass without snagging her dress, pricking herself, and above all without screaming, Tina said, "If there's a lamp, all we can see is ourselves. I want to watch the storm."

She sat down, feet and knees together, her hands on her lap, no doubt picking at the wan little violets she herself had sewn onto a handkerchief.

Shivering in my wet clothes, I sat in silence. I could hurry up to my room and change, but I was afraid to leave the room for one moment. I watched her. In the darkness she seemed to narrow, shrink into herself as if right before my eyes she were shriveling. I blinked, and she was again herself, or at least what I could see of her.

I crossed the room with excessive and unintended slowness to the lamp. I discovered my matches were wet. Of course. I turned to ask Ursula Dolmon for hers. Ursula Dolmon and Mrs. Sheehan sat in the darkness of their chairs like sphinxes sinking back into the sand. Tina sat bent forward like a dark *C*, a doll frazzled and funked by too much rough play. "It's time." I went to the French doors. Thunder journeyed across the sky, shaking the glass. Hugh Venolio crossed the sky in the yellow cone of light from the lamp he had lit in the room, reflected in the dark pane and obliterating the world.

He put his arm around my shoulders and said in his tight, odd voice which always reminded me of an oboe, "Who are you?"

"Oh cut that out."

"I mean are you Cooper Goggins, Vance Green, Jimmy McJames . . .?"

"Vance Green."

"Ah. My favorite."

I whispered, "You should have waited. We had a chance for something better. If you had only waited."

"There, there," he said. I was crying. Nuzzling me with his great proboscis, he breathed in my ear, befuddling me, spinning everything until it came unnotched and slid off, and while his bright eyes stared down his nose, I found myself alone on a street, narrow and endless, the sounds of the city cupped by the sky and muffled to an ethery *wah wah wah.* In my hand was a card: *Miss Sondra Padilla,* and the address was the place across the street. A face, small and vague, was stuck in a window on the second floor. I took off my hat and waved it.

"Be good," Venolio murmured and with a shove sent me forth.

But I turned to them and said, "What do you think of your outdoorsman now?"

Mrs. Sheehan and Ursula Dolmon stared right through me! But Tina crooked her finger. I went to her and leaned down. She whispered, "Hugh tells me you must be off for an appointment with a certain Miss . . . Pudolla?"

"No," I said. Venolio coughed peremptorily behind me. "There's plenty of time," I said, glancing at him. He stood with his hands clasped behind him and leaning slightly forward like a banker pondering loans, foreclosures, evictions. "I am still their guest," I whispered.

Walking by me, and mumbling what was either "Rather" or "Blather," he went to a sideboard and poured a drink.

"Dear Mr. Venolio," Mrs. Sheehan said in a lutey tremolo. "I do hope you will favor us with one of your songs."

"He sings?" I exclaimed. "He has told you he *sings*?"

Venolio bowed his head modestly. He downed his drink, dabbed his lips with a blue silk handkerchief, and strode to the center of the triangle formed by the ladies' chairs. He tooted a pitch pipe and, lifting his great nose as if sniffing the note as it hung in the air, launched into a blasting rendition of "I Dreamt I Dwelt in Marble Halls."

Mrs. Sheehan clasped her hands ecstatically and at the sadder parts hid her face with a hankie and whined. Ursula Dolmon closed her eyes and nodded in full agreement with every note and sentiment; she even hummed along loudly, which didn't in the least bother Venolio. The third lady nodded her head and for a while patted the arm of her chair roughly in time with Venolio's music, until this tired her out; then leaning back, her mouth opened like a dark hole, she breathed loudly and unevenly.

When Venolio finished the song, they applauded at length and he bowed a dozen times. It didn't take much coaxing to get another song from him.

"Wait!" I said. "Listen! I . . . ."

Venolio launched into "Captain Hornsby's Ride":

Oh the cruel and wintry vigils keep the soldiery heart aloof,
Hey nonny ru, ta-rah, ta-rah,
Till the dauntless lads salute the dawn and then fall off the roof,
With a waldy way, a waldy woe, a waldy waldy wall.

I stumbled from one of them to the other, tugging at
their sleeves, putting my face in theirs, calling in to them. I
knocked Ursula in the shoulder but couldn't get her attention. I jumped up on the arm of Tina's chair, climbed onto
the back of the chair as if I were crossing a stile from one
field to another.

Venolio finished his song and began another. I collapsed
on the carpet but watched every move until they broke for
lunch.

From the kitchen I went into the dining room with my
pockets stuffed with carrots, celery, and radishes. I ate standing behind them at the table. "I can't begin to tell you how
pleased I am, Mr. Venolio," Mrs. Sheehan said, "that my
niece has found such a gentleman."

Venolio, picking his teeth with the prong of a fork,
mumbled, "My pleasure," looking across at Tina who had
once again assumed her beehive, pink dolly dress, and green
hose.

When they finished, Venolio scooted back Tina's chair
for her, and as she rose, nudged the back of her head with
his nose.

As they processioned into the parlor I threw radishes,
popping them off Venolio's head; they bounced helter-skelter
and Mrs. Sheehan almost tripped on one.

"Do tell us of travailing in Tibet," Tina said.

"Traveling, dear," Ursula said.

"Above all," Venolio said, "I am an outdoorsman. My
heart is always in it, no matter where I am. So Tibet was inevitably the place for me. Just as"—he thumped down on his
knees before Tina and took her hand in his—"it was in-

evitable that I should pluck this prize and take her for my own."

I ran up and jumped on his back. I hoped to send him down face first to the floor and pummel his head, bash it in if I could—and if I couldn't, I would try to steer him down the lawn and into the creek. I pictured myself straddling his neck and holding his head as we sank into the depths.

But when I leaped onto him, he merely hunched slightly and didn't miss a beat of his spiel. As he stood, I climbed onto his shoulders.

Now Venolio was gibbering in Tibetan. He did a little jig from the hills, knocking my head on the ceiling. Then he taught the ladies a Sherpa nursery rhyme:

Hup toppa yurka
Puka pow, puka pow.

Which he translated If you're good, when the yak dies we'll eat him, eat him. Venolio then had them dancing with him in a circle. When they sat panting, I climbed off his shoulders.

On the terrace rain dripped from the eaves, but the storm was over. Ursula's dogs came running across the lawn and skidded on the wet marble, surprised to find me out here, their big ears pricking, their eyes round and questioning. "It's all right," I said. I glanced into the parlor: he had brought out a Maori game, and they were chasing him with feathers and bones.

We found the cart. Ecstatic, they faunched and gamboled and I could hardly get them in the traces. I checked and still had the address card, and with a click of my tongue we were off.

It was slow going, across the lawn, but at the bridge we took to the road and made excellent time. They fairly flew, their ears down, their long bodies stretching into the smooth rhythm that promises eternity.

K

Who really knows him? Of course there are countless stories about him, articles, interviews in journals, popular magazines, and on television, and a dozen people are writing books about him. Though these books will focus on his work, hopefully they will also explore the man himself.

It is doubtful, though. For if he has a hand in doing these books he will most certainly mislead the authors. That's his way. And it's that which mystifies us, and which we love. That and certain other qualities.

K.

With all its literary echoes.

And he is the outgrowth of that literary past, just as our era is the outgrowth of the strange eras preceding it.

He is invited to a party; he does not go; those who do attend are butchered. The case is famous, an achievement in disgust. It is the kiss-off of an era, a very oral era, no doubt the most remarkably oral era in recent history. The murderers drank their victims' blood. They would have eaten parts of them, had they the imagination. They would have left mouth prints in blood, had they the imagination. They would have performed oral sex on the dead bodies, had they the imagination. The murderers were morons. K. should have been at the party. He would have shown them a thing or two, made life exciting for them, really turned them on, really given them a red white and blood bang up blow out whammo bammo crammo, he would have blown their minds, rung their chimes, shown them some changes, some flashes, some phases. Because K. invents that country, K. lived there before those shambling yahoos were even born, K. was surviving there while those little Americans were not yet even glistening sparkles of spittle on their mothers' crooked teeth.

K. our hero our modern man our leader in times of madness, would have ruined it all for us, though, because none of that night's pranks would have happened, had he been there. But what *would* have happened? Think of it as an assignment, our first of the semester. Remember, among his numerous identities and disguises, he is a professor: he stands before young men and women and *lectures* to them; sits cross-legged on a desk and *chats* with them; explains, hypothesizes, spins, weaves, lures . . . .

Have you heard the one about the beginning of his Individual Will and Society? It was to be a seminar, but 300 students showed up for the first meeting. Unperturbed, K. greeted them and with his vulpine smile explained what they would do in the course. Each student must murder someone.

Ha ha.

Ha ha ha.

We turn and nudge each other and grin and wink and are all in all very much satisfied that this is the real thing, the real K., living up to all the stories we've heard about him, just as far out as his books . . . . He waits until our shuffling and nudging and tittering are finished. Staring implacably he goes on to say that we will submit a paper following the murder, giving in complete detail the method and execution. This time no tittering. K. may be outasight but maybe he is also just a little poor in his judgment of timing, for the class has that feeling an audience gets when a comedian has pushed a joke just a little bit farther than it can go. But that's all right. After all, K. is K. the Writer. The class is tolerant, though already there are expressions of condescension, impatience, showing on our young American faces. K. further explains that this will be the sole basis of our grade in the course and that he will give only two grades: A and F. A, if the murder is performed and verified by the police investigation and news coverage; F, if a murder has not been committed by the last day of class. He asks if there are questions. There is a nervous silence over the 300 people. K. dismisses class. We sit there blinking at him. We wait for him to *explain.* He stares at us. Even when not smiling, his expression is . . . wolfish. It occurs to many of us young ladies and young gentlemen that he has a decidedly foreign look. K. was not originally an American, we recall. For a full minute, going into two minutes, the class remains seated and silent, waiting. Then we stir. Squirm in our seats. We look at the persons sitting to our left and to our right. Over our shoulders. We're waiting for our spokesman. It is a girl. "Are you putting us on?" she says clearly and rather brashly, a with-it young woman. K. assures her he isn't putting us on. His expression is unchanging, his eyes are truly impenetrable, the girl doesn't like him at all and she liked his books so much, she wonders why she is wasting her time, he's a creep. Other spokesmen pitch in, one after another, pursuing K., for he is elusive, cryptic, and he sticks to what he's already said. We're hoping to get him on to the next step, for we have a hunch that this is a trick and he's just waiting for the right person to say the right thing to nudge him on to the payoff, the punch line, and then the next point. But he sticks with that by now stupid, by now quite a pain in the ass statement about . . . . What was it . . . ? Already some of us have put it out of mind, we're already out of this auditorium and strolling to our next class which we hope will be more entertaining and intelligent and challenging than this one. This shit is boring. We think maybe this isn't really K. We wonder if K. really exists. You know it could be that publishing companies put out books by so-called "authors" whose names are put together in a way which the publishers' research and marketing departments assure them have the right sound, the right combination of consonants and vowels, to trigger the best possible sales. So they use this name or that and their art department and cover design people, who are skilled moneymakers in their own right, come up with exactly the right face to put on the dust jacket of a book, a face that fits this season, a face that will compel the folks wobbling through the bookstore to zombie-like reach out and pick the book off the shelf and carry it to the cashier and shell out the cash or slip the old credit card across the counter the whole fucking system stinks . . . .

Unreal, someone murmurs, and all 300 of us feel the word throb in our subconscious the same way we sometimes feel the thrumming whir that dully vibrates the bedrooms of our little houses and apartments as we lay sleeping, a vast subliminal perception that slowly blumbles up from under our pillows, *Unreal* . . . . Yes, right on. That's it and that takes care of it. Just look straight ahead but it's unreal so be cool, show nothing, walk through it, everything is cool . . . .

But this fucker isn't kidding. He means it. This is too much. Someone should report the motherfucker. Someone *will* report him. None of us has ever reported anyone. Laissez faire. But this fucker should be reported and maybe someone will report him.

Because he *means* it. *Murder* someone.

That's 300 dead people.

He is crazy, not just crazy but what you call Truly Insane. How did he write those books, get a job teaching at this so-called university, become a famous person who Dick Cavett has on his show? The answer to all of the above is: Young Americans, You Have Been Tricked Again. Which also means: Young Americans, You Have Been Fucked Again.

We young people yearn for meaning, insight, truth, wisdom. And the system keeps putting fuckers like this phony fuck K. in front of us. We young people feel that old American forlorn folklore feeling in our bones and along the backs of our ears and down the insides of our thighs. Used to be, young Americans like us could listen to the whistle of far off locomotives in the nights. Nowadays kids have to just sit in silence and look out a window or stare at a wall and feel the old American forlorn loss of it. K. is talking, explaining to a question what he has already explained. More bullshit. What are we *doing* here? At precisely the same instant 30 of us, maybe 40, picture ourselves Killing Someone. We do it a la TV gangster stuff. Bang! Bang! Run and jump in the black sedan idling at the curb (Who'll drive? Roomo.) Or the old bomb-under-the-hood-of-the-sucker's-car: big bubbly orange explosion of gasoline, black smoke at the top of the flames; cut before the black smoke comes down and hovers over the fire and the car . . . . Some guy asks Can we get credit for already killing someone in Vietnam? People laugh, we all know the guy is telling K. to kiss his ass. K. is not amused. He says no, though he says he must admit Vietnam vets have an advantage over students whose study of life has been limited to books. Are you putting down books!?!? someone, outraged, asks him. He shrugs. No, he's not putting down books. He grins. It's not as unpleasant a grin, under the circumstances, as you might expect. Fucker he is, but maybe a charming fucker. We remember the Cavett interview. Cavett had seemed fascinated by K.—or at any rate Cavett told us, over his shoulder, that he was fascinated. But when Cavett says it he means it, not like with Carson who when he says something means always just the opposite and always it's utterly cynical . . . .

Someone asks What if we get arrested? K. replies That will not affect your grade, though you should avoid arrest. We stare at him as if he has just laid on us some great wisdom.

More and more people are disgusted. You can feel it in the air. This whole scene is just typical of the waste of time, the bullshit, the . . . .

People are walking out and they're not trying to be quiet, they're going out in twos and threes and talking and laughing as they go and letting the big doors slam, and the whole scene is a joke, the whole fucking routine is falling apart, and he's still sitting up there on the desk with his legs crossed in his tweed suit and his vest and his narrow black tie and his forehead intensely wrinkled just as before and he looks even more like a wolf even though the people are telling him he's a fake. He is talking to someone in the front row, and doesn't seem aware that his "class" is walking out on him.

Next week eight people show up, four guys and four gals. K. passes out a reading list, they go down the hall to a seminar room with a round table, and K. asks them to introduce themselves and as they go around the table K. listens with an intensity which exhilarates his students. And though they are kind of frightened of him, as K., as the man who has written the books and who has actually done no telling how much of what he has written about, already they love him, for they know he is K., *the* K., the one and only *K.*!, who will teach them about themselves and about their world and about the terrible world he has known and survived and also about the world which they think he shares with them.

C.

Creepy crawling. We love it. Imagine us all in black with black on our faces crawling along suburban lawns through rose bushes under hedges burrowing through those little wood chips which suburban Californians put around their trees and bushes, and then, the real test, we jimmy the easy lock on the back door (or the front door—why not?) and while one of us stays at the door, lying flat, with a knife or a gun, usually a knife, we have this thing about knives, the rest of us, usually two or three, crawl right through the door and into the house.

Imagine the darkness of crawling into a house you've never seen in the light of day! We crawl with immense slowness. The slower the silenter. We learn to see in the dark, too. Hard at first easy after only a time or two of practice especially when you know there's a houseful of people you can hear them snoring usually the old man and sometimes another man maybe the son, once when we creepy crawled a house in Beverly Hills the place was full of snorers, it was really too much but we went right on in and did the whole thing.

We girls do the creepy crawling. Save the guys for the heavy stuff. The you know what. Heh heh. Slowly through your typical hypothetical suburban living room like crawling down into a cave. That cave part is good, we tell our old man C., it's like crawling into caves and he nods, his eyes half closed, as if this too he has already thought of and also known even more profoundly than we shall ever know it yea though we do creepy crawling until we can't drag our weary little twats across the Karastan and Dura Weave. We go slow and find the corner of the sofa, the easy chairs, once even turn on the big color television set with the sound off and watch Susan Hayward and her big solid knockers do a vigorous five with a john who one of us suggests in the softest whisper must owe Hayward a shitpot load of money and one of us shakes her head and says No, Hayward wants more of the take she's bringing in from peddling her ass. Look at those jugs. How'd you like a suck at those? We all agree that would be something like peace on earth and we go hi ho back to our duties, switching off the set and crawling down the darker than ever hall, straight down, or so it seems, toward where something, it sounds like maybe a minotaur, is snoring and growling and snorting and carrying on like sleep is some kind of slow gruesome fight.

Oh the carefree life of the creepy crawlers. We take off our clothes on the floor and kiss and diddle right beside the bed of mister and missus. Naked we crawl, one right behind the other sniffing and nose-goosing and giggling in a silent way we have perfected, into the bedroom of junior miss and kneel in awe beside her bed. Junior Miss is beautiful, they're always beautiful in the dark. She is sleeping on top of the bed-covers and her baby doll has worked up. She's sleeping in what C. calls the nimbus, he says it's the most powerful far-going of positions, and we put our arms around each other in reverence and love of Junior Miss. We silently yearn to wake her with the softest and sweetest of kisses and while she is thinking that she is having one of those evil little dreams Junior Misses sometimes have, we will spirit her away, or at least spirit ourselves into bed with her. But that's a no no. We wouldn't do that, anyway. We are infinitely smarter than that. What crap to even think of such a thing.

Once while we are creepy crawling, the old man the bear of the woods snaps off his snoring and gets up, comes down the hall, his footsteps vibrating the floor and the whole house, we can feel the earth shaking, the vibration and rippling and undulation of the air which his moving down the hallway causes, and the two of us like gliding cats of shadow ink into the lumps of deeper darkness of the sofa and one of us along the wall right under the front windows, which is a very dangerous place to be for he might come to the window for a midnight peek out and if he does he will step on her stomach and wonder why the carpet is so lumpy, warm and squishy. But he goes into the kitchen for the all-time all-American favorite treat the midnight snack. No, tonight it's the old drink-some-milk-right-out-of-the-carton-in-the-middle-of-the-night. From the front room we can see him in the light from the refrigerator, a large man in red pajamas. It's one of those open houses in the suburbs, not unlike the ranch house where we creepy crawlers and T., who is of course standing in the foyer with a knife so long and so sharp the old-fashioned fellow glugging his grade-A homogenized would never never never believe it even when and if he felt T. putting it all the way home—and where a dozen others live in sweetest harmony around our old man, our lover provider guiding light C. We watch the old man drinking his milk, tilting the carton up, really going after it, and then he stops, we listen to him breathing deeply, and we like that just as we liked watching Junior Miss, we get to feeling almost possessive about these people, and we nod wisely as the large man in red pajamas belches and it bumps and thuds throughout the dark house. Then he comes into the living room. The one who was under the window crawled across the room while he was in the kitchen and now she's in a ball on the floor at the end of the sofa, maybe he won't notice there's one too many hassocks in his living room.

He comes into the living room and sure enough he goes to the front window and hooks back the curtains and stands there. From the outside light, moon, far off street-lamp, we can see his face clearly, a thick heavy face, he looks like he's still asleep, and he looks out at the black blue gray front lawn, he sees but doesn't see the van parked right across the street. Maybe he *does* see the van. Maybe that's why he's standing there so long. No, now he starts scratching his balls. Good sign. Best of all possible signs. He lets the curtain fall into place and he shuffles back through the living room to the hall and we hear him in the john having a good old noisy piss, he doesn't flush the toilet, then far away we hear the sigh and grumble of springs as he climbs back into bed.

Come on, we hear though it isn't spoken. It's T., he was here in the room with us and the big man in red pajamas and we girls didn't know it, we tell this later to C. and he praises T. The creepy crawlers were creeped! And it's even scarier than crawling down the black hole into a house, that T. was right there with us in the room, he could have reached out with that knife and touched either of us or the man in red pajamas . . . .

We leave without marking that place. Marking the place is something we usually do at the end. Some little thing so next morning the folks will discover they have been visited so to speak. Put all the food out of the refrigerator onto the kitchen floor. Leave some poetry or some lipstick art work in some quaint place like on the ceiling above Junior Miss. The best ever was when one of us was having her period we found a Bible, don't ask how, we got so good at creepy crawling we could just sink into a house and whatever we wanted or needed would just come floating through the dark into our hands. So we leave a nice pussy print in the middle of the Bible, let it dry, then put the book mark to the place so when they pick it up they'll open it to the right page. Later in the van T. said it was a wrong move. They could turn it in to the police and the police would turn it over to the F.B.I. and the F.B.I. keep files of everything. Now there would be an F.B.I. file with her pussy print. But when we told C. he laughed and thought it was the funniest most wonderful thing he had ever heard, and for several months after that when all us girls at the ranch had our period we'd make pussy prints and send them to our boyfriends and girlfriends, and we compared prints. It was like a contest to find the weirdest print. Sadie of course had the weirdest print. C. awarded her the prize. He said her pussy print was the Rorschach that shows the Devil in bats.

But creepy crawling is only training. We all knew it was from the beginning. But only C. knows what the larger plan is. He only tells us a little at a time, though he keeps giving us the whole philosophy all the time, C. stresses it over and over until everyone not only knows it both awake and sound alseep but it is like something that is in us, it is our bones, it has taken the place of our bones and blood. This is why some of us are of the opinion that we are C. When we sit down to look out a window or to just sit, we find our minds sliding down like little metal filings to clickety-click to a magnet and C. is the magnet. C. is the philosophy. It is C. is. C. is *is*, if you get what I mean. We can't say what the philosophy is in what you would understand. That's not my fault that's *your* fault. *We* know. Words aren't necessary. None of that matters. Just open your mouth, whatever comes out that is what is. Yes and no are the same. When we think or when we close our eyes or when we ride in the van and look out across the desert we see C. Sometimes I feel my face, I go and look in the peephole of the painted mirror and squeeze the cheeks and the flesh that move so loosely under my fingers, and under my face is C.'s face.

The larger plan is coming, we all know it, we can feel it in our faces, a numbness, something coming up inside us. We have stopped talking. We wait, watching C. move around the ranch. He is restless, angry. Little, hunched, his eyes so small they aren't eyes at all but black light, glints that come up from Hell.

He takes T. aside, and Sadie, and three of us others. The rest sit along the walls of the big open room of the ranch house, their skirts pulled down over their knees and down to the floor, silent, watching and listening like little lady gargoyles, as C. explains what T. and Sadie and we are going to do. The planning takes days and nights and then a week and it runs into two weeks. T and Sadie and the three others of us follow C. around everywhere, and sometimes when T. or Sadie or one of us wakes up in the middle of the night C. is leaning down whispering already before we're awake, his beard brushing our cheeks as he whispers *if when you get there there's more than what we thought, what are you going to do then, you hold back and wait and see how many's there before you go in, see, so there's no surprises, but the more there are the better it is, that's why I'm doing it, see?* yes we see, we know it all by heart, we're doing it over and over all day long with C., C. gives T. a new knife, one which none of us has ever seen before, a bowie at least a foot long it looks even longer. There's silence as C. gives it to T., everyone grooves on it, we're all there, it's night and we've been listening to C. play the guitar and sing and now he gives T. the bowie and everyone watches and holds their breath. We all know this is it. It's very spooky just thinking about it. Each night we all ride in the van and go through the gate and stop at the little house down by the gate and we imagine we sit in the van and watch T. go up to the gate house and go in without knocking, no need to creepy crawl this night . . . .
Even those who won't be going dream about it every night and it's worse as we imagine it than it ever could be when T.

and Sadie and the others actually do it. And who knows maybe the whole thing is just a trip that C. is taking us on. There are all kinds of knowing, as C. has told us a zillion times. It means what you think and dream is what you do. What's out here, the ranch, the fire, the guitar, all these faces that look just alike, all this is not real except in the head of C. as he imagines it. We are all of us in his mind and nowhere else. It's the greatest trip imaginable.

K.

These "writers" hire expensive automobiles, drive onto the campus, perform coyly, inappropriately, smugly, in interviews with deans, and are hired to teach courses in "The Modern Sensibility" and such. One may, and often does, slip down the darkening corridors late in the afternoon (for that is when these individuals prefer to "teach" their "courses") and in passing the classroom (he never closes the door, implying "I have nothing to hide!" and, even more arrogantly, "Stop and listen—learn something!") one catches snippets of "earnest dialogue," for these classes are never lectures— how, after all, could lectures be delivered on a non-subject? Moreover, or haven't you heard?—the lecture is dead! Along with God, etc. One presumes God is somewhere delivering a lecture on etc. The universe does not listen.

But come, the room is down this hall. Late afternoon. It is in fact the last day of the semester . . . .

Well, what a surprise. 'K. is conducting his class. One would have thought K. had already left for California where, rumor has it, he plans to spend his summer, hobnobbing with Hollywood types, "doing" a film script, and exploring the California "scene." And, we must assume, he will inevitably do a "book" on the subject.

Let's stand here around the corner from the door. Very difficult to understand his accent. It's rather odd the students don't complain, except they never complain about what they

don't understand. So they listen all semester and don't understand a word, but wouldn't under threat of death admit it . . . .
    What's that—he's onto death again! He's obsessed with
the subject! And . . . yes, it's *murder* he's talking about!
Not only does he write book after book about the most
gruesome matters, but he drags his preoccupations into the
classroom where he pours the noxious potion into the students' sleeping ears—(Quote here precisely the lines from
Hamlet.) A few years ago it would have been so easy to get
him fired. But now the administration is powerless. Think of
the furor! The students would rise up like locusts. But fact
could be marshaled, powerful facts that in a fair fight would
crush K. Shrinks could testify that he is obviously, surely,
purely mad: his works, his teaching, his suspicious behavior
prove it unequivocally. Not only could he be fired, he could
be locked away for observation. There, in solitary, somewhere in the bowels of an institution, he could "rap" . . . .
    K. helps a young man find his way out of a long-winded
and increasingly hazy point concerning isolation, paranoia,
and murder, and the class gets back to Jung's discussion in his
memoirs of angels as entities who, when they appear in the
wrong time and place, cause cataclysms.
    A young woman, who sits opposite K. at the table and
who hasn't spoken throughout the semester and won't speak
on this last day either, sits thinking of the isolation of the
terrible heroes of K.'s books. They act in vacuums, worlds
that don't exist, where the gray settings sink into the gray
hearts of the characters. She has read and re-read his books
so many times this semester she believes she at last knows
K. *I have entered his fantasy*, she wrote in her journal. (K.
assigned them to keep a daily journal; he would glance over
them at the end of the semester, he said, though this is the last
meeting and he hasn't mentioned them again; will he call for
them? will he actually read them?—no, she is certain he won't,
he won't even call for them to be handed in, he has forgotten
he made the assignment. But she brought her journal today

just in case, though she has kept it in her book bag so when
he doesn't call for them she won't be embarrassed in front of
the other students.) *I live with the terrible people he puts in
his novels and who are part of him. Some days I cannot
separate the world in his novels from what I see around me.
Which proves his fantasies are the truth.* Her fantasies have
their truth too, as when she idles away thirty or forty minutes
making love to K. in her mind. She has done it three times
this semester; afterwards she took a sleeping pill and floated
away into long complicated novelistic dreams which she
could only vaguely recall in bits and pieces when she woke,
though their mood was distinct. One of these dreams had her
going with K. to California—he had mentioned to the class he
was going there after the semester ended—and the mood of
the dream was terrible. *No,* she said in her dream, *let's not go
to California . . . .*

He is agreeing with the point that the mood of an era
informs the private and solitary acts of the individuals in a
society. A young man, while he is listening to K., is staring at
the young woman who hasn't spoken all semester. Though he
hasn't spoken to her nor she to him, and though he believes
she is stuck up, he is in love with her. Even though it is
clear to him that she is in love with K. It is clear, he thinks,
to everyone because she very innocently doesn't try hiding
it because she very innocently isn't aware that it is showing.
Though I am trying not to, I must come in here to say that
this big tall beautiful girl looks remarkably like Sadie Mae
Glutz who at this moment, out on the ranch in the Panamint
Mountains above Death Valley, is sitting on the slanting back
porch which was ruined one day when some of the guys
tried to drive a dune buggy into the kitchen. Sadie is smoking
a joint and listening—inside the house someone is noisily
frying something on the stove, someone is playing a guitar,
someone is playing a jew's harp, some children, one of them
Sadie's, are playing with wooden blocks wired together
to make a train. Out there on the back porch Sadie believes

she is listening to C.'s voice, just as her look-alike Ms. College-Student -wearing-a-halter-and-cutoffs -and-rubber-thongs-and-that's-all sitting in a seminar room at a big round table, believes she is listening to K. In Ms. College's recent dream, which she is vaguely recalling, she rode slowly down into the smog-filled bowl of Los Angeles. She and K. are going to a house in a canyon, far from other houses, and at that house K. will arrange for wild dogs with huge red dicks to fuck her . . . .

Another girl in K.'s class, one who talks a lot, says that Jung foresaw World War II, for so many of his patients, ordinary little people, were dreaming chaos, people tearing each other apart . . . K. is familiar with this in Jung. He thanks the girl for the substantiation of the idea that the mood of an era informs . . . .

". . . all the ears deformed," someone says in the kitchen. Sadie murmurs, "Far out." She tokes and watches the same sun slowly sinking which slowly sank in that other place, ending the course and the semester, and ending a period of K.'s life and that of his students.

Though not quite. K. doesn't forget the assignment he made about the daily journal! And not one of his students forgot the assignment—they all produce notebooks, some ordinary bookstore notebooks, some more individual, one is a grocery bag full of little pieces of paper covered with writing, this one K. nods at and grins as he hefts it. The girl who looks like Sadie Mae Glutz hands in her notebook, two six by six inch pieces of pine decorated with little blossoms lacquered forever to the wood, drilled with two holes which she made herself with a knife (it took her forever: imagine her bearing down on the handle of the knife and slowly turning the blade back and forth to force the point deeper into the wood; see her face which is the same beautiful face as Sadie Mae Glutz's, who has often imagined her own face and how it looks when C. is eating her, and how her own face will look when she holds in her hand the knife). Inside the journal

which the girl passes to the student next to her and watches
as it moves up the table and finally into K.'s hands, the
margins of the pages are decorated with little drawings, men
and women with flowing seaweed hair, long arms, flowers,
grinning automobiles lying down in grass and giving up. She
watches as K. opens the front board cover and reads the
first page. He looks up directly at her. He has read the
dedication, an unabashed statement of the girl's love for K.
She and K. look at each other in the by now very nearly dark
seminar room, and K. winks.
    She grins a big happy grin.
    K. winked at her!
    Where oh where did K. learn to wink!?
    She will wait a long time before she finds someone to
whom she can tell the story of her seminar with K. and how,
at the end, he looked up and winked at her. The person she
finally finds, who will understand and fully appreciate the
story, is of course the person she knows she loves.
    K. takes all the journals with him and tells the class they
may pick them up next fall. But now—he stands, the great
bundle of their journals, their dreams, their confessions, their
criticisms of the universe, under his arms—but now farewell!
And he is the first out of the room and they hear the sharp
click of his leather heels as he goes down the dark corridor,
on his way to California.

                            Kalifornia
    How important are the facts? K. is famous for blending
his own biographical facts with those of the people he invents: his central characters are intriguingly similar to K.,
coming to the United States from an Eastern European
country which after World War II was closed behind the Iron
Curtain, he later slipped out of that country by clever subter-
fuge . . . . But how much of this is true, one wonders as he
reads the amazing cryptical biographical notes which are as

someone has pointed out the final chapter of K.'s first novel?
Some facts: K. flew cross-country to California. Or he
purchased a new car, or a customized Ford with a Ferrari
engine, and motored across America, stopping along the way
to spend a day here, a day there, digging the American scene.
(He loves Kansas!) Or he rode a Greyhound bus, for the purpose of even more deeply digging the American scene. Or he
rode a train and read three books, eleven essays, and the
journals of his students—and he didn't dig the American
scene one iota, not once looking out the window of his
private compartment; in fact, he pulled the blind on the
window!

At any rate, once he is in California, what are the facts?
We see K. everywhere: he pops up in the backseat of a
day-glo '52 Chevy loaded with teeny-boppers so high on pills
they believe they are on the moon. K. is almost invisible in
the backseat, buried by teeny-boppers: we can see only his
wrinkled brow, his pinched, determined smile-which-isn't-a-
smile . . . . We see him staring coolly through a hassle being
thrown at him by a pimp in front of a club on the Strip called
All Girl Vu. We see him, in black gown and mortar board,
and surrounded by one hundred surly academicians moving
into an auditorium on the campus of U.S.C. . . .

The previously private, almost reclusive K. is now the
ubiquitous K.: we see him poolside at a midnight party. The
youths are naked, some are in bikinis. A group of older
guests haven't taken off their clothes; K. is among these. We
watch K. on t.v., giving interview after interview—for the
California media are abuzz that the famous K. has come to
California. "Are you working on a novel about L.A.?" "What
are your views on modern youth?" "Why are your books so
violent . . .?"

But all this is public. And those first weeks in California
K. does lead a marvelously public life.

But then he retires to the privacy which is so much the
essence of the man. He becomes intensely selective of invita-

tions. He has serious matters to deal with, work to do, special individuals he must see, arrangements to keep of a rather peculiar nature and which we, yearning for the facts, must merely grope for . . . .

One invitation is phoned to him, late in the summer, and the answering service explains that due to the complexity of the message a tape recording of it was made and that K. will have to pay an additional fee for this special service. K. assures the officious woman that he doesn't mind whatsoever paying the additional fee, and encourages her to play the tape for him. It's in Polish! From P., the movie director—K.'s compatriot and friend! K. returns the call—and must pass through the befuddled hands of P.'s answering service which, because of the special nature of the message, put K.'s Polish on a tape recording for P. In this message K. says he will of course come to P.'s the evening of August 9.

As K. accepts the invitation does he feel any shivers down his spine? and later, half-asleep near dawn after a long night's work, does the invitation worry its way through the multitude of details, useless and useful trivia, scraps of ideas and blurs of scenes? Does the invitation keep coming back to K.'s mind with strange urgency . . .?

Of course not. Such things only later are recalled as being immensely important and peculiarly sinister because of their seeming innocence, like timebombs inside the blithe rubber heads of dolls, like *plastique* packed among bags of mutton, beef, and pork, and placed on the top shelf of a refrigerator.

More facts. Other guests who are invited to the party. They are not who you think they are. One is a 35-year-old sculptor whose work hasn't caught on. He comes, leaves, no one seems to notice he was even there. Another: Marti Green, 30ish, tall and slender, married numerous times, a free spirit, mentioned often in columns as a fun person. Paul Vumee, 41, an extremely successful gambler, nimble guitarist, and in recent years the manicurist and "specialist" of an incredible number of people. He, too, is discussed in the columns, as is

Kirstin, the wife of P. She is a singer, a beautiful woman with long blond hair, a strangely somnolent expression which has for several years now mystified men, much to Kirstin's amazement and delight. Is Kirstin pregnant? (Why does that question arise?) No, Kirstin P., formerly Ms. Kirstin Michaels, isn't pregnant.

Suddenly it is the night of the party and we are there. We are the first to arrive. Kirstin opens the door, gives us that sly, sad, rather wistful, rather forlorn smile which could (and perhaps will) someday become her "trademark." We are duly mystified by the smile. Which delights Kirstin, who is not at all self-conscious about her beauty. She laughs easily and often, though never to the point that one feels there-Kirstin-goes-again. It is a light, quick, alert laugh, and, like two or three birds, it accompanies us down the short hall from the front door to the large open living room, where Kirstin offers us drinks, hash, kif, Acapulco Gold, whatever we prefer . . . .

Paul Vumee comes in from the hall which leads into the house, and for a moment we are stunned by the resemblance of Paul to Kirstin and to P., whom we have met before though he isn't here now—and, for that matter, to all the others of this circle. They are blond, fair-skinned, and, yes, beautiful. But the resemblance is so strong it is as if they are all members of the same family, a very successful family which is somehow able to totally self-contain itself, so that its members need never leave their own territory, so to speak, their own homes. . . . Such is great and unusual success that it creates in the outsider(s) an awe and envy which seeks and finds conspiratorial significance in the most innocuous of details.

Paul Vumee speaks quickly, his accent giving a mellifluous lilt to everything he says, causing his meanings to sometimes slip by even those who have known him long enough to know they must listen very closely to him. Paul greets us with a hearty muscular handshake. The pupils of his eyes are tiny.

Seated on the long leather sofa, we tell Kirstin and Paul about our trip out. The usual amusing anecdotes—a highjacking scare at the airport, and later a drunk on the plane who theatened to blow himself up. His finale had been to hold his breath, bulging his beefy red cheeks, his eyes bulging, until with a wet explosion of breath he burst open for air and announced, "Damn. It *never* works."

We drink some J.B./Wild Turkey or we smoke some grass/hash. Kirstin, who isn't drinking or smoking, tell us P. won't be here this evening. He had to rush off to Palm Springs at the last minute. A crisis involving backing for a film. What is the new movie? Discussion of the new movie. Oddly familiar theme and subject matter, which surprises us, for P., like K., is alarmingly original. The new movie—from what Kirstin has been able to piece together from overheard conversations between P. and his writers—has to do with the man who killed all the nurses . . . . what's his name? None of us can remember his name. Anyway, P.'s film will fictionalize it all. That is why she and the rest of us have already forgotten the name of the killer. P. will change what happened. "Will it have a better ending than the reality it's based on?" Kirstin laughs her brilliant soft laugh. She shakes her head. She isn't smiling. "P.'s films are terrible," she says. She has already told him countless times! They are beautiful but terrible. He will not leave behind his childhood in Poland. Ah ha! Undo what happened in Poland, undo the whole war, undo the 6 million, undo the slow and steady grinding in Vietnam, and P.'s movies would be not only terrible, they would be perverse. As they are, though, they present tamed, understated, tastefully subdued vignettes of town and country life . . . . "Richard Speck!"

Then we hear Marti Green's sports car raging along the winding road through the canyon. We stop talking, listen. Paul shakes his head in amazement. The engine revs higher and higher, then the car is suddenly so close we can hear the

squeal of tires as Marti pushes the car through the curves,
taking up every available inch of road surface. "If anyone is
foolish enough to meet me on a curve we're all done for!"
she once shouted to a passenger who what-if'd while riding
with her to P.'s. Doing 60 m.p.h. she hits the narrow chute-like
groove through P.'s stone gate and she immediately stomps
the brakes, shutting down the car to a stop in less distance
than is actually possible.

Kirstin lets in Marti and she greets us with a calmness
approaching remoteness, indifference. This often puts off
people first meeting her. She *is* quite wealthy, eveyone knows
that; and she *is* beautiful, anyone can see that. People often
assume her uncanny calm is old-fashioned superiority. She
wears a see-through blouse, large amber beads. Wonderful
breasts. Black slacks which accentuate her long slender legs.
Our eyes return to her breasts, quite beautiful, with large
nipples. Paul, too, is looking at those breasts. Kirstin, too, is
looking at them. After our helloes, we are all, except Marti
herself, gazing at her breasts. We sit down and Marti accepts
a drink.

"Are we all here?" Paul asks. "K.," Kirstin answers.
"Oh," Marti says. "K." She closes her eyes. "How wonderful
of you," and she rises and goes to Kirstin and kisses her on
the mouth. Kirstin returns the kiss.

Marti paces about and immediately the large room is
filled with her nervousness, though her expression remains
unchanged, and we know that even as she drives her furious
gray Porsche at its top speed in fifth gear which is a true
calibrated 178 m.p.h., Marti has this same expression of
pellucid calm, insufferably otherworldly dignity, a grace too
exquisite for mortals . . . But now she paces about the room.
She is humming! Paul and Kirstin watch; they are grinning.
Paul winks at us.

"Oh," Marti says and turns to us, "what will I *say* to
him?" They laugh, Paul claps his hands. "Oh," Marti says,
and now she too is laughing, "I can't stand it, I just can't

stand it . . . ."

There is music; we all go out to the kitchen and dig into the refrigerator; Paul makes a torpedo; Kirstin puts bean burritos in the oven for Marti and herself . . . . Other guests drop by and stay a while, friends of P. who had hoped to catch him at home: the sculptor mentioned earlier who has no future; a poet who leaves a book P. was interested in reading; Dennis Wilson of the Beach Boys; three or four others who just seem to wander in and wander out again . . . .

The night has slipped by. It is midnight. Past midnight. Kirstin has gone to bed. Paul has gone into her bedroom and given her a massage and then gone across the hall and lain down in his clothes and closed his eyes and slipped off onto a smooth complicated ocean which will incorporate sleep in a form that Paul by now is familiar with and which doesn't bother him in the least. Marti Green and we remain in the living room, talking, listening to music, reading.

Marti goes out to the kitchen. We lie down on the sofa.

Then Marti is standing over us, though we can hear her out in the kitchen, hear her running water to rinse her wine glass, but Marti is leaning over us, we see the outline of her head, we see her arm as we look through our half-closed eyes, we open our eyes wider and see that the woman standing over us is not Marti Green, she is a coarsely beautiful young woman with her hair tied back, her eyes shining, she has a great knife in her hand and in one numb unbelievably calm still endless moment we realize that the young woman is not threatening us with the knife, that she is not leaning down over us but that she is lunging down and that the knife is not poised over us but making its swift movement through the short space between where we see it and our stomach and then we feel the blade, a sensation that is not at all a surprise, and in that long moment we amazingly have time to store away the reaction that, though we have never before been stabbed, the sensation of being stabbed is not in any respect a surprise, that being stabbed feels exactly as we knew it would, no more but certainly no less. The pain goes all the way in. The arm behind the blow—we immediately know and hate that arm, for we know the blade is a thing of great deep pain but the arm, that strong lean arm is the real enemy. We are in that long moment staring into the eyes, of the young woman who has stabbed us, a look that is flat, uncommunicating except in its flatness, or at least that's what we see in her eyes; what she sees in our eyes, no doubt, is predictably surprise, pain, dismay . . . . The look which we exchange with Sadie Mae Glutz lasts long enough for this— "Why? Who are you? What are you doing? You've *stabbed* me!" But there is no intention to discuss on Sadie Mae Glutz's part, and the long moment which has involved so many words here and which involved echoes over several generations much too rapid even to be aware, is brought to an end when the young woman, with both hands, jerks the knife out of our stomach and draws the same long slender powerful arm up over her shoulder and brings it down again, though this time she doesn't have a clear shot at our stomach, for we shoot up our left arm—why the left? because we instinctively know that our right arm, the stronger, must be saved as long as possible, and that the arm that is lifted now will take a wound, as it does, deflecting the knife at the cost of a long slice down the forearm clear to the elbow, cutting down to the bone and shearing off a more perfect slice of flesh than you could ever imagine . . . . now we may stop. This happened but it didn't happen.

We feel our stomach. It is intact, wonderfully intact. Our left arm is intact, not bleeding. We run the fingers of our right hand along the smooth firm flesh of our forearm.

We are safe and alive and none of it happened because K. arrived—shortly after Marti. In fact Marti has the odd sensation of listening to her own arrival of a few pages earlier, the vengeful roaring of a sports car tearing along the winding canyon road.

But this time the roaring sports car doesn't swerve off the

road and come bouncing through the gate—we all listen as it
goes raging on by, we watch its headlights sweep and cut as
the car rounds a curve that takes it off into the night. And we
turn again to the living room . . . . There is K.! He sits at the
end of the sofa in a tweed suit, bow tie, vest, frowning at us
in his best vulpine manner. Kirstin, Paul and we, too, experience a moment of shock that is more than simply shock, it is
close to fear. For a moment we are afraid of him. Then he
smiles that wry, academic, bitter smile and speaks Polish, his
voice rising at the end. Kirstin answers in Polish, and turns to
tell us K. has asked where is the host . . . . Now let's go back
to where we were before the evening became vague and dis-
jointed, and before the uninvited guests glided into the house
like bumblebees descending on blossoms.

An Evening with K.

We assumed he would dominate the conversation. And he
does, at least for a while. He knew Paul Vumee before this
evening but not Marti Green, and not us, though he is so
generous as to say he has read one of our short stories. In
the conversation with Kirstin and Paul he does all the talking,
telling about mutual friends in New York, and updating
Kirstin and Paul on his own doings this summer in California.
Then he asks about them and he is quiet silent and attentive
while they speak. He smiles in a way that is different from
what he uses in his classroom; it is a smile that is almost coy,
arch, as if he doesn't really believe what he is hearing but will
indulge Kirstin and Paul because they are friends. It is the
closest he comes to laughing. When the rest of us laugh at the
stories Paul tells about some of his more famous customers,
and at Kirstin's funny story about her and P. being locked in
a jewel vault at Tres Chic in Hollywood, K. gives the silent
coy smile that purses his lips tightly and twists his mouth
slightly to one side. His black eyes are, though, merry, and
we soon are no longer bothered by his not laughing; we

stop feeling as though he is an adult and we are children . . . .

Kirstin doesn't ask if he will drink or smoke, but goes to the kitchen and returns with a small pot of coffee and a green and golden cup which shows a densely tangled forest. "Ah," K. says, "you haven't forgotten." He lifts the cup and turns it slowly. It is our guess that this cup reminds him of the forests where he spent his childhood, and as Kirstin pours coffee into the cup we believe we hear K. chuckle! A very low, very distant sound that seems to come from the forest on the cup (though maybe he has somehow read our mind and is laughing at us), and he says, very softly, "Indeed," and noisily sips the steaming coffee.

He turns to Marti Green. Kirstin, Paul, and we turn to each other and have our own conversation. K. and Marti, talking quite intently from the very beginning, cross the room after K. finishes his coffee, and stroll out onto the terrace. The three of us in the room pause and look out at them as we would look at young lovers we are chaperoning.

But they are not talking about love. Out the corner of her eye Marti is aware the three of us have stopped talking, paused for a moment, and are staring at her and K. She says to K., again looking into his unblinking black eyes, "But I would need to be more *human* to wait." She pauses to give him an opportunity to respond, to perhaps tell her she doesn't need to be more "human," or to tell her, Yes, Marti, *be* human, give it a try . . . . But he says nothing. She is getting the impression that his manner is something like that of an analyst—intent waiting. It is a manner she has grown to detest. And in that instant she easily proceeds to a quite definite detestation of K. (Don't assume that because she so quickly jumped to this conclusion that it is any the less serious or complete on her part; Marti makes all her decisions with the dreadful ease of a chess wizard. Indeed, Marti plays an excellent game of chess. Later she and K. might discover that they both play chess, and like two wolves who have caught the same scent at the same instant, their heads will lift and they will smile slyly, keenly.) Marti has known a dozen analysts and general shrinks. She is fond of luring them into their poses and drawing from them their performance. Marti is convinced as she talks with K. that soon now *his* performance will begin. She hopes it will at least compare well with that of the famous shrink, Bergen, whom Marti met at a party in Boston a few months before the great man's death at the age of 77; Marti had let the old fellow feast on her . . . She realizes at this point that she is assuming she and K. will spend the night together. It seems the whole evening was set up with that in mind, as if P. weren't here this evening so that K. could spend that much more time with Marti, as if K. had come to California specifically for this purpose, as if Paul and the others had been invited to mask the coming together of K. and Marti . . .

The question still hanging between them is that of whether she should attempt to be more "human" and wait. At last K. informs her that staying alive is no easy proposition, that the ease of her life has apparently given her many pleasant illusions, but that she must never cease being aware that they are illusions and that her relationship to reality is so deliberately ludicrous that her choices and all possible actions which she might perform, including, by now, the act of suicide, are airily remote from what could be in any accurate context with reality considered in any fundamental sense "human."

She takes this as coolly as she would take a 45-degree turn wide-open in second gear of her beady little Porsche. *He is not interested in balling and he won't let me talk about myself.*

"So," she says, "I suppose *you* are more human because of what has happened in *your* life."

"Absolutely not," K. says. "If we are both born humans, we remain humans until we die and our atoms are free to re-group."

"You are playing semantics with me," she says, her voice

rising.

Not at all, he assures her. Any behavior performed by human beings is human behavior. But her suicide would be extravagant and aimless, though characteristic and perfectly appropriate to what she has dedicated her life so far, based upon what she has so openly told him in the last twenty minutes.

She tells him that, like all other men, he is outraged by the fact she is immensely wealthy.

K. shakes his head. Frowning, he says, "I am not interested in your wealth. I do not even know, other than what you have told me, that you are in fact wealthy. The fact or illusion is important to you, though, and it is the basis apparently of what you claim are the alternatives open to you. Conceivably, you are lying about this wealth; perhaps you are lying about your interest in suicide–though I believe you aren't. As to your wealth, I am unconcerned with it other than as its being an element in . . ."

"You talk like a machine."

Turning his back to the glass doors of the terrace, he reaches into his jacket, under his left arm, and slides out a Mauser. He flicks off the safety and offers her the gun.

"You are absurd," she says.

"You were tired of talk."

"Why should I kill myself for your sake, to prove something to you?"

"Then all this has been a hypothetical exercise." He switches on the safety and returns the pistol to its holster. She asks why he carries a gun. He arches his eyebrows as if her question quite surprises him. She asks does he feel insecure without a gun. Does he need two pricks? Why is he afraid?

He lets her finish. She says it all quite coolly, her voice as level as before.

"I am carrying this pistol," he says, "because a band of maniacs might come into this house to kill us."

"What an interesting world you live in, Mr. K.," she says.

She turns and walks from the terrace into the living room. Putting on her leather jacket, she says good-night to Kirstin and Paul, ignoring us as if we are in with K. Kirstin asks why she must leave. "Because I cannot stand to be in the same room with him." She looks at K. who has come into the room.

She leaves, her car roaring furiously as she pushes it through the first sharp curve in a four-wheel drift, her face expressionless, her eyes nearly closed as if dozing off, and she sees the van parked by the side of the road, its lights off and several people looking through the windshield as if in shock, Marti Green's reaction is to briefly muse that if they had left only one second earlier from wherever their starting point was, they would have met her in the curve and that would have been that. Though of course the van wasn't moving; it is parked at the side of the road, its headlights off.

C.

They lie awake listening to him prowl through the house, out the back door and around the side, kicking tin cans, talking out loud to himself. Around to the front porch where he stops and listens to a coyote cry far off. He laughs. They know he has understood, that the coyote has passed on a message to him. Maybe the message was *They are there. Now they are going in* . . . . Or maybe the message was more important. Will he come in and tell them when he knows? Or will he wait until T., Sadie and the others come back? He stops on the front porch and sings. He comes in and they see his body gleaming as he passes the window which he doesn't allow to be covered at night. He is naked. He goes to the window. From here he can see all the way down to the road, ten miles away. Others need binoculars to see the infrequent cars, but he doesn't. Not only can he see the headlights at night, he can tell what kinds of cars they are, or so he says, and he proves it by predicting within a few minutes when one of the dune buggies will reach the ranch. He is seldom wrong. He goes outside again and the rest of them pass into shallow sleep that takes them in the van down the hill up the road to the highway into the city . . . . They wake hearing him running, he is outside running around the house. They hear him panting on the front porch when he stops.

For him this night lasts forever. He has thought ahead to when they return and they have gone over with him again and again what happened, how they did this and how they did that, and each time there are more details, and as he lives it again and again the night lasts forever, the details slowly well up and color the black sky, he sees it all happening again and again, slightly different each time . . . . Time is something they, the others, have. It is their invention but he is outside it. He is here always in this night where coyotes tell him *Now. Again. Again. Be. Go.* The others, they, make clocks. They would put him inside a clock and let it grind and chew him. But they can't touch him! He climbs up onto the roof and masturbates, watching a tiny seemingly motionless point of light on the road over ten miles away.

Inside the house he goes around the large room and counts them. They aren't sleeping. He sees their eyes glinting as he passes by. He walks off a ways into the desert and hunkers down, smoothing his hand over sand, closing his eyes, the sand is cool, with his eyes closed he sees a hand, Sadie's hand, cupped and sliding along a stomach to catch blood running down it . . . . He slowly lies down on his back in the sand and looks up into the motionless sky. God is up there and he grins at God.

Time which is their invention passes as if they willed it to, just as they try to impose their will on all things and all people, and the desert comes up from darkness and there again is the ridge behind the ranch, a line of three cars' lights on the road shrinking farther as do the stars like the eyes of fish which had come to the surface of a pond and stayed hanging. It is day and they haven't come back in the van.

They should have been back by two a.m., three at the latest. He goes into the house. Some of the others are sitting up, whispering, though most of them are still asleep. He looks at the clock which they keep in the store room. It is six o'clock, straight as a long black One. He drops the clock, it bounces, doesn't break.

He goes out and sits on the front porch staring down at the road. Later when he hears them moving around in the house he goes off into the desert.

They don't talk, they wait, going to the window and looking down at the road. This is very bad. What will he do? Someone says he has gone in to town already to do something. Someone says that's crazy. He will have all of them go together with guns and knives. No—and they all know that this is actually what he will do—he will send two of them as usual down to make the garbage run and while they're down there they can find out what happened. Of course they will find out nothing. But that's okay. T. and Sadie and the others are just waiting . . . .

But the day passes, a night, another day, and still they don't return, and still there is nothing in the newspapers O. and R. bring back from the garbage run. T. and Sadie and three others went in to L.A. and just disappeared.

He doesn't talk to anyone. When they ask him a question he stares through them as if they aren't there. He doesn't eat. He doesn't laugh or sing.

Then one morning when they get up they find something on the front porch. He is asleep and they wake him and take him to the front porch and he looks at it. Rolled in a ball, it's about the size of a basketball, immediately he knows what it is—he laughs, a high yipping laugh. Then cuts it off. Looks around the horizon. "Guns," he whispers. They all go into the house, get their guns, load them, for a few minutes the house clatters with the steel snicking of loading.

They bring in the ball off the porch. It is naugahyde, pale, tied with heavy twine. They snip the twine and unroll the ball. There is a debate—it is naugahyde, it is not naugahyde. It is a pelt. It is T. They sit around it, silent. C. doesn't leave the house. He sends out the men to patrol with guns and swords and knives.

But the next morning they find another big pale ball on the front porch. This one is Sadie. The third morning another pelt and so on until all five have returned.

"What's *happening* out there? How could those fuckers *do* this to us?

C. knows. He knows he is being toyed with. Already he sees them on the next morning rising in a ring around the house, steel heads and steel shoulders, black armor, robots that will come straight down onto the ranch. In this dream he is skinned alive, he is certain Sadie and T. and the others were skinned alive, for now that they, all of them out there, are no longer playing civilized they can do anything. In his dream he is fed to rats and burned up and dropped into a big pool of fish and at the bottom of the pool there is a huge man, God, with a gigantic open mouth waiting to chew him up . . . .

They load the truck and in the middle of the night drive off, not down to the road but toward the ridge. At the base of the ridge they drive without lights, a caravan with the first dune buggy mounted with the .50 caliber machine gun, and the truck, in which C. is riding, in the back hiding buried under the bags of beans and flour, proceeds in the middle of the caravan, and at the end of the ridge they turn south and head into the desert toward the silver moon grinning down on them.

K.

K. returns in the fall a week before classes begin. About him there is an unusual spritely energy. His friends are impressed that his summer in California so revitalized him, though he tells them he got little rest in California, in fact he was very busy.

The semester begins. The past is a mutable dream, the facts of the past are no surer than the minds and hands of the present, consciousness is the stutter of phenomena . . . .

THE ATTACK ON SAN CLEMENTE

O'Connor's agent dropped him off at Theodore's restaurant. At his agent's insistence he had put on the black beard, his auburn mane was stuffed up into a gray wig of conservative length, and he was wearing the security suit, as his agent called it, a pocketless blue plastic suit and a paper shirt with a red tie painted on it.

O'Connor was studying Theodore's menu when a large man came over and told him there was a phone call for him.

"This way," he said, and led O'Connor to the men's room where another big fellow was waiting. They introduced themselves as Walt and Ernie, and said they were his transportation.

The three of them sneaked out the back door of the restaurant to a shiny black Volkswagen bus waiting in the alley. After they were on the freeway and heading south, Walt and Ernie confided to O'Connor that they were private dicks and they'd gladly tell where they were taking him, but they didn't know. All O'Connor's agent had told him, when he tricked O'Connor into this damned package deal, was that his client lived in or near L.A., and that he was willing to pay—"I mean like *pay*, man!"

Walt, Ernie and O'Connor stopped at a Jack-in-the Box and bought a big sack of hamburgers and three strawberry shakes, by remarkable coincidence the favorite of all three of them!

They got back up on the freeway and followed the directions which they dug out of the bottom of the sack. They cut off the freeway, backtracked north for a while, south again, then zigzagged back and forth across it, and up and down the streets of beach towns along the way. The directions left them at a gate at the end of a road where three young men in tan uniforms and mirror sunglasses invited O'Connor to step out of the bus. Assuring O'Connor this was part of the plan and everything was all right, Walt and Ernie drove off and one of the guards took O'Connor through the gate into a garden. They passed through a bougainvillaea wall and entered a small side entrance to a Spanish style house. They left O'Connor in a room empty except for a recliner in which he was allowed to doze a while. A man woke him by tickling a nostril with a broomstraw. He introduced himself as Horace Pardee, and said Mr. Nixon was waiting.

The next day while O'Connor was poking through cartons of documents, correspondence, photographs, and scraps of paper covered with indecipherable scribbling, he heard voices from the South Wing carrying on the still air, laughter, then shouting, followed by crashing furniture. Later, Horace Pardee came floating around the corner patting sweat and spittle from his face with a paper towel. Ignoring O'Connor's greeting, he surveyed the mess spread on the table and floor, sighed, and told O'Connor he could use the pay phone in the Press Room if he had to make any outside calls.

Horace Pardee wore a security suit and paper shirt identical to O'Connor's. He was fiftyish, tall thin and very pale, an Anglo Dracula with an arrowhead nose and a neat, straight, lipless mouth.

"Also," Horace Pardee said, "if I were you I wouldn't try anything cute on the phone. It's tapped, of course. For security reasons. Okay?"

"Okay."

"So. How did it go last night?" There was a skeptical slyness in the way he asked, as if it were a loaded question, or as though he expected O'Connor to come forth with a transparent lie.

Last night had gone all right, O'Connor supposed, though how does one judge such things? Mr. Nixon and O'Connor had settled down to get something done. (That was how Mr. Nixon put it, with gruff heartiness: "All right, O'Connor, let's settle down and get something done.") Mr. Nixon had worn a short-sleeved blue, red, and yellow flowered shirt with the tail out, white Bermuda shorts that came just below his knees, and black plastic thongs. O'Connor couldn't help but notice Mr. Nixon's feet. They were nice feet, very shapely feet. The toenails were neatly trimmed and had the soft satiny sheen of a recent pedicure. More than once Mr. Nixon caught O'Connor staring at his feet, and O'Connor could tell by Mr. Nixon's demure expression that he was quite proud of them.

Mr. Nixon paced slowly about the study, his hands clasped behind him as he delivered a long monologue, glancing often at a tape recorder slowly spinning on the desk. He told O'Connor he expected him to take good notes; now and then he looked over O'Connor's shoulder at what he was jotting down. "Even though all I'm doing now at the start is what you might call thinking out loud"—he paused to give his ear a thoughtful tug—"you never can tell. All of this is important, you know. We never know when I might say something, if you get what I mean. Even the little things are important in their way. That's something most people never seem to realize, how even the little things count and have to be taken into consideration. That's what this is all about, to let everyone see how there's always more than what you think."

He talked for about thirty minutes, then stopped and stood gazing out at the garden, its paths dimly lit by knee-high gaslights. "Give your notes to Mrs. Pardee. She'll see that they're typed up," he said without turning, his voice trailing off. Then he went over again some of his points—the need to get straight the general philosophical terms, the scope of everything general that's involved in any situation. "Then we can start breaking it down and putting in the smaller things, the parts that always get overlooked and cast aside but which are so important. Something like this might make a good introduction, you know. But maybe that's what everyone does. But if I don't say something about the general philosophical overview of things, then they won't know how everything else is fitting in. They might think something is wrong, that it's just . . . here and there."

He turned from the window and stared at O'Connor. "I'll be back," he said vaguely and left the study. O'Connor waited, helped himself to the liquor, then went next door to his room.

Horace Pardee nodded at O'Connor's account of the evening. "About your notes and all the rest of this"—he made a dismissive downward waggle with the long fingers of his left hand—"my son Perry types everything up but you're to have nothing to do with him. Is that clear? Give your notes to my wife, Lurla, and she will take it from there.

"Now. Do you want a word of advice?"

O'Connor said he did.

"Listen but don't listen. You know what I'm saying? And don't push—not that I'm implying that you would, but it needs to be said. And if he offers a cigar, politely refuse. Don't interrupt, ever, even when you think he has stopped or completely lost the thread. If there's a word that seems just out of reach, don't hand it to him. That's called prompting— you know what I mean? Don't do it, ever. Not that I think you would do any of that, but a little friendly word of advice never hurt anyone, did it?"

O'Connor agreed, then accepted Horace Pardee's offer of a nice bath.

That became the routine. O'Connor would rise about two or three P.M., wander off to the nearest kitchen where he would breakfast lightly, and spend the rest of the day doing some researching, some catnapping, and some gazing out at the garden.

Mr. Nixon and O'Connor got down to work evenings after Mr. Nixon's guests left and the South Wing was quiet. On the intercom Mr. Nixon would beckon O'Connor to the study and after O'Connor took up his pen and pad, and after the recorder began its slow spin, Mr. Nixon would discuss philosophical general terms. Each night these led more directly and more frequently to lengthy and thorough analyses of the theory of football, with illustrative references to recent games on television which Mr. Nixon would play back from a video tape machine. There were discussions of movies.

Once Mr. Nixon discussed O'Connor's books on the boyhoods of famous generals. O'Connor's own remarks on the books Mr. Nixon seemed to find rather drifty and beside the point, which indeed they were, and several days later Mr. Nixon asked O'Connor to confide in him and admit that he had used a ghost writer to do the child-generals books. O'Connor gladly confided and, going further, said that all his books had been done by subcontracted ghosts. For a moment Mr. Nixon seemed puzzled and almost suspicious. O'Connor allayed this mood by saying, "All my own work, the work I do myself, goes into what I ghost for other people."

"Ah," Mr. Nixon said, slowly nodding. "Now I get it."

A wide range of matters wove in and out, though O'Connor continued taking notes since Mr. Nixon's glance at the pad on O'Connor's lap indicated he was expected to keep jot of it. But after a week or so the note-pad was left behind as their discussions took them deep into the South Wing where they shot some snooker, while continuing discourse, and played some ping-pong, and in a converted greenhouse full of mirrors played a game new to O'Connor.

Mr. Nixon called it darts, though it was unlike any darts O'Connor had played. The game involved motorized wheelchairs, welder's goggles, all the large stationary mirrors and numerous little hand mirrors for defense scattered along the "tracks" through the maze of mirrors, and "stingers," as Mr. Nixon called them—submachine gun-shaped weapons that emitted intense beams of light which popped when they hit their target and stung sharply if that target happened to be human. A shot to an opponent's ear (worth five points) was so intensely painful it usually ended the game. Not infrequently Mr. Nixon and O'Connor were up until dawn, and several daybreaks found them haphazardly chipping onto a practice green adjoining the compound, while security guards moved among the shadows of the palms beyond the sand traps.

Every two or three days Horace Pardee took O'Connor to his own cramped quarters where he was allowed to shower and shave, and Pardee provided him with clean security suits and paper shirts identical to the others. Horace warned O'Connor against lounging around with his mustache off and his hair down. "Don't get me wrong, chum. It's beautiful, truly beautiful," he said, stroking O'Connor's hair. "But if the boss sees it, you're finished."

That same evening, when a hard knock on the wall by O'Connor's head beckoned him to the study, he forgot, of course, to put on the mustache and wig.

"That's it!" Mr. Nixon said, gawking. "I couldn't put my finger on it at first, but you look just like what's-her-name. Are you related to her?"

O'Connor said he wasn't as far as he knew. Mr. Nixon insisted O'Connor leave off the wig and mustache from now on. "Usually I find long hair on a man sissified. But you look so much like . . . oh, you know who I mean . . . ."

"Barbara Walters."

"Right! You look so much like her . . . well, that makes it another matter."

That night they didn't bother with philosophical general terms but talked about actors and actresses and TV personalities. Sitting with O'Connor on a sofa Mr. Nixon called him Clive and said it was okay to call him Dick.

The next morning when O'Connor was sleeping it off, he woke to the abrupt chuffing sound outside of what he took for the report of a gun being fired with a silencer, followed by a ping. He leaned forward but saw nothing unusual in the garden. There was another shot, another ping—and this time O'Connor detected movement in some foliage above which some big white blossoms jiggled nervously. A round gray object bobbed among the flowers, then disappeared. Suddenly a Japanese gardener wearing a helmet jumped up and ran. From next door there were five rapid shots but no pings as the gardener ducked around a hedge. O'Connor went back to sleep and was awakened again by the chuffing sound, which he now recognized as the report of a BB gun, and more pinging. Knowing what to look for, he soon spotted the helmet moving through the flowers as the gardener tried to stay under cover as he did his weeding.

Horace Pardee and a large fellow in a gray suit brought a crate of papers into O'Connor's room. This was Jose, Horace Pardee said, the chief of security. Jose winked at O'Connor. People were always winking at O'Connor, but there was something about this fellow that was vaguely familiar. Perhaps O'Connor had encountered him on one of his deeper penetrations into the bowels of the city. It wasn't until a day or two later, when O'Connor saw Jose rip out the seat of his pants while kneeling down to retrieve a remote-control rat which Dick Nixon had misrouted under a sofa, that he recognized Jose as the guy O'Connor had taken for an agent from Downey, Bollege, Tinkin, and Wu during a dawn raid on his place at the Jardins du Grandiose.

The cartons Jose and Horace Pardee carried in were full of documents, letters, coded notes, and hundreds of telephoto-lens shots of Asians wearing sunglasses, short-sleeved shirts, combat boots, and toting machine guns. Horace Pardee explained that all this material was documentation and substantiation for the memoirs. O'Connor seemed not to have got the point, so Horace Pardee explained that O'Connor was to go through all this stuff, decode what needed decoding, index it, put it in order, learn it by heart, and separate the parts that would be useful as footnotes to the memoirs, from the parts that were too sensitive security-wise.

The next morning when O'Connor tottered forth for another day, soggy from yesterday's work and last night's gin, he heard the steady tapping of a typewriter coming from the cubicle which he had assumed and hoped he would find stonily empty so that he might catch some rest, though waking now and then to leisurely sort through a ream or two of documentation and substantiation, until he would be called out for a conference with Dick and the drink or two that would lead to the real conference that would last into the wee hours. As O'Connor paused outside the cubicle, his hand on the doorknob, he entertained for a moment the eerie sensation that he was already inside, unhungover and hard at work.

Cracking the door, he was further lured into the sense of spying on himself, for at the little desk sat a fellow who, if O'Connor had ever asked himself what he might look like if he could turn himself wrong-side-out to let the actual inner guy come out, roll his sleeves up, and sit down at a typewriter, that fellow would look exactly like the narrow, intense, black-haired stiletto of a lad pecking away at the typewriter.

Even when the fellow was clearly aware that O'Connor was standing behind him, he kept typing. Reading over his shoulder, O'Connor saw he was typing from a handwritten account on a yellow legal pad, making some changes, X-outs and adding a word or two along the way—

> and using that pressure, that vantage, I succeeded in keeping it from the press. For I knew they would choose to misconstrue, going for the wrong meanings, the wrong values, going

for inflaming the folks out there in the public body with my heroism. I can almost see the headlines now: *Nixon saves Girl Scouts from Crazed Zoo Ape Attack.* There would be photos, even, I'm sure of it, though there were no photographers present, thank God. But the press corps would somehow come up with half a dozen pictures, half of them staged, like that phony shot of Mao swimming, and claim they were authentic snapshots taken by visitors to the zoo, tourists from out of town who happened to be passing by when the ape scrambled up the wall of the moat surrounding the ape grounds or whatever it's called, straight for the Girl Scout troop that was standing there looking down at him, and there would be the photos, embarrassing to a modest, fundamentally self-effacing person such as myself, of the President, who had sneaked off from his Secret Service bodyguards for a moment of privacy, some solitude and meditation in the zoo, taking a stand between the screaming little girls and the ape, frothing, enraged, *crazed*—there's no other word for it. I cannot imagine what provoked the ape to such fury, unless the girls had unintentionally, innocently done something to give the ape the wrong impression. And there would have been two or three shots of the struggle between Man and Beast, taken from angles that would have shown my face in dynamic profile and

O'Connor tiptoed out, shutting the door behind him. He started around the house and met Mrs. Pardee wearing another of her daringly short skirts, this one a shiny green with taunting little yellow flowers. Her brilliantly red hair was titilated and frilled into hundreds of excited little curls. O'Connor had met her a couple of times and found her perversely attractive. In spite of himself, and in spite of all signs and signals which Lurla Pardee so directly blared his way, he found the fiftyish, severe woman almost painfully interesting. I can sure pick 'em, O'Connor told himself for the thousandth time, and put on a friendly expression—not too lovestruck, he hoped.

"Where are you going?" Lurla Pardee said, her gray eyes twitchless and level as a hawk's.

O'Connor explained that Dick had apparently replaced

him with another ghost. "He's back there working away like the blazes," O'Connor said.

"Oh," Mrs. Pardee said. "You mean the young novelist, Mr. Coover. He's Mr. Nixon's guest."

"Oh. Then he's not on the payroll?"

"I really don't think that concerns you, but I don't suppose it will hurt if I tell you he's here doing some special interviews of Mr. Nixon."

"How much is Dick paying him?"

Lurla Pardee arched her brows. "My! Aren't we the inquisitive one this morning!" She cutely, cruelly crinkled up her nose and pursed her lips. "How do you know Mr. Coover isn't paying Mr. Nixon? Had you thought of that?"

Thinking of that, O'Connor went to the kitchen with Lurla Pardee and had some tea and she let him suck up some sloe gin which he found in a broom closet among the wax, Lysol, and ammonia. Feeling worlds better, O'Connor went into a book-lined study and was settling down for a nap when he saw Dick Nixon and young Coover strolling in the garden. Dick was wearing a bright red and white Budweiser sport shirt and Bermuda shorts, and he walked with one hand in his pocket, the other in constant movement as he gestured. He smiled frequently and laughed as he spoke. Coover, in a black turtleneck and scruffy jeans, swaggered along with his hands in his hip pockets. He winced as Dick, distracting him with an upward spiraling of his left hand, jabbed him in the kidneys with his right and laughed. O'Connor decided Coover had been walking with his hands behind him to protect himself from these rabbit punches. But it was hard to outwit Dick.

That evening O'Connor, Dick, and Coover drove down to Dana Point for posada at Rosita's. Dick went around to all the tables and shook hands, and he had Rosita bring drinks for everyone in the house. Then he went back to the kitchen to say hello to Rosita's mother and sister. "They still believe in me," Dick said when he came back and sat down. "The little people have always believed in me and they always will." He took out his handkerchief and blew his nose.

O'Connor and Coover immediately got into an argument. It was a trifling point concerning a line by Gertrude Stein. O'Connor himself never quoted, considering quoters as fundamentally pompous, though he had to hand it to them on memory and their knack for skewing others' ideas into conversation. Anyway, nine times out of ten O'Connor had no idea whether they were quoting correctly, not that he gave a damn, but incredibly on this particular occasion he was familiar with the Stein poem, the one about her meeting Picasso for the first time. O'Connor recalled vividly that it ended with a couple of lines about what history teaches.

"You've got that wrong," O'Connor told Coover.

Coover's black little eyes tightened, he leaned forward, and if O'Connor had been in any other place with any other people and had seen that expression, he would have grabbed the nearest object to defend himself against the knife that was surely on its way out of the little rat's boot. "It goes like this," O'Connor said. "'This is what history teaches: history teaches and preaches.' The way you said it, 'history teaches, history teaches,' doesn't make much sense."

Dick Nixon agreed with O'Connor that it didn't make much sense. "It's what I'd call a redundancy," Dick said. "But with preaches in it, it makes pretty good sense."

"But," Coover said, his voice very low, "the poem ends with 'History teaches.'"

"Tell me, Bobby," Dick said, "are you sure you saw the final version of that poem?"

Coover thought a moment before he spoke. "What do you mean?"

"I mean writers are always going back and changing what they write. Surely you know what I'm talking about—you probably do some rewriting yourself."

"No," Coover said, shaking his head with a jerk, "I get it right the first time."

"I do too," O'Connor said and smiled sharply at him.

"Right the first time, every time."

"But most writers," Dick said, "do lots of changing. I know *I* do. All my speeches—lots of rewriting. When I was writing *Six Crises*, why I made all kinds of changes as I went along. A writer *has* to change things, I mean the wording and this and that. A writer who doesn't take advantage of the prerogatives to change things, well, he just isn't taking advantage of things."

"I agree wholeheartedly," O'Connor said. "Come to think of it, I seem to recall that Gertrude Stein kept going back and changing her work, sometimes for the better, usually the other direction."

"You're thinking of someone else," Coover said, pushing back his chair, turning, and staring across the restaurant.

"You know," Dick said, laying his hand on O'Connor's arm and leaning toward him, "I just this minute had a very interesting idea. Excuse me, gentlemen." He hurried across to the pay phone up by the pinball machines.

Coover looked at O'Connor out the corner of his eyes. "Just who the fuck are you?"

"Mr. Coover, I am the single girl who wrote Helen Gurley Brown's *Sex and the Single Girl,* and I'm the naked dude who finished Norman Mailer's *The Naked and the Dud* for him, and I'm the Humbert who drove home the bolt of every other chapter of Saul Bellow's *Humboldt's Gift,* and the nouveau noir who wrote every other sentence of *Roots.* I authored *The Towering Inferno,* the remake of *King Kong, Star Wars,* and believe it or not, while William Faulkner was out to lunch at Random House I wrote like crazy and piled up a stack of manuscript by his typewriter so when he came back he thought he had written *A Fable.* But my most satisfying feat was that I was the fourth-echelon editor at Doubleday who rejected the manuscript of your baseball book by running it through a paper-shredder!"

"Why, I know who you are." For a moment Coover's face twisted up horribly. "Now I know," he whispered,

leaning slightly forward as if to get an even better look at
O'Connor. He spoke again, mumbled, too low for O'Connor
to hear.

But what he said caused O'Connor to lean forward until
their faces were close. "Who knows what evil lurks in the
hearts of men," O'Connor whispered. "The *Shadow* knows."

Coover's twisted-up expression slipped down and off. His
face relaxed strangely, went quite blank, as if he had completely left. He rose and walked over to Dick Nixon. Dick
covered the mouthpiece of the phone, nodded as Coover
whispered in his ear, looking over at O'Connor. Dick nodded,
patted Coover's shoulder, and called, "Later, Bobby," as
Coover walked through the cafe, glancing at O'Connor with
a completely blank expression.

Rosita brought the posada and chorritos. "Will Señora's
little boy be coming back?" she said."

"No," O'Connor said, "but leave his plate. I'm ravenous."

"Very honored," she said with a curtsey. "I'm Rosita."

Dick came from the phone rubbing his hands together.
"Ah. Posada and chorritos." He took Rosita's thick little
hand and kissed it, getting a smear of grease on his chin.
"Best posada and chorritos in town."

They ate a while, then Dick leaned over to O'Connor and
whispered, "Great idea. The one, you know, my idea about
rewriting? *Wonderful* idea. You know, I get my best ideas
when I'm around you imaginative types. Looking back . . .
Well, anyway, I just put in a call to Boops Rink. Do you
know Boops?"

"I've met her."

"Wonderful girl. Just wonderful. She's going to help us
on this with some of the actors in her agency. We'll get cooking on it tomorrow!" He rubbed his hands together. "Bobby
will have cooled off by then." He leaned over and nudged
O'Connor in the rib. "You know what that little shit told
me? He said you're a Democrat."

"That's a filthy lie," O'Connor said sincerely: he was an

Eisenhower Republican.

"I know, I know. He just said it because he's jealous because I picked you to be the head ghost on the memoirs and because you caught him misquoting Gertrude Stein. But he'll be happy when I let him in on this next thing. In fact we'll have to put aside the memoirs for a while."

O'Connor sighed deeply.

"I know, that's frustrating to a writer. You like to stick with something till it's finished and all that. But this new thing is going to take all we have."

"What exactly is this new thing? I mean, I hate to bring up such matters, but . . . well, can I shoot straight with you, Dick?"

"By all means."

"Well, I was contracted to do your memoirs. My publisher said there might be other areas involved, but he was vague about the arrangements and how the terms would be negotiated."

"Let me put it this way," Dick said and laid his hand on O'Connor's, "have I *ever* done anything to lead you to think I was trying to pull a fast one on you?"

"No," O'Connor said.

"Right, and I never will. You can be sure that you'll do well by me, *very* well, like in the ballpark of something like triple what you're presently contracted for on the memoirs. Do you get me?"

"I get you."

"And how does it sound?"

"It sounds wonderful, that part. But the other part is still a little unclear. I mean, what exactly is the writing . . . ."

"Rewriting."

"What exactly is the rewriting we'll be doing?"

"It will involve a little more than your basic simple rewriting. We'll get to do some acting, too."

"Really? Hm. On the stage?"

Dick chuckled, then laughed. And harder. He laughed so

hard his face turned red and his eyes watered. He put his hand to his face. When the laughing subsided, he winked at O'Connor and said, "What's amazing about you writers and artistic types is that you're so goddamned imaginative but you can't put together how to *use* something. No, we're not going to do this on the stage. We're going to do it on tape!"

The next day they went to the golf course on the Marine base at El Toro. While Dick waited for the men he was going to play with, he knocked some practice balls off a tee. O'Connor and Jose watched and offered some advice. Jose said Dick was looking up. O'Connor thought that wasn't so much the problem as a little dip that Dick gave on his down-swing. "I do that when I want to slice," Dick said. "Look." He did the little dip on his down-swing and sliced again.

"How do you keep from slicing?" O'Connor said.

"I turn the club like this." He turned the head of the club, drew back, started his swing, gave his little dip, and looked up before he had even hit the ball. The shot took off like a low-inside drive down the third-base line, then lifted, bending in a hook, but then corrected itself, straightening over the fairway, then warped around to the right into an even more severe slice than the others.

"Gee," Jose said. "That was some of everything."

"Hey, O'Connor!" It was Coover up at the clubhouse, yelling from the terrace outside the bar. "There's a long distance call for you."

"You go with him, Jose," Dick said, "show him where the phone is."

Jose accompanied O'Connor up the lawn. On the terrace Coover was having a large Bloody Mary. "Sounds like trouble, old fellow," he said, slapping O'Connor on the shoulder as he went by. "Too bad for you."

Inside, Jose ducked through a side door behind the

bar. O'Connor picked up the phone and waited for the
click of the extension being picked up before he said, "Hello.
O'Connor here."

"Clive! Do you know who this is?"

"Yes, I think so." It was his agent, Auric Twant.

"How wonderful! And how are things going down there?"

"Things are going just fine."

"I'm so happy to hear that. Say, I bet you don't know
where I am."

"You're right."

"Guess."

"I have no idea."

"Try a guess, anyway."

"You're in New York."

He laughed. "You're *cold*. Guess again."

"I have no idea."

"You've got to guess again or I won't tell you why I
called and it's *very* important."

"You're in Boston."

"No."

"Philadelphia. Baltimore. Norfolk. Charleston. Jackson-
ville. Miami . . . ."

"No, but you're getting warmer!"

"Havana. Rio de Janeiro. Montevideo . . . ."

"Sao Paulo," Jose mumbled.

"Who's that?" Auric Twant said. "Clive, are you still
there?"

"I'm still here. That was just some interference. Listen,
Twant, I must get back to work. So good-bye."

"But you haven't guessed where I am and if you don't
guess I'll not tell you the important news I have about you-
know-who."

"Who?" Jose said.

"*You* know." A pause, then, "Clive, who *is* that?"

"It's no one, Twant. Just tell me why you called."

"I called to tell you that our plans might be changing

momentarily, so finish off there and be ready to jump on a plane and fly south."

"You've got it all wrong, I'm afraid," O'Connor said. "I won't be finishing off here for a long, long time. It looks like there's more work here than we expected."

"Like how much?"

"Like I think I'll probably not get away from here for five or six years, maybe longer."

"*What?!*"

"That's right. This is some package deal you got me into."

"But six years isn't in the contract. Why, that's out-*rageous!*"

Coover put his arm around O'Connor's waist and whispered in his other ear, "They're ready for you."

O'Connor covered the phone. "Tell them I'll be right there."

Twant was saying you-know-who was going to be in Key West doing some water-skiing and it looked like there was a good chance for O'Connor to pop into the picture. Coover was sliding his hand up and down O'Connor's ribs and blowing in his ear.

"Cut that out!" Dick Nixon yelled from the terrace door. He lifted his nine iron and came charging. Coover ducked away and Dick chased him down the bar and out the front door.

Dick came back—O'Connor had hung up on Twant—shaking his head and apologizing to O'Connor. "That little sneaking faggot. I'm sorry that had to happen, Clive. If I'd known he was a sneaking little fag I'd never have brought him in to work with you. Why, who would have thought of it!"

Dick put his arm on O'Connor's shoulders and they went out of the bar and down the lawn.

The men O'Connor and Dick were going to play with were large Italian twins. They wore white silk shirts and black trousers and black and white golf shoes. Their bodyguards were slender young wasps in three-piece suits and crisp straw hats with feathers in the crowns. One of them carried what looked like a clarinet case; the other carried what looked like a trombone case.

As soon as Dick's friends saw O'Connor their eyes lit up, but when Dick introduced him to them, they squinted and got crudely suspicious looks on their faces. "Hey, Dick," one of them, O'Connor didn't quite get the name, it sounded like Guido Montefeltro, said and cocked his head to the side, "you're putting us on, eh? This here's Barbara Walters, eh?"

Dick laughed heartily. "That's what everyone says—isn't it, O'Connor?"

O'Connor said it was indeed what everyone said.

"This is Clive O'Connor, the famous writer," Dick said.

"Oh." Guido and the other one—Giuseppe?—nodded with due respect and suspicion.

Dick teed off, slicing viciously off onto the green of Number Eighteen. His second ball was another slice and stopped within three feet of the first. Guido hooked into an arroyo. Giuseppe sliced powerfully beyond Eighteen, beyond a row of trees, and beyond the road to the golf course. O'Connor hit his ball straight down the fairway about thirty yards.

"Hey, Barbara," Guido said as he and his brother and the bodyguards piled onto their cart, "nice shot, but put more meat into it." Giuseppe said something in Italian and Guido and the bodyguards had a good snigger as they drove off.

Driving his cart en route to his balls on the Number Eighteen green, Dick asked O'Connor who that was on the phone from South America. O'Connor told him it was Auric Twant.

"Nice boy, that Twant. Has lots of good ideas and he knows how to set things in motion. That's what I like." He waved to the players on the Eighteenth fairway who had stopped their carts well back to let him play. "I'd like to put him on my payroll, but he's got his own projects going. He'll go far, I'm sure. What would you use here, a two iron or a driver?"

O'Connor said it was a hard decision. Dick got out and using the driver scooped a great hole in the green. Glancing over his shoulder as he picked up the divot to replace it, he saw that a hillock on the fairway-side of the green concealed the green from the players waiting down the way. Winking at O'Connor, he packed the divot into the cup and spiked the Number 18 flag into the divot he had made. "Come on," he said, hopping into the cart, "let's get the hell out of here!"

Guido Montefeltro, Giuseppe, and their slender young bodyguards exposed themselves to O'Connor in a bunker back of the Number Nine green. He should have seen it coming, but nonetheless it surprised him. He had hit into the same sand trap where Giuseppe was already stuck, whacking away with his nine iron trying to get out. Guido, seeing O'Connor knock into the sand, picked up his ball while Dick Nixon was looking the other way, and threw it into the same trap. The four men stood in a row facing O'Connor, making water into four rings in the sand.

"How do you like our action?" Guido said. "You think you could get us on TV?"

"I bet those network guys got nothing like this, eh?" Giuseppe said.

"Well?" Guido said. "Whadda ya say? Which one of us you want? Giuseppe or me? These other two jack-offs don't count."

"Gentlemen," O'Connor said, "please put those away and let us finish our game of golf."

"Aw, come on, Ms. Walters," Giuseppe whined, quickly putting his away. "Guido is a slob." He hit Guido hard in the stomach, knocking a grunt and a sharp laugh out of him. "This wasn't my idea. I'm ashamed of myself and these guys, really I am. Let me make it up to you tonight, okay? A nice dinner, some dancing, none of this crude shit, okay?"

On Number Fifteen. O'Connor and Guido Montefeltro were in the rough together. "Hey, Barbara," Guido said. "Just between you and me, tell me about Nixon. You're the first woman I've ever known him to mess around with. I mean, Lurla Pardee's just like one of the guys, if you know what I mean. But I mean a real woman like you, you're the first. You must be really tops. So tell me, what gives with Dick?"

"He's a real man."

"Yeah? Hm." He scratched his head. "I don't know how to ask this, but . . . well, like a *man* how is he? I mean you seen Giuseppe and me back there, and for that I must say I am very much ashamed of myself and that rotten Giuseppe, but now that you seen us you *know* us, if you get what I mean. So how does Dick Nixon, you know, compare?"

"I've seen few horses with prongs as big as Dick Nixon's."

Guido's mouth fell open. "God's truth?"

"God's truth."

Guido shook his head. "Well, that just goes to show, you never can tell."

"There's only one problem."

"Problem?"

"It's too big for his own good."

"How could that be?"

"It's so big that when it's up, Nixon's down. All the blood rushes to it and Dick passes out."

"My God! I've never heard of such a thing."

Guido's game was off the rest of the round. In fact, he picked up his ball and didn't play the last three holes, riding in his cart with the bodyguards. Riding back to the compound, Dick Nixon asked if O'Connor had any idea why Guido turned sour. "He wouldn't speak to me the last three or four holes," Dick said.

O'Connor said he had no idea.

Dick sighed. "Well, I guess that shoots our hopes of getting their backing."

"Backing for what?" O'Connor felt a surge of anxiety stronger than any adrenalin.

"A little something I have cooking on the back burner. I'm sure we could drum up some interest in a film."

"A what?"

"You know—a movie. I think it's a swell idea. You know, give the other side, the unknown side. It could come out about the same time we release the tapes. Think of that! First—wham! the tapes. Then—bam bam! the movie."

Dick leaned forward and had Jose hand him the telephone from the front seat. "Do you know David Frost, O'Connor?"

"Sure," O'Connor said limply. "Everyone knows David Frost."

"I think David just might be interested in a deal like this, don't you?"

He placed the call but had to wait for a line to London. "Drive around, Jose," Dick said. "I like to be on the move when I'm setting up a deal." He leaned back, the phone in his lap, and put his arm on the back of the seat behind O'Connor. "You know," he said, turning to O'Connor and smiling, his eyes set and a little watery from the whiskey after the golf, "I think our relationship is going to be very nice." He gave O'Connor's shoulder a little squeeze. "What do you say?"

In the rear view mirror O'Connor saw Jose staring at him. He gave O'Connor a big slow wink and mashed down on the gas, the limo surging past car after car on the fast lane to L.A.

O'Connor was sleeping, more or less, in the game room when he became aware of the presence of something in the darkness, a slow movement of shadows pushing across the floor in that portion of the room not lit by the moon. Maybe it's death, O'Connor mused, and gave a slow sigh.

Earlier he had decided to leave Casa Pacifica—this after realizing that if all went according to plans, he would probably never be able to walk out the door in broad daylight.

But when he looked for his shoes and blue plastic security suit, everything was gone.

That stunned him—and angered him. But he wouldn't be held against his will! If he had to, he would hitchhike on the freeway in his BVDs. He was slipping down the hall toward the kitchen with the thought in mind that the best escape route was out the back door, when none other than Dick Nixon himself popped around the corner.

"Oh. Clive!. Well, how lucky. I was just thinking a while ago. You know if *Vengeance Is Mine* does even half-way decently at the box office, we ought to start up a movie company. Really plunge in. Do the whole thing. I have lots of ideas. Come to think of it, I had an idea about a movie about these kids who live on the beach. You know? No hippies or anything crappy like that, but these really decent, beautiful kids who live in the sun. I was thinking of the young man as someone like Troy Donahue or what's his name, that good-looking blue-eyed Jew. Paul . . . ."

"Paul Newman?"

"Right. He would be the star and there would be this really nice girl for him to meet and they could fall in love. You know the public wants things like that. Wholesome. And interesting, too. There could be lots of interesting things to work into something like that, don't you think?"

O'Connor had told Dick he thought it was a basically sound idea though there were some problems here and there, and he got away from him as quickly as possible.

He tried sneaking out the back way, but a security guard popped up out of a rose bush, the floodlights came on, and in seconds flat there was Jose with what O'Connor ridiculously thought was Dick Nixon's BB gun, until he saw that it had a long clip hanging down below it like a big black schlong.

"Hey, man, take it cool, you know?" Jose said as he led O'Connor back into the house. "You want to take a stroll in the evening, you do it inside the house. That's a good place, you know? Okay?"

So O'Connor had sat in the game room trying to resign himself, as the old saying goes, and marveling at what an inane concept that was, to *resign* oneself, how impossible, how utterly intolerable . . . when he became aware that a wide section of the floor unlit by the moon seemed to be lumpily moving toward him. I am asleep, O'Connor told himself, and this is what happens to the world around us when we resign ourselves. But he knew he wasn't asleep. Those lumps, that movement, were real.

O'Connor. It came up from the darkness, maybe from the darkness inside O'Connor, less than a whisper, maybe it was the beginning of the murmur of conscience which O'Connor had read so much about, his poor secret inner self was going to ask if he could hide in O'Connor's closet. . . .

"Psst. Come down here," the lump of darkness whispered —and O'Connor recognized Coover's voice!

"Coover! I thought you had got kicked out!"

"Shh. I got kicked out but he changed his mind. Come down here. We've got to stay low."

O'Connor got down on his hands and knees. "This is worse than I thought," Coover said. "Do you know how bad it is?"

"It's pretty bad. Yes. I've known that all along. But what exactly are you talking about?"

"I'm talking about him. He's got us by the nuts with both hands. Tonight I told him I was leaving and he told me I wasn't. He's got the idea he can tell us what to do."

"He's given Jose the same idea."

"And the rest of them, too. Was that you out there a while ago?" Coover asked.

"Yes."

"How far did you get?"

"To the end of the garden."

"Is that all? Christ. Maybe if we set up some kind of diversion on the other side of the compound, a fire or something, then I could go through the garden and out that way."

"I'll go with you."

"You're giving up?"

"Yes."

"Good. Then you can do the diversion. Start the fire. It doesn't need to be anything big, just wad up some newspapers . . . ."

He broke off when they saw through the patio doors a figure moving up from the hedge bordering the garden. All in black, he came up onto the terrace and to the doors. Nixon! No—the man was too large, a very large man, over six-foot-five, with a huge chest and square shoulders. But the head and face were Nixon's. The man was one of Jose's security guards wearing a rubber Nixon mask! He cupped his hands to the patio doors and looked in, then turned and passed across the terrace and out of sight.

"At night they all wear Nixon masks," Coover said. "Okay. So get newspapers and wad them up . . . ."

"There are no newspapers here."

"No problem." He slithered across the floor to a bookcase and came with some books. "Rip these up, wad 'em up, put it all in a waste can, soak it with lighter fluid—there's a can in the drawer by the sink—then light the paper and throw the whole can onto the roof of the garage."

"That won't make much of a fire."

"So what? It'll be enough to get Jose and the others to come around to that side of the house for a look. It'll give us a minute or two, that's all we'll need. Okay?"

"Okay."

The luminous face of a watch appeared before O'Connor. "It's a quarter past two now," Coover said. "Go out and throw the can on the roof at exactly fifteen till three. Use the clock in the kitchen stove, I've synchronized my watch with it."

In the dark Coover reached out and found one of O'Connor's shoulders. He gave it a squeeze. Then Coover was gone.

O'Connor went out to the kitchen with the books and sitting down at the table began ripping out pages and wadding them up. He found the lighter fluid in the drawer where Coover said it would be. He doused the pages and looked at the clock in the stove. He had only a few minutes to spare. He went out the back door. The night was immensely silent. He tiptoed down the flagstone path to the garage, counted ten, then struck a match and dropped it into the can. A tame blue flame hovered over the wadded pages. Maybe they would burst into raging yellow flame when they hit the air and scattered. O'Connor heaved the trash can onto the gargage roof and high-tailed it back inside. He had just shut the door and was by the sink when a Nixon entered by the hall door. This was the real Dick Nixon, O'Connor believed; he was in pajamas. "Oh. Hi, Clive. You still up?" He got a glass out of the cabinet and went to the refrigerator. "I like some buttermilk when I wake up in the middle of the night. Care to join me?"

"Thanks, Dick, but I believe I'd better hit the sack."

"A little buttermilk will make you sleep like a top."

"Well . . . all right."

Turning from the refrigerator, Dick glanced out the window. "Look at that! Looks like Saint Elmo's fire." He went to the sink and leaned forward. "Say," he whispered, "what if it's a UFO . . .?"

From the other side of the house, outside, they heard muffled yelling, then a sharp whap as something struck the house by the kitchen window. "Down!" Dick said and squatted with the buttermilk tucked in close. O'Connor, too, recognized the sound of ricochets clanking stone out by the garage.

"Jesus Christ," Dick whispered, grabbing O'Connor's arm with a tight grip. "UFOs. We're under attack! Follow me." He yanked O'Connor in the direction of the hall door. They went on their hands and knees. Outside, people were running.

"Run for it!" Dick said when they reached the darkness of the inside corridor. O'Connor got to his feet and ran after Dick down the hall and into Dick's quarters. Dick slammed the door after him, locked it with three big bolts that banged into place steel on steel, then he ran across to the windows, threw a switch, and a steel shutter slammed down with a deafening clang.

Dick then switched on a light, ran to his dresser drawers, and fumbled with some keys to a bottom drawer. A bullet struck the steel shutter. "Oh Christ," Dick muttered. "Sweet Christ this is *it,* this is *it* . . . ."

From the drawer he took a machine gun and a steel helmet. "Bring that one," he pointed to another helmet in the drawer. O'Connor picked it up and put it on. "Take that off your head!" he shouted. O'Connor took it off. "Follow me."

O'Connor followed him across the room to a large leather sofa. Dick flung aside the cushions and lifted a steel trap door where the springs should have been. "Come on." He went headfirst down the hole.

They emerged in Mrs. Nixon's room. She had closed her shutters, too, but she was working at her drawing board, a cup of coffee on the little stand beside her, and smoking a meerschaum pipe. "What is it this time?" she said.

"The UFOs are here!" Dick yelled.

"The UFOs?" Then—"What's he doing here?"—frowning at O'Connor.

"Clive and I saw them land," Dick said.

"How many are there?" Mrs. Nixon said.

Dick looked at O'Connor. "How many would you say?"

O'Connor shrugged. "Two or three at least."

"At least. But who *knows*?" He paced about, gripping the machine gun. "Check the door," he told O'Connor.

O'Connor went over to the door, turned the knob. The door wasn't locked and, moreover, O'Connor unwittingly swung it wide open. There stood a Nixon in black holding a very large, very unusual sort of pistol unlike any O'Connor had ever seen and with which he immediately fell in love.

"Aiieee," the real Dick Nixon yelled behind O'Connor as the other Nixon fell back and out of the door. O'Connor instinctively dived away from the door just as the room erupted with the incredibly loud steady endless head-hammering sound of Dick Nixon's machine gun firing off more rounds per second than O'Connor thought possible, making him wonder, as he lay as flat as he could, his arms over his head, holding his breath, why he, O'Connor, had ever taken such a permanent and long-lasting fancy for small arms when in fact there is nothing equal to fully automatic water-cooled high-caliber weaponry.

Next morning at breakfast Dick told O'Connor that he had fired Coover again, that sneaking little faggot, and that now they could really get down to work. Which O'Connor took to mean that Coover had made his getaway. No mention was made of the UFO attack. The security boys put on overalls and got to work restoring the West Wing, and for three days the tapes had lots of hammering and sawing in the background. "That's all right," Dick said. "We'll use that. Clive, you work in something like some remodelling."

"Sure," O'Connor said, and jotted some notes to the effect that the floor boards in   Lincoln's bedroom were loose.

"Good," Dick said, "very good," and on the tapes, in a conversation with John Dean (played by Jose), Dick commented on the noise in the background and how it was necessary to prevent an international incident. "Why, just think what might happen if some foreign dignitary got a toe pinched off while trying to sleep in Lincoln's bed!"

They were through taping for the day, stopping earlier than usual because they had been hitting the sauce a little too hard. In fact there was a good chance that the last two-thirds of what they had done today would have to be erased and re-done. But Dick believed it was some of the best stuff they had done so far, especially the part where he got out his BB gun and started plinking away at Cato-san out in the garden.

"But I think we're mixing up these tapes," O'Connor said. "You didn't hire Cato-san until you left the White House. People'll listen to these tapes and wonder who that really is out there in the White House garden."

Dick brushed this aside. "That's fine. Let 'em wonder. After all, who knows *what* I had in the garden—right? Anyway, if these tapes are going to, you know, be halfway effective, they're going to have to give the people, the public, ah . . . a sense of feeling that they, that there's . . . ."

"Yes," said Irwin Ott, who was doing Bob Haldeman, "a sense of discovery, revelation."

"Yes," Dick said, "that's it exactly. See, they'll listen to these tapes and they'll hear these little things that they didn't already know about and that'll be something for them. They'll get that, that Bob was talking about."

"The same with the drinking," Irwin Ott Haldeman said as Dick loudly clinked his glass as he poured another drink. "That's already out of the bag, the public's already well aware of that, so when they listen to the tapes and hear that we're drinking they'll be reassured that we're not trying to cover up anything."

"Excellent," Dick said.

"I don't know," said Hugo Halloway who was doing John Erlichman. "I think we're running the risk of some contradictory overlap."

"Well, yes," Dick said. "Hm. I'd thought of that, yes, but that overlap, well, what can you do about that, there's always some overlap no matter what. That will make it seem more . . . authorial, more authentadictive."

"What do you mean about the contradictory factor in the overlap?" Irwin Ott Haldeman asked Hugo Halloway

Erlichman.

"It's a small matter, in my opinion," Dick said.

"I simply mean," Irwin Ott Erlichman said, "that when they check the events of the day on which certain tapes were made, they will find that maybe we weren't talking about what we should have been talking about."

"Why, that's the whole idea!" Dick said. "They think they know every goddamned thing that was going on and this will by God show them that they didn't know anything. That's the main, the whole idea. That's . . . it."

"I see your point," Hugo Halloway Erlichman said.

"And it will be contradictory," Irwin Ott Haldeman said, "especially if the sequences are disarranged."

"They will disarrange everything, it's their penchant for doing everything. They were disarranging before I ever came along, by God."

"That's right," Irwin Ott Haldeman said. "After all, the whole idea is to give the idea that we're playing right into their hands."

"Hm," Hugo Halloway Erlichman said. "Perhaps. Let them think that the jumble and general incoherence is to their advantage, right?"

"Right."

"That's what I intended all along." Dick said. "In fact I think it would be a damned good idea if we had several different tapes made, like you know half a dozen or so, for the same date."

O'Connor groaned, "But that would take forever," he said.

"So what?" Dick said. "We've got all the time in the world. As far as I'm concerned this can go on forever. We'll wear the bastards out. Once we start coming out with these tapes and they get before the public, the public will want more and more."

"That sounds very good," Irwin Ott Haldeman said, "don't you think?" he asked Hugo Halloway Erlichman.

"Yes, and in those various installments of the tapes there could continue to be the overlap."

"Right. And the quality of the overlap being contradictory could be less contradictory than interpretive."

"Of course," Dick said.

"Each new section or installment of the tapes that is released can have several new versions of the tapes made on certain dates that have already been released."

Hugo Halloway Erlichman said, "Comparison, shades of subtle difference . . . ."

"Gross contradictions which would throw into question interpretations and positions which they took when they got their hands on earlier segments . . ."

"Great!" Dick said. "I love it!"

"I can see it now," Irwin Ott Haldeman said. "Dan Rather and Robert Pierpoint and all the others will have to eat their words because their earlier interpretations and pronouncements won't make sense in relationship to the new tapes that are released."

"They'll get into it, too," Hugh Halloway Erlichman said. "The whole thing will run into a continuous re-evaluation and re-analysis and re-interpretation of not only the tapes but their own positions."

"There's a question, though," Irwin Ott Haldeman said, his tone quite unenthusiastic and somber, and the rest of them quickly calmed down. "How can all this *hurt* us?"

"The re-evaluation and re-interpretation . . .?"

"Right. How can that maybe work against us in the long run? We need to consider how they can turn that against us."

"Yes," Dick said. "I was already wondering about that, especially when you mentioned Rather, that dirty little son of a bitch, he'll do anything he can to . . . ."

"They can say we're shamming," Hugo Halloway Erlichman said.

"By shamming," Irwin Ott Haldeman said, "do you mean they could somehow come up with the idea that the overlaps and seeming contradictions, the reviews, the . . . what would you call it . . .?"

"Criss-crossing," Hugo Halloway Erlichman said.

"The criss-crossing was an effort on our part to create an aura or . . . an atmosphere of . . . ."

"Diffusion."

"An atmosphere of diffusion which is aimed at creating in their minds an aura of . . . ."

"An aura of confusion."

"An aura of confusion which would in the end, in the long run, place us in a position of being in, or of seeming to be in, control."

"Yes," Hugo Halloway Erlichman said. "That's what they might think."

"But they're going to think that *anyway*," Dick said.

"That's right," Irwin Ott Haldeman said. "They're already there."

"They're already there," Hugo Halloway Erlichman said, "but they might pounce on these tapes and say, 'Look, here's proof of what we've been saying all along, they're shamming.'"

"I don't like that word, shamming," Dick said. "It sounds . . . ."

"We could say in reply to that, that in all openness we are opening up everything, revealing the very worst, the most ordinary and banal and everything imaginable, and if they don't want to accept it on the terms of the openness with which it is offered, then . . . well, we can say they aren't receiving these tapes in the proper spirit."

". . . fake," Dick said. "It sounds fake and like there's something that isn't . . . well, I just don't like it and I don't think we should use it in these tapes"—he looked over at O'Connor who was sitting behind the big desk—"switch the machine off." O'Connor realized the machine was indeed running. He switched it off immediately. "Becuase if we let that word out in these tapes, I know those bastards will

pounce on it and they'll throw it back in our teeth. I know
these bastards so well I know what words they'll latch onto.
They just love a word like that—shamming. It sounds . . .
nasty."

"The tape was running," Irwin Ott Haldeman said to
Hugo Halloway Erlichman.

"We'll need to erase all that."

"Don't erase it," Dick said. "Don't erase anything. We
want this to be *honest,* for Christ's sake."

"But what we were saying wouldn't sound very good
if . . . ."

"You don't get the idea, somehow," Dick said. "These
tapes aren't going to sound very good no matter how we
do it, don't you see? They're going to say this and they're
going to say that. My God, I can't imagine what they'll do
when they get their hands on these tapes."

"But we were talking about these tapes," Irwin Ott
Haldeman said.

"They'll immediately recognize that we were aware that
what we were saying was going to reach their ears," Hugo
Halloway Erlichman said, "Which will cause some credibility
problems, unless they consider the possibility that perhaps all
along there was an awareness on our part that the tapes were
being made, if you get my point."

"How far back?" Irwin Ott Haldeman said.

Hugo Halloway Erlichman shrugged. "All the way back
to the very beginning of not just these tapes we're making
but the other tapes, too."

"Do you mean . . .?" Dick started, then stopped. "I
wonder what if we *had* been aware that everyone was listening to what we were saying, if we would have, how it would
have been, there would have of course been some differences,
but I don't see how that would have changed all the *other*
things."

"I think it's a good idea to keep it running all the time,"
Hugo Halloway Erlichman said. He turned to O'Connor and

nodded at the machine. O'Connor switched it on. "If we knew from the very beginning that it was running, then we have nothing to hide, right?"

"I've never had anything to hide," Dick said, turning to the machine as he spoke. "I have always said that. It has from the very beginning of all this always been my main point."

"And later," Irwin Ott Haldeman said, "if we change our minds . . . ."

"Right," Hugo Halloway Erlichman said, "we can go back and do some editing here and there."

"No," Dick said. "I don't want any gaps. No gaps."

"That's no problem," Irwin Ott Haldeman said. "When we erase, we can fit something new into those slots, for the sake of continuity."

"On the other hand," Hugo Halloway Erlichman said, "maybe we should consider how we could make the gaps advantageous to us. Because they're of course going to be expecting gaps, so if there are none, they'll be suspicious, right?"

"Right," Irwin Ott Haldeman said. "I see your point. That's really the truth."

"I see your point," Dick said, "but it's those goddamned gaps that . . . ."

"Here's a scenario," Hugo Halloway Erlichman said. "I see them finding gaps and saying, "What's been cut here?" We come back with national security, but—and this is the big difference—we say that we have the deletions on a separate set of tapes!"

"I like that," Dick said. "Yes. I like that a lot. How about you, Bob?"

Irwin Ott Haldeman said, "I think I like it. The multi-dimensionality of it is good, the national security, at the same time the thoroughness of the Office in taking the precaution to put all the deletions on a separate series of tapes. But they're still going to wonder what's on those separate tapes and they're going to wonder if they really do touch on national security."

"They'll want someone on the inside to listen to them," Dick said. "I could talk to John Stennis . . . ."

"We could handle that, too," Hugo Halloway Erlichman said to Irwin Ott Haldeman. "The separate national security tapes could have actual national security items on them. As simple as that."

They sat in silence.

"What kind of stuff?" Dick said.

Hugo Halloway Erlichman shrugged. "We could . . . well, you could give us a run-down on some things that were national security, and we could talk about them in the time segments that would fit into the gaps that we put in the other tapes."

"Wonderful idea," Irwin Ott Haldeman said.

Dick was sitting silent, slumped down.

"What's the problem?" Irwin Ott Haldeman asked him.

"I don't . . . well, let me put it this way. Those national security issues . . . . Hm. Well, to put it in a nutshell, I can't seem to recall anything that, you know, we could fit into what you might consider, well, national security."

"That's no problem," Irwin Ott Haldeman said. "Do you think that's a problem, John?"

"Not at all," Hugo Halloway Erlichman said. "We'll talk about SALT, NATO . . . ."

"Some personalities, too."

"Right. Trudeau, Somoza . . . ."

"If it's personalities you want," Dick said, paused to chuckle, "we have no problem there at all. I've known them all, known them all."

Hugo Halloway Erlichman turned to O'Connor. "What do you think of this, John?"

John Mitchell O'Connor cleared his throat with a rumble. "Well," he said, getting the quaver going, "I'll go along with whatever the President says."

They all turned to Dick who was slumped in his chair

grinning into his glass. "I say it's time to load up and see if we can get old Cato-san on the run!"

"Here, here!" Irwin Ott Haldeman said.

Leaving the recorder running, they got their BB guns out of the gun cabinet, freshened their drinks, and took their places at the terrace turrets. At first it appeared Cato-san wasn't on the job. But then Dick, the keenest eye in the bunch, spotted some movement among the roses. "Little fucker," he whispered, lifting his gun to his shoulder, aiming at a spot that to the others was merely foliage. He fired— pink!—and the helmet popped into view and started bobbing through the roses toward a hedge while the rest of them loosed a barrage.

HEROES AND VILLAINS

Murna heard a calliope, the ripply booping like great blue bubbles floating up, and beneath her sleep mask she wondered if her daughter, Eileen, had at last revived from her trance, slipped out of the hospital, and brought this music home with her. But the calliope was so faint perhaps it was the soundtrack of a lingering dream in which cheetahs passed airily through a conversation Murna was having with policemen. The cats looked over their shoulders with black, insouciant eyes, listened to Murna and the police, then puckered their lips and precisely whispered the same word again and again—a word Murna couldn't hear and which the police, ignoring the cats, missed. Murna believed she could solve the mystery if she could only hear that word and pass it on to the right someone. The calliope faded and the dream slipped away.

Removing the mask she sat up and looked about, amazed to find she had slept in the large, high-ceilinged gallery. The walls were lined with old books which gasped and pow'd when opened. Above the books badly foxed engravings hung among portraits of whiskered worthies from another century; according to the yellow velvet booklet which Murna's son-in-law, Mickey Vozzio, acquired with all the pictures at an auction in Hollywood, one of these mutton-chopped notables was a descendant of the Sheriff of Nottingham! The picture which enjoyed prominence, though, was a huge and murky landscape by a fellow inspired and cursed by the conviction that his best work came to him late in the afternoon just as everything was sinking away. His hillsides, millstreams, and meadows, presumably immortalized, were again sinking as the painting faded into itself, suggesting things beyond what the artist could have found even in his finest fits of melancholy. Inevitably someone, maybe Murna herself, would someday stand before the picture and, after first seeing nothing but a vast brown and black rectangle, and after then penetrating her own dim reflection on the protective veneer, see at last movement, deep and vague . . . . Gypsies slipping across the fields at night, the ponies' bells muffled, the wagons' wheels greased so the sheriff and his ruffian posse wouldn't hear . . .? Or would she see profounder, more sinister doings? All enclosed by a wide gilt frame in which rampant cupids blasted clarions at the backs of each others' heads and sent doves surging determinedly through the molten sky and over the antlers of stags, tangled in the golden underbrush of cupid hair, on the trail to Sherwood Forest.

In a far corner was a large leather chair, Mickey's, though Murna had seen him sit in it only once. (She had in fact seen her son-in-law that one time only, except when the police let her peek into a brown paper bag containing what she was told was Mickey Vozzio.) The walls in that corner were badged with breastplates, broadswords, battle-axes, spiked truncheons, and muskets—all plastic. Beside the chair a Duncan Phyfe table with Mickey's short-wave radio waited his return: here he would sit with a cigar and brandy, and get the results from Caliente, Del Mar, Hollywood Park, and tune in police calls from all over the world . . . .

Morning had entered the house, proceeded from room to room and now stood in gray clumps and columns in the gallery like a tour of ghosts ready for the next spiel: "Here sat Mickey Vozzio on the fateful evening when a mysterious call beckoned him to affairs that ended with his untimely and incomprehensible death. In this recliner Mickey Vozzio's new wife, Eileen, sat knitting a sweater for her cat. While across from her, on the same sofa where just last night she struggled through the crowded, churning, rackety sleep which poets suffer nearly every night, sat Murna Pooley, *the* Murna Pooley, known here and there as the author of such volumes as *The Bawds of Baffledom, Oh Sweet Mystic Halloweenist,* and *The Albatross and Other Heavenly Birds,* herself a tourist of sorts, bon vivant, sometimes lecturer, but currently full-time grieving mother-in-law and worried mother of a terrifically sick daughter. That evening, just before the phone rang, Ms. Pooley looked up from the book on her lap and with that gaze easily mistaken for the foggy mood which verse evokes in gentler readers, she wondered if Mickey could use the excellent tax write-off of publishing a poetry magazine . . . ."

Murna sat up and tried a quick fantasy: Eileen and Mickey were upstairs in the master bedroom and all the rest was a bad dream . . .

But she knew she was alone. Last night returned on great black wings. Murna saw herself roaming through the house. She was looking for something, and though she found a great deal of everything, she couldn't decide what was a valid clue and what wasn't. All this was of course quite new to her, especially the telephone calls.

The phones kept ringing and she had answered them in this room and that as if she were hearing one by one from a chorus. With her notebook in hand, Murna at first tried to take messages; she would give them to Eileen when she left the hospital. But her notes were too bizarre to pass on, though they might someday provide a poem of two. The phone calls were vortexes into which Murna sank deeper moment by moment, the callers talking with speedy incoherence and a desperation which Murna recognized though she understood nothing of what they were talking about. They talked on even when she tried to interrupt, their words racing faster as Murna softly repeated, "Good-bye for now.

Good-bye . . . ." and lowered the phone to its cradle. There were several calls in a foreign language, but not Italian. Listening dutifully to the deep-voiced fellow, Murna tried to feel through the totally alien words to the basic human hiding, she trusted, beneath it all. But she could make absolutely nothing of it, and after several of these calls it occurred to her that the fellow was merely gabbling. When he called again Murna launched into it with him, coming forth with wild nonsense at which she discovered she was quite fluent and in which, she further discovered, she had a great deal to say. When the fellow hung up on her, she stood waiting for him to call back and was rather disappointed he didn't. Murna had continued roaming through the house, waiting for a phone to ring, but none did. She at last picked up the receiver of one and found the line was dead.

She has started upstairs to bed when there was a knock. And the man at the door—Murna was fairly sure this wasn't a dream, though now in the gray gallery it all seemed tremendously far away—was he a taxi driver? He wore shabby khakis too big for him and a billed cap with a badge. Maybe he was a Mexican policeman. As Murna expected, she couldn't understand what he said, though it sounded vaguely English. She was distracted in part from understanding him by his remarkable face, yellow and protuberant as if his head had been squeezed from behind, bulging his eyes, jutting his lips, and creating at least three handfuls of nose. She let him talk a while and then slowly shut the door in his face and went into the gallery, dragging behind her a polar bearskin under which she snuggled on a sofa. Just as she was slipping away, the thought floated through that the man, though unusual, apparently knew Mickey, was perhaps even his friend, for people do befriend taxi drivers and Mexican policemen, and then Murna realized that while listening to the man she had noticed out the corner of her eye, without actually seeing, that his pants were unzipped. Were they really? Yes, she was certain. Perhaps he had been asking to use Mickey's bathroom.

Tinkling cheers, delicate with distance and the ambiance of dawn, came through the sound- and bulletproof gallery windows. She went to a window, the bearskin around her shoulders. The sloping lawn sparkled with dew. Large trees stood about, involved in that long and dour confabulation of trees. Around the lawn a fifteen-foot hedge concealed a fence which Eileen had told Murna carried enough juice to roast all the rhinos in the L.A. zoo.

Cavorting on the lawn was a troupe of small, nearly naked people. Murna smiled, blinked several times, and decided they were actual people, though they were quite successfully coming across as elves, limberly cartwheeling, bobbing, and tossing each other about. They sprang off a blue trampoline and sailed blithely through the air, arms tight to their sides—to be caught at the last moment. They spun each other into somersaults and flips that zipped them across the wet grass like water bugs skimming a pond. To the side stood a red wagon with two white ponies in the traces; in the wagon was a calliope, and at the keyboard, with his legs crossed and buffing his fingernails, sat a little man in jockey boots, cap, and silks. When the tumblers saw Murna, they gave a cheer, formed a circle, and did a frisking, lissome dance, glancing toward the window, their black eyes glinting with that sure slyness of persons who have already gone too far but intend to go even farther. A young man, naked except for a G-string and shiny with dew, came up the lawn, his lips flared back from a large mouth of exceedingly white teeth, many more than most people have, his long blond hair flaming from his head as he ran. Under the window he flung open his arms and addressed Murna. But Murna heard only a cottony muffle of words—and, dimly, the calliope as it started up. Under the window the young man grimaced in a dramatic agony, his neck bulging. Murna tried lipreading him. It seemed he was singing the same words over and over.

Murna wondered if the young man and the rest had heard the news about Mickey. She smiled, then said silently but exaggeratedly, enunciating as though speaking underwater, *Mickey is gone.* The young man stopped swaying and gesturing; the frenzy knotting his face vanished. *What?* If only Murna had a sheet of paper, but she had misplaced her notebook. With a finger she wrote the message on air, realizing as she did that to the young man it was of course written backwards: he frowned; Murna shrugged. *Good-bye,* she said and backed away from the window.

She went to the gallery door and peered down the dark hall. A suit of armor lurked half-sunk in shadows, the slits in the smug beaklike visor staring at the opposite wall while at the same time leering sidelong at Murna. The mesh fingers of the right hand seemed to curl tighter around the grip of the mace they held.

Murna hurried by the armor, through a door, and down a narrow passage. She entered the kitchen just as Pusser Boy was coming in by another door. Seeing her, he stopped and backed out. "Well," Murna said. "Could it be someone wants his breakfast?" She went to the refrigerator and got her yogurt from the top shelf. The other shelves were filled with baggies of kidney. While she was peeling one open, Pusser Boy looked around the corner and slipped into the ktichen. He rubbed against the backs of her legs, then stepped inside the bearskin with her and stood with his tail between her thighs. She put the kidney down for him and, climbing onto a stool with her yogurt, watched him eat. Twice he paused, licking his lips and staring at her.

When they finished, Murna waited as Pusser Boy paid a visit to his box in the utility room. Then she went down the hall to the staircase, looking back and seeing Pusser Boy was following but at a distance, stopping when she stopped. Upstairs he followed her down the hall to the master bedroom.

A purple arm stuck from under the closet door. Murna

opened the door: a tuxedo wadded on the floor shimmered silkily within itself like a fermenting jellyfish, and the closet had the fecund, rather rotten odor of the sea. On the racks leather jackets, vests, shirts and slacks, that appeared hacked from wood, hung among dresses, full-length gowns, and a dozen or so dungaree jackets stitched with big black apples, yellow-green sun bursts, tarantulas with baby faces, and, covering the back of one denim jacket, a maroon rubber vulva drooling candlewax into the motto *Pussy Power*. Murna again searched pockets, finding rainbow condoms and toothpicks, pop-top rings and worry beads, hairpins and nine-millimeter bullets, lire, pounds, pesos, dollars, cents, and several grand in play money, and a hard as rock, mustarded, ketchuped and relished hotdog bun sans wienie.

Murna put the clothes away and shut the closet door, convinced she had again let the clue she needed slip through her fingers.

She went to the cluttered dressing table where Jacqueline Onassis smiled from the cover of a movie magazine, her eyes large and oddly blank. On the front of a detective magazine the gray sky covered a shirtless, thin-chested boy being dragged through a ditch by large men in slickers and cowboy hats. On another, Charlie Starkweather and Caril Fugate sheepishly looked out at the world. There were racing forms with bilingual scribbles, lace bikinis, a fifty-dollar bill folded into a dense square and bound with a rubber band (Murna refolded the bill and looped the band around it again) and a pair of white silk boxer shorts monogrammed with a lavender V looping and swirling like a pretty worm wriggling into flight. Jewelry boxes tried to outdo each other before an audience of coffee cups which, gaping with awe, revealed thick black residues caked in their bottoms. Murna opened a box of chocolate-covered cherries and found among the crinkly wrappers a cigar butt, a jack of spades, and a Richard Nixon wrist watch. She replaced the lid and put the box on a rubber glove pointing to the tip of a lipstick poking out from a folded racing form. Murna picked up a pair of yellow plastic opera glasses which, she had discovered the first time she looked into them, didn't give her a better view of things but showed her a tangle of two women, a man, and an object nearly as large as a fourth party which surely wasn't what it semeed to be, though now as Murna took another look into the glasses (for even in there she might find the clue) she acknowledged that the object was indeed that.

In a drawer she found Eileen's big jar of pills with a masking-tape label penciled with an unending indecipherable sentence winding through itself and covering every square centimeter with words. Murna unscrewed the lid and again was surprised by a familiar nose-tingling smell. This time she stirred around in the jar and uncovered a great white pill. She got it out, sniffed it—a moth ball. She dropped it and Pusser Boy trotted over and, as Murna dug out a pill, a blue one big as a thumb and soft and wrinkled, Pusser Boy swatted the moth ball under the dressing table.

When Murna returned from the bathroom, Pusser Boy let himself be picked up and carried to the bed. He lay stretched down her side, not purring, and though cheek to cheek with Murna, Pusser Boy's amber eyes were sternly averted—not to the door but the wall as if he knew that when trouble comes it doesn't saunter through the door or pop through windows, but bulges out of walls.

Murna hummed as thick blue welled up and she murmured in Pusser Boy's ear, "Oh silly goose, what shall we do, stick it down with paste and glue?" which wasn't exactly what she meant but as she tried to hear it again, the minnows flitted away and, leaning out too far after them, she glided onto the lake and lost herself.

That afternoon Murna dressed in a rush and ran from the house. When she arrived at the hospital she was informed by Nurse Hudlow—an exceptionally tall person with a tendency

to roll her eyes up, perhaps from habitually ducking door-
ways and checking the whereabout of ceilings—that a group
had tried to visit Mrs. Vozzio that morning. But Hudlow and
the other nurses, who at that moment stepped from a room
behind the nursing station, two powerhouses with oversized
plastic tags on their uniforms announcing *Spaag* and *Muldoon,*
had thrown them out: visiting hours weren't until one-thirty.

"Were they tumblers?" Murna said, imagining that
morning's troupe of little people tumulting down the corridor, the white ponies' hooves clattering, the calliope sending
its hopeful tootle echoing through the hospital.

"Tumblers?" Hudlow said. "Ah—" rolling her eyes up—
"no. More like actors. Actors being ordinary in gray suits.
Ah—actors in politics, dicks and goons."

"Some of Mickey's friends, perhaps," Murna said. The
nurses walked down the hall with her. "Is Eileen resting
well?"

"She—ah—remains catatonic."

Spaag leaned to Murna. "That's resting very well."

They reached Eileen's room, all white except for furry
shadows gathered in the corners and under the bed. Murna
entered and, stepping onto a stool, leaned over the guardrail
and kissed Eileen. The smooth eyelids didn't flicker.

Turning, Murna saw a young woman, a girl actually, no
more than twenty years old, behind the door, squeezed in a
corner beside a cart of blankets and rubber hot water bottles.
The girl put her finger to her lips.

Murna smiled at Hudlow, Spaag, and Muldoon, shoulder
to shoulder in the hall, and said, "Thank you so much for all
you've done." The three moved off.

"What . . .?" Murna started but the girl shook her head,
her finger still to her lips. Her face was gray and thin, with
the wistfulness of an ascetic waiting for the moment that
would spring her into being someone else, or something else,
or let her vanish altogether—and Murna realized the girl bore
a disturbing resemblance to Eileen! Did the hospital substi-

tute dejected look-alikes for patients who were beyond fixing? But maybe the girl's vagueness had nothing to do with Eileen. Had this girl been irreparably shamed? Had she just recently and barely survived an onslaught of love fought with strange acts? Had she on a dare given herself to a giant? Or was she the sister of louts who gorged on pails of oatmeal, guzzled honey, then dragged her to the basement for a rampage . . .? She wore a brown sack with *Idaho Spuds* arching a dark figure in a field. Her legs were long and bony, and ended in big gray feet. She wore gold rings on her toes. What mysteries we are, Murna thought, and with a smile whispered, "Hello, my darling."

The girl made an indistinct sound—sigh, groan, or grunt—and, turning to the cart beside her, tucked in the blanket.

Going nearer, Murna saw a yellow rubber water bottle at the end of the cart; the blanket's lumpiness suggested there were more. Then Murna realized the blanket covered a person, soft and slick, the vague nose, mouth, and closed eyelids floating on the flat yellow face. "Oh my," she said.

"They cut him in half," the girl whispered.

"He must have been terribly sick."

"Huh?"

"I mean, for the doctors to perform such drastic . . . ."

"It wasn't the docs. It was *them*." Murna looked into her half-closed eyes, purple-gray, remote. "I guess you know they got the husband of that one." The girl nodded toward Eileen on the bed. "Crunched him down to a boullion cube. But my Robert they sliced off half of him—the back half, from the head straight down. If he ever walks again he'll have to tiptoe everywhere—no heels." With a Kleenex she dabbed the yellow lumps which were Robert's eyes. "Do you have a cigarette?" she asked Murna.

"I think . . . ." She dug into her purse—or rather it was Eileen's purse she was carrying.

The girl lit a cigarette and blew a cloud of smoke toward the ceiling. "Sorry I brought Robert in here. I mean it's

her room. But I gotta keep moving him around. If they get
their hands on him again I don't know what they'll do. Slice
off some more. Or do it to me . . . ." She stared off. "I wish I
hadn't thought of that, because now they'll think of it too.
And they'll cut me in half and make movies of Robert
and me tiptoing down the street. They have a big sense of
humor."

"You *know* these people?" Murna said.

"Sure I know them. Like the back of my hand. Everybody knows them. It's no secret any more."

"I'm glad I found you," Murna said and touched the girl's
cold cheek, "for I am gathering material on the death of
Mickey Vozzio and the mysterious shock that has driven her"
—nodding toward Eileen—"into this deep sleep. You're certain the same people are involved in Mickey's death and"—
she glanced at Robert.

"Who else?" The girl limped across the room and got an
ashtray. Coming back, her hand on her side, she said, "I got
a game hip. Say, I don't guess you could spare some change,
could you?"

Murna gave her some quarters, dimes, and pennies. The
girl quickly counted the money and stashed it in a leather
pouch hanging around her neck. She rubbed her hip and
suavely said, "I'm a little stiff from balling." She leaned
against the wall and, slowly scooting down, sat on the floor,
her thighs against her chest. She pulled the sack over her
knees and down to her ankles. "So you want some information. Are you a detective?" Murna said she wasn't. "Okay.
Just an interested party. So. The first thing you gotta learn is
information without proof is nothing. You need evidence."

"Where can I get it?"

"Don't worry. I can give you all the evidence you will
ever need. Enough for you and a dozen interested parties.
I'll fix you up with Mr. Stein. Soon as I finish this we'll take
off." She inhaled on the cigarette. She stretched out her long
thin legs and rubbed her hip. She breathed out the smoke. "I

don't think it's my hip at all. It's my membranes. Look." She
pulled down her lower lip. "Touch," she said through her
teeth and, taking Murna's thumb, ran it across the lip. "Too
slick. Uh? Do you have membrane problems?"

"No," Murna said.

"You're lucky. Sit down." She patted the floor. Murna
sat, her legs tucked under her, her skirt—or rather it was one
of Eileen's—hiking up. The girl put her cigarette in the ashtray and, reaching right up, touched Murna's lips. Her hand
smelled of smoke and metal. "I . . . ." Murna started and the
girl slipped a finger into her mouth. She felt along the lower
lip, then the finger slid in deep, along Murna's jaw, turning
and probing while the girl and Murna stared intently at each
other. "Nice," the girl said. "Real nice." She reached down
with her free hand, took another puff on the cigarette, and
ground it out in the ashtray. Then the finger came out of
Murna's mouth with a soft plop and swiftly, like a fish leaping from a pool directly into one's eye, slid up between
Murna's legs. "Please," the girl whispered. "I'm all alone
now."

Murna clamped her thighs together, stopping the hand.
"I'll help," Murna said.

"Good." The hand squirmed.

"But . . . ."

"You draw the line on that?"

"I don't draw lines. But I want material and evidence."

"Okay. But you must pay the piper, and that's me." She
leaned slowly forward, her eyes closing on their purple-gray
crowd of villains, giants, wolves . . . and Murna licked her soft
blue lips and narrow tongue.

Pusser Boy was licking Murna's lips, or rather Murna
and Pusser Boy were tapping tongues as if trying to put the
other's back where it belonged. Murna removed her sleep
mask and Pusser Boy jumped off the bed and ran from the

room. Then far off, as if from a hollow wooden planet, Murna heard someone knocking.

She put on one of Eileen's gowns and hurrried downstairs. Looking out the tiny glass peephole in the front door, she saw the world not as a convex night, sleek and bulging, but a soupy, gray convex day. But she saw no one. She opened the door a crack. "Hello?" she whispered. Pusser Boy pushed his way out and slipped into the bushes.

Murna shut the door and went from room to room looking out. From a rear window of the east wing she saw a large man who looked like Oscar Wilde sitting in a lounge chair by the pool. He wore a green velvet sports coat, pearl gray slacks, and white patent leather shoes with gold buckles. Before him a tall youth with spriggy red hair was stripping. Murna believed she had seen the youth before. Down to his shorts, he bounded to the edge of the pool and, sticking in his foot, stirred a hole in the moss. He grinned at the man in the lounge chair, and now Murna was quite sure she recognized the boy—that wide square mouth like a slot where one might sock in a cassette, and all those big teeth: he was the large-mouthed lad with flaming blond hair who had performed on the lawn with the tumblers! He dived into the hole.

His head popped up in the middle of the pool. He laughed and shook back his moss-streaked hair. *It's cold. It's green,* Murna lipread as he called to his friend. He climbed out and with a whoop ran down to the far end of the pool. He bounced on the diving board, his arms lifted. *Look. Look.* His companion waved a large, long-fingered hand, and the boy dived in.

And the thick carpet of moss remained unbroken beyond the time he should have come up. Maybe it was so thick at the deep end he couldn't break through: Murna pictured him suspended in blackness, butting his head against something like the sky.

His companion lit a cigarette and leaned back his head,

large and shaggy, with black curls hanging down to tease his cheeks and nearly conceal his long ears. He closed his dark-ringed puffy eyes, and on his face settled a bloated serenity that was disturbed only by an occasional quiver of the chin and a petulance of the lips.

Murna cranked open the window. "Yoo hoo!" He opened his eyes. "What happened to your young man?"

His forehead creased, his lips pursed with a pensive, weary irony, and he stared at Murna. She felt he was seeing quite all of her. "Should I send for an ambulance?" Murna said. "A doctor? The police . . .?"

"No need." His voice was as effortless as a cloud. "I am the police."

He took a book from his pocket—Murna's first slim volume! A collection she shared with the McCoy sisters, Beryl and Ida, with whom she skipped arm in arm, nude and gauzy, on the cover as if to refute the title, *We Wiser Disguisers!* "Is it true that you are Murna Mina Pooley?" he said. She affirmed she was. He rose slowly and with difficulty. He slipped the book into his pocket and, his heels clicking on the patio, walked to the window. Looking up, he said, "Well, are you going to unlock the door, or let down your hair?"

Murna hurried to the nearest door. When she opened it, he was waiting, even larger than he seemed before, and there beside him, moss-smeared and dripping wet, was his sidekick, who wasn't at all a boy but a wiry thirty-year-old man standing with his clothes wadded in a ball. "Hi," he said and Murna saw within the slope of his forehead, in his perfectly round gray eyes and gaping square mouth, an awful resemblance in the two men, as if they were grotesques of each other.

The gentleman in the green velvet sports coat spoke. "I am Basil Stein. I am inquiring into the death of Marvin Foster, a.k.a. Michael Fogstar, Mick Fallo, Mickey Nozzolio, Mickey Vozzio."

"He was Mickey Vozzio to me. Please come in." She showed them to the gallery where Basil Stein lowered himself onto a sofa and crossed his trunk-like legs. His companion stuffed his clothes in a vase and went about the room opening drawers and digging under the cushions of chairs and sofas. He found a stick of chewing gum which he unwrapped and stuck in his mouth—then he found some change! Laughing loudly, he brought it to Basil Stein who slipped the coins into his coat pocket.

Murna said, "I was afraid he had drowned in the pool."

Basil Stein closed his eyes and slowly shook his head. "Roy can hold his breath for ten minutes, perhaps longer. Anyway, he found a room under the diving board." He opened his eyes and looked at Murna. "Were you aware there is a secret room under the pool?"

"No. What is in it?"

Roy, on his hands and knees with an arm stuck to the elbow in the bowels of a sofa, said over his shoulder, "Nobody was home. It's just a little place with a little door."

Basil Stein took out *We Wiser Disguisers,* read a line or two, then looked up. "Why are you interfering in these affairs, my dear?"

"I happened to be in the country to see my publisher. A wire was waiting for me there from my daughter informing me she had gotten married. I left New York immediately and arrived here in time to say hello to my son-in-law, see him off to his death, and put my daughter in the hospital. Now I am doing what I can to get to the bottom of it all."

"Then you're willing to cooperate with us in every way imaginable?"

"Yes."

"Hmm. Good. But need I point out that you're hardly adept? For instance, we were here earlier, spying, and you didn't know."

"It's true that it didn't occur to me that you were spying that morning. But I did recognize him"—nodding toward

Roy. "Were you out there too?"

Basil Stein looked away aloofly. "In the calliope. But I have more important matters." He took out a notebook, glanced into it, put it away. "Have you ever been Murna Cooney or Irene Rommel?"

"No. I have always been myself."

"You've never disguised, done a poem or two under a nom de plume, or chanced an afternoon as someone else?"

"Well . . . ."

"Okay." Covering his eyes with one hand, he held up the other as if he didn't want to know. He patted the cushion beside him and looked out from between his fingers. Murna sat beside him. "We shall wait," he said. Reaching his long fingers into his hair, he began scratching his head. He closed his heavy-lidded eyes; the movement of the hand, hidden to the wrist in his hair, slowed, then ceased. Murna believed he had fallen asleep. Then he spoke, but barely louder than a whisper. "Mickey's death was a shock to us all. In truth, I find it quite impossible to accept that he is really dead."

"I barely knew him," Murna said. "I have tried to piece together his life with my daughter so that I might understand why she . . . ."

Basil Stein began speaking while Murna was saying this; she trailed off and listened.

". . . and even earlier, I knew him as a child, we were school chums, following each other about the schoolyard, in the winter waiting around the corners for each other in the dark hallways and in the basement under the gymnasium. We laid traps for each other." Basil Stein chuckled. "His were always best. Such as the time he and his gang caught me in the storage room above the auditorium. They nailed me to the floor and wrote their names on me with burning sticks, and drew arrows and hands and naked women. Mickey was on the chess team and the night he won the state championship I caught his sister and made her eat stuff and she was in the hospital for a month. On graduation day Mickey and I swore to be enemies to the end. We wanted to choke each other to death right there in the middle of the football field, but of course they wouldn't let us. I went to the Korean War and was a hero, while Mickey stayed home and made three million dollars in hot cars, whores, and smack. When we won the war, I came back and sneaked into his house—not this one but the one in Trenton—and sprayed kerosene everywhere, and I was there waiting when Mickey came home. I shot him in the stomach, but just once and with a twenty-two caliber so he would live."

Basil Stein sighed and, opening his eyes, looked around the room. "But that was years ago." He smoothed down his hair and sat up. "Nice place he has here. I like the art work. Especially that big piece with all the niggers hiding in it." He crossed the room and stood before the dark landscape. "I wonder what they're doing in there."

Roy, who had joined him, cupped his hand to Basil Stein's ear and whispered, rolling his big gray eyes at Murna.

"Hmm," Basil Stein said. He turned from the painting. "Anything to eat around here?"

"Yogurt. And Pusser Boy's kidney."

"He's the cat, right?" Murna confirmed this. "I find it strange that Mickey would leave his cat behind, to fend for itself and to ultimately starve." He took out his notebook and a pencil. "Cat . . . still . . . living," he said and dotted a period with a jab. "Okay." He yawned widely, causing Roy to yawn. "Give me the yogurt and what's-his-name's kidney."

When Murna returned from the kitchen with a tray of food, thirty large men were wandering in the hall and milling about the gallery. They looked at her out the corners of their eyes and ignored her when she said hello.

Basil Stein ate the yogurt with a tablespoon. "I love it. This stuff is so good," he told her, looking up with his large dark eyes. But he had her throw out the kidney which he claimed was tainted. He said the pissy smell alone would make everyone sick.

Basil Stein and his men tuned in Mickey's short-wave and got the results from Hollywood Park. Between races they picked up signals from abroad, listening a while to a man distressed in the Indian Ocean.

For supper Basil Stein sent out for Chinese, and afterwards had Murna sit with him and the others in the dark gallery. The curtains were open, and two or three men stood at each window, cranked open wide, with rifles and machine guns; the rest sat in chairs and sofas, and some sat on the floor, whispering. Around nine o'clock they heard the thrumming of a diesel: a huge fire engine with its lights off sat in the driveway. The driver switched it off and Basil Stein and his men squeezed the truck through the narrow space between the swimming pool and the house, and pushed it down the lawn to the trees. By the light of the moon they camouflaged it with branches and rose bushes. When they finished, the fire truck looked like a great pyre ready to be lit. As they went back into the house, Basil Stein slipped his arm around Murna's waist. "We might need it," he said. "If not tonight, tomorrow for sure,"

Back in the gallery Basil Stein ordered a movie projector to be set up, and they watched jerky silent movies, grainy black and white, from Mickey's film library. Murna recognized some downtown streets and buildings: there was the public library with Basil Stein himself trudging up the endless steps with an armload of books and nodding to the uniformed guard who opened the door for him. Basil Stein went in—and in a moment came out, crouching, gun in hand, grinning Roy's huge square grin. He jabbed the gun in the guard's back and sent him tumbling down the steps. There was the hospital: inside to the lobby where row on row of black people slumped against each other; then down a corridor to the door of Eileen's room. The door opened a crack and Basil Stein looked out at the camera and silently said, *Leave me alone.* In the ensuing fracas Basil Stein, Roy, and several other men were knocked about and thrown out by the nurses. More street scenes. A young woman in a short dress was yanked in a delivery truck by a large hook. An extraordinarily thin, literally flat, man and woman came tiptoing down the sidewalk. Several times Basil Stein told the projectionist to run something by again: the men roared when a huge truck spat a patrolman from its grille onto a wobbly motorcycle which straightened itself by bumping a curb and then zipped backwards down the street. Later, a dozen policemen sprang from a pile on the sidewalk and allowed a little person wearing a ski mask, with a round awed mouth, to pop up and back briskly into a bank.

Basil Stein sent out for sandwiches, and the projectionist showed color movies. The men came down from the roof and up from the basement and from their posts at the windows, and drank milk with their sandwiches and watched movies of naked people playing croquet, oiling each other, doing the twist, frug, and bunny hug, and rolling around with ponies and dogs. Basil Stein's men laughed, groaned, whistled softly. Then Mickey Vozzio, wearing the same purple tuxedo which lay on the floor of the master bedroom closet, bowed to the camera and welcomed them to the very room where they were sitting: it was filled with as many men and women as there were now policemen, but in the movie everyone was naked, gold, and sported glass phalluses.

Basil Stein and Murna went up to the master bedroom and sorted through the things in the closet and drawers. On Basil Stein's suggestion Murna tried on a pair of jeans and a red tank top. "Good," Basil Stein said. "Excellent." Next he picked the denim jacket with the big maroon vulva on the back. She put it on and walked about as Basil Stein lay on the bed, his hands clasped under his head. "*Tres bien,*" he said. "But you need a wig." She tried one. "No." A long black one? "Ahhh." He smiled, his eyes nearly closed. "Come here." He unzipped his fly, reached in, and pulled out a snubbed-nosed revolver. "Here, Patty," he whispered.

"Don't let the schmucks take you alive."

They ate breakfast at Denny's, then drove across town in a caravan of twenty patrol cars with red lights flashing, the fire truck bringing up the rear. Murna rode in the lead car with Basil Stein. Roy, who had donned some of Eileen's clothes and an orange afro, rode in the backseat.

Basil Stein listened to dispatches, then switched to a rock station on a.m. He checked his watch, then nudged Murna. "Get this." The disk jockey cut off the Beach Boys and announced that Patty Hearst and other members of the Symbionese Liberation Army had been seen leaving a local restaurant, and police were tightening a ring around them.

They were driving down a street of bare yellow houses. Black people looked out the windows as they passed and their front doors slowly closed. Basil Stein pulled off and stopped at the end of an alley. One other patrol car stopped, and the others went on.

Murna got out with Basil Stein and Roy, and with the patrolmen from the other car they walked up the alley to a house with a low stone wall. "This is it," Basil Stein said and the patrolment went in the back door.

A woman yelled, a pan clattered and a chair was knocked over. The woman said loudly, "What you . . .?"

Murna and Roy followed Basil Stein in. The patrolmen were handcuffing a black woman to an old washing machine. Two black men came in from the next room, their eyes big. "Down," Basil Stein said and pointed to the yellow linoleum floor. The men lay down. Basil Stein, Murna, and Roy stepped over them and went in.

The walls of the small dining room and living room were covered with framed photographs of black people standing in front of their homes with their cars, arm in arm at reunions in the park with tables covered with hampers and big bowls of food. There were pictures of black people with their children, with their dogs and cats, black soldiers grinning in Germany and Japan, and there was a picture of a stern old man with his mule. Football and basketball teams of bright-eyed boys stared confidently at Basil Stein. Everywhere there were big happy girls—girls with sticks ready for field hockey, girls in prom dresses with corsages, girls in ballet slippers and frazzled tutus, girls with new bikes.

In the front room, wearing dungarees and a denim jacket, was the young woman from the hospital—or half of her, for now she was as thin as her Robert had been. She sat on an old brown sofa, weighted down with a shotgun across her lap. "Hi," Basil Stein said. The girl didn't answer or look up.

The patrolmen came in and after shutting the windows, pulled the blinds and curtains. Immediately the house became very hot. Basil Stein sat on the sofa, tilting the thin girl toward him. "How about a snack, uh?" he said to Murna.

She went out to the kitchen. A policeman sat at the table staring at the woman who was now handcuffed, both hands and feet, to the washing machine, and at the two men on the floor. Murna looked in the refrigerator and cabinets and all she could find were a jar of peanut butter and a box of animal crackers. Basil Stein, Roy, and the patrolmen ate all of it and drank a gallon of water from a plastic pitcher with little cheese spread glasses.

Basil Stein brushed crumbs off his jacket and dabbed his mouth with a black silk handkerchief. He stood and nodded to Roy. Roy jumped up. "Good-bye," Basil Stein said. They shook hands.

Opening his mouth wide, Roy laughed and cried. Basil Stein turned and motioned to Murna. She went to him and he put his arms around her. He kissed her and murmured, "It's a whole line of nature, there'll be peace in the valley." Then he and the patrolmen ducked out the back door and ran up the alley.

The girl turned on the t.v., a big color set: there was a small yellow house with a low wall around it. The afternoon sun slanting down the street made the house, the few runt trees, the sky itself, parched brown. "That's us," the girl said. She hooked back a curtain and up the street Murna saw the t.v. men behind an old car, the camera on a fender. The men ran between some houses and, turning to the set, Murna saw hundreds of policemen milling on the back porches and in the yards across the street. Some sat on the hoods and trunks of patrol cars eating from lunch pails; many had taken off their shirts and were putting on vests of linked steel. Several pitched horseshoes in the alley, while others had spread army blankets and sat cleaning their machine guns. More motorcycle patrolmen and several patrol cars full of men came up the alley, and these joined the others without speaking, though the camera caught the sidelong glances, winks, and secret smiles the officers exchanged.

"Here," Roy said and handed Murna a machine gun.

"I know nothing about these things," Murna said.

"It's easy." He picked up another gun, crammed in a clip, wound the strap around his left arm, brought the stock to his shoulder, flicked off the safety, and with the snout of the gun hooked back the curtain. While he stared at Murna with his depthless gray eyes, he pulled the trigger.

Instantly the air solidified. Continuous, profoundly dense noise locked thought. Murna dropped her machine gun and covered her ears. She kept moving her feet up and down even after she had backed against a wall, and there she stood, holding her breath, until Roy emptied the clip.

Through the numb ringing Murna heard gunfire across the street, loud but strangely hollow.

The window panes shattered and the curtains and blinds twitched like skirts on the hips of mad dancers, and everything in the house was jerking, spurting into disintegration, chairs and little tables hopping and kicking over as pieces spewed out of splintered gouges. The sofa disgorged clots of stuffing. Pictures flew into pieces and hunks of plaster crashed to the floor. The t.v. set took a shot in the side and went red, gave a powerful moo, and exploded. In minutes the curtains and blinds were shredded, and in the brown light Murna watched the living room and dining room become a long box of dust and rags.

"Whooee!" Through the dust Murna saw the two black men stumbling through the kitchen and out the back door, carrying the washing machine with the woman riding on it.

The girl crawled through the debris, and Murna got down on her hands and knees and followed her. They had just reached the bedroom door when a red-hot tin can came spinning through the window—then another, then all at once half a dozen more, all skipping and leaping about, butting into what remained of the walls and spewing tear gas.

In the bedroom closet the girl opened a trap door and crawled down the hole. Murna followed.

In the crawl space there was the cool smell of earth and dry wood. The shooting was so remote Murna wondered if the police had decided to attack the house next door, having finished with this one.

But when the girl and Murna reached a vent in the foundation, Murna saw that the police were still across the street and still firing—and the day was becoming even browner as smoke buried the sky. The girl poked her shotgun out the vent, fired once, and the recoil kicked her skimming like a board back into the darkness. Immediately there was a steady thudding against the foundation and some bullets zipped through the vent and gouged up puffs of dust in the sandy earth.

Roy came down through the trap door. "Everything's on fire!" he shouted and crawled up beside Murna. "What will happen?" he yelled.

The floor above was hot and through it they heard fire, a steady, increasingly loud rumble. "Dig!" Murna yelled and clawed the sand. Roy dug beside her, scooping out sand between his legs like a dog. He shoved his face into the shallow hole, and cupped sand over his ears and neck.

Murna climbed onto him, her back nearly touching the floorboards, and to her amazement in an instant all the air went straight up through the back of her head, neck, through her back, buttocks, and the length of her legs. It went out with a stunning suck that left her cold and expectant, her mouth open but airless, her eyes open and for a moment seeing nothing.

But then the vent was darkened by the shadow of an animal. Through the smoke, and looking out from such a tremendous distance within herself it was as if she were looking up a misty forest path, Murna barely saw the animal but knew it was a cat and knew it was of course none other than Pusser Boy! He stood in the air vent sniffing with that patient interest of cats, then he came slowly in and began licking Murna's face. *More,* Murna urged. *More* . . . . And it was over, the cheetah trotting smoothly away, not glancing over its shoulder. Murna leaned back and found as she expected, in the corner of the armrest where she would have left it, a slim volume with a slick black cover. She opened it and read the first lines, casually metered and rather obscure, rather private, concerning her life with the heroes and villains.

POPINJAY'S
AFRICAN NOTES

Two hunters came into Hofmockel's and told the bartender they had seen a cougar. They had been out just after dawn, and while one of them stopped to take a dump, the other smoked a cigarette and enjoyed the scenery. He saw the cougar staring at him across a field. "Look," he said. When his buddy stood up, the cougar slipped into the woods. They crossed the field and studied the tracks. Making parentheses with his hands, he said, "This big." I didn't set them straight, but the paw that made a track that big was larger than a cougar's.

The bartender announced a round on the house. There was lots of loud talk and excitement. The hunters had tracked the cougar for three miles but it easily outdistanced them. "Don't feel bad you didn't get a shot at it, because that's no big deal," the bartender told them. "What counts is the cougar itself, the idea of it. You know what I mean?" They thought about that, then nodded, and we let the rest go unsaid, since clearly everyone already knew: having a cougar out there was just what we needed.

The woods surrounding town are full of animals that reached through their bars and unlatched their cages. Farmers and even people in town are always finding big three-toed hoofprints in their turnip patches. And essing troughs, belly-wide, wakes in the dust left by an anaconda which for years has crawled back and forth from one end of town to the other under houses, giving dogs and cats the willies when they hear the nearly imperceptible slithering under the floor-boards, and once a jumble of old books in the library base-ment indicated the snake had spent some time deep in the Depsweth archives. And an elephant, even, sighted usually late in the fall, though the people who see it don't realize for a day or two what they have seen and, invariably, mis-taken for a haystack or the shadow of a cloud, gliding through the woods with the absolute silence which amazingly only the elephant, among all beasts, is capable. And apes—hundreds of apes, which winter in barns on deserted farms, sometimes going so far as to break into farm houses and sleep in the closets, and, come spring, leave mounds of garbage on the porches and thoroughly vandalize the houses, break the windows, rip through the walls, and sometimes burn down the houses after they're sure the warm weather is here to stay.

I was looking out Hofmockel's front window, watching our first real blizzard of the season, when rumor came in con-cerning a murder. A dead man had been found, naked, in someone's garden.

The bartender tried to get some details by phoning his cousin, who was a sheriff's deputy; no luck—he was out on patrol. Then a Hofmockel regular brought in word that a prof at Depsweth had got himself killed by another prof for raping his wife four times. They all turned and looked at me.

Then who should blow in through the door but the bar-tender's cousin with the news that the dead prof was my mentor, colleague, and old friend, Louis Haup. Someone had shot him out of a tree.

Though I didn't ask, I was told, as I tried to make my way to the door (they blocked me, delaying me until I heard it all) that Haup had hastened into the tree from a third-storey bedroom window. I see it all, the slow, clumsy fall as Haup tries to grab a limb, then another, then gives way and goes crashing from one limb to the next, his gangling pale scarecrow body even whiter, blue-pale and almost shiny, phosphorescent in the snowstorm, his arms flailing even after they no longer try to grab the limbs, as knocking against the limbs makes him flop and flail like a big puppet, head over heels, until with one last thunk he solidly kisses the lowest limb and enjoys the silent, cold, unimpeded distance between that branch and the already snow-covered ground where he lands with a muffled bump. He lies facedown, his body pressing into the snow, as if intent upon getting into the earth immediately.

And standing straight from the back of his head, sticking straight up with unspeakable arrogance, is an arrow tipped with bright red and yellow feathers, the shaft bright clean wood newly cut. For in my version of things the man who shot Louis Haup is not a Depsweth prof, but one of the local idiots who, considering themselves true hunters, spend days tracking their prey before closing in for the kill with bow and arrows.

With the map which Fancy Nagel sent in reply to my note to Haup, I had been the first to venture out to their new place following their return from Africa. After turning off the highway, in the afternoon of one of those November days when half the sky is blue while the other half recedes in grayness as if Winter itself were watching, I followed a gravel road along the edge of a woods overlaid with bright autumn colors until I came to a fork that wasn't on the map.

I chose the way that went into the woods, on the assumption that wrong roads don't go far before they run out. I must have driven twenty miles before I realized I was lost, on a road hardly wider than a footpath with tree limbs and brush leaning across the hood of the car. Ahead there was a clearing. I drove into it and was turning the car before I saw the old house backed against the woods. Haup stood on the porch.

Haup! Just as I remembered him—tall and leaning, his

arms swinging even while he stood still as they prepared to gangle into flight to help him grab his meanings out of the air as he would stride up and down lecturing, his sharp nose, sun-blistered and peeling, swinging east and west, providing a most unwelcome view of nostrils, his head tilted back as if, even in the lecture hall, he kept watch for what might come swarming over the horizon. . . . He called my name with that unique voice of his, high and hoarse, the voice of a person who in his time has shouted down thousands of people.

Francine "Fancy" Nagel came out wearing a brown gingham dress with a white lace collar. Her face was thin and pale, without lipstick or other make-up, and her hair, that beautiful russet cascade into which I had stared so often, was knotted in braids and tightly coiled around her head.

Then a tall black woman wearing a tight shiny green dress came onto the porch and stood behind Haup and Fancy. A bat was clamped head-down on her nose, its greenish blue wings spread across her cheeks and eyes! No—she was wearing a mask. No again—it was a tattoo, gleaming as if just before stepping from the house she had oiled it or laved it with spit. As I got out of the car and started toward the house, she waved so widely I glanced over my shoulder to see if it was intended for someone at the far side of the clearing.

"How good to see you, old fellow!" Haup said, coming off the porch and shaking my hand and pounding my back. His eyes were bright with tears and I smelled whiskey on his breath. "You're the first. And probably the last!" He laughed loudly.

Fancy nudged Haup aside. "Dear Goody," she said, taking my hands and holding them tightly. She smiled her serene, competent, knowing smile, the same smile I always see when I think of women in the abstract and the general. We kissed. Then the black one stepped up for her turn.

Such breasts! I looked away, grinning foolishly. Haup laughed, literally whooped, and slapped his thigh. "This is my wife, Utowoga." To her—"This is your new friend, the Sleep

Man, Goody Sherwin."

Encased in the metallic green sheath, it was as if she were a great naked reptile. And her face was incredibly beautiful—not despite but because of the tattoo, which seemed not to have been nicked and gouged into her face, but to be emerging from beneath the surface of the skin, and even as we stood quite close, I didn't see her nose and cheek, as such, but the densely gleaming blue-green bat. And there were smaller tattooes, red and yellow figures so small one would need a magnifying glass to see what they were, though at a glance I realized they were placed with such perfect symmetry on either side of her nose that half of her face seemed to be the reflection of the other. "You boop the radio," she said, or that was what it sounded like. Stepping even closer, she waited for a kiss. I glanced at Haup and Fancy. They waited, smiling.

Very well. On the cheek. I lifted my hands to place them on her shoulders. But Utowoga dipped one shoulder forward and slid into my arms. And there we were, nose to nose. Or rather my nose to the solid beady head of the bat which had squeezed itself under the skin of her nose, and as I skidded down the blue-green incline of her cheeks into her eyes, I saw the yellow and red figures were little people and beasts floating beneath the glazed surface. We kissed and something slipped through my lips into my mouth. Her tongue, of course—but once in my mouth it was larger than a tongue, a powerful lizard, probing left and right, then starting down my throat.

I squeezed off my throat and tried to force out the thing with my tongue. I couldn't. And I wouldn't bite down, for I didn't want to hurt Utowoga. After all, it was only her tongue. But it was working deeper, and I had absolutely no doubt that it would have gone down my throat if Haup hadn't pulled us apart.

"Here, here," he said. Utowoga released me and I released her, for in my panic I had held her as tightly as she held me.

Haup started talking about the interesting features of their new home, pointing across the clearing to the dead tree where an owl had its roost, and the rusty barbed-wire fence which some optimistic soul had put up years ago. I tried to share Haup's enthusiasm for the place, especially its inaccessibility. "Shall we?" Haup put his big hand on my shoulder and, squeezing hard, turned me to the house.

But we couldn't enter because three big dogs were wedged in the doorway. Huge, morose things. Mastiffs, Haup said. They were sick, he told me, gravely ill. And the veterinarian in town couldn't seem to put his finger on the problem.

Fancy freed the dogs from their predicament and we all went in. "Well, my dear fellow," Haup said, "here it is!" With a sweeping motion he offered me the crates, trunks, and bales stacked from one end to the other of the long, high-ceilinged room. The place was aromatic, to say the least—a smokily urinous, goaty, wet-straw odor—Africa, I supposed, quite overpowering, reminding me of a peculiar experience I had while taking some students on a zoo tour. Pausing to deliver a brief commentary, I noticed the students were staring behind me with their eyes wide and their mouths hanging open. I turned. Beyond the waist-high fence I was leaning against, an enormous black Cape buffalo surged up out of nowhere, its massive head and horns coming within inches of me. Then it sank back down the wall of the dry moat bordering its pen. Again it came up, as suddenly and silently as before, its great withers and neck straining, its nostrils flaring, its intense square eyes fixed on mine. I have no idea how long I stood locked there, or how many times the Cape buffalo loomed up, then vanished, before I moved from the fence. But I wasn't freed until I actually smelled the animal and felt the heat of its breath and heard the beast—not its hooves, which were utterly silent as the great thing charged up the wall, but the grinding of its teeth.

I had wandered into the next room. Leaning against one

of the crates, I felt the rough wood through my trousers. A narrow bed was crowded in among the crates. Beyond the walls I heard the wind move through the woods; a tree limb rubbed against the roof. I returned to the front room. "Well, Haup, I hardly think you brought back enough."

They stood at the far end of the room, each looking off in a different direction as people will who have been so long together that with a flick of the eye they can be miles apart. Or were they listening for something? All I heard was the wind. And I heard Haup loudly breathing through his mouth, wheezing. Perhaps being confined with so much of Africa sent their needles spinning. Or as hypnotics will shudder and lose track of things each time they pass the spot where they first gave themselves over to a stronger will, Haup, Fancy, and Utowoga seemed to have quite left me behind.

"She gets the dirty part," Haup said, nodding toward Fancy. "She's doing the sorting and cataloging. A terrible job. And I'll get all the glory!"

Haup and I straddled crates. Fancy and Utowoga rode an ancient brown sofa which came with the place, Fancy cheerily informed me as she served us: whiskey for Haup and me, wine for her and Utowoga.

Also it was Fancy's job to nurse the dispirited dogs, who had come in and collapsed at our feet. Twice that evening we stopped talking and watched as Fancy got down and baby-talked them into letting her spoon gruel past their great teeth and down their throats. I asked Haup if maybe the dogs were discouraged by the chaos into which he had brought them. He had considered that possibility, he said, but rejected it because dogs don't mind chaos; in fact they're quite keen on it, liberty hall and all that. Such a fine place for dogs, way out here—they could roam through the woods, run after rabbits, chase squirrels up trees, and do all the other things dogs thrive on. But they never ventured into the woods, and once that night when they accidentally got shut in another room, they whined piteously and clawed the door until Fancy opened it.

We got around to Depsweth talk. First, the gossip—all the tidbits who had danced and fluttered around the flame of notoriety, featuring the several tragic-comic figures who had had their dazzling, madcap moments, then flown straight into the fire, and including the more numerous others who had risked a loop or two but back-pedaled at the last moment and hung up their wings for the season.

Then to various colleagues and how their work was coming along. Not surprisingly, all this was covered quite quickly, and Haup and Fancy asked about this person and that, scattered individuals who, apparently neither succeeding in arranging any juicy or even faintly untoward doings, nor in accomplishing anything in their work, seemed to have spent the year in suspended animation: one saw them shut away in basement laboratories in Depsweth's older buildings punctuating lecture notes they had taken in their youth.

Fancy said, "How is Ludy? And the children?"

"Ludy is well," I lied. "And I will tell them that you are, too," I lied again. "And the last time I saw the children they were all healthy and . . . active."

"Are you still stringing him along as your lab assistant?" Haup said.

"Well, he is still my lab assistant. However, I certainly don't feel that I am stringing. . . ."

Haup laughed. "I knew it! Nagel's reached his limit, his level of . . . level of. . . ."

"Incompetence," Fancy said softly.

"Yes, incompetence. You ought to fire him, Sherwin. Kick him out on his can! Make a man of him!"

"Please, Louis," Fancy said. Then to me, "I'm coming in to town to see them as soon as I can arrange for a car. Would you tell Ludy. . . . Tell him I'll be in as soon as I can." A sigh. Then, with a surge of enthusiasm, she asked about my research.

I brought them up to date instantly, for there was nothing to tell. I had gotten bogged down in sleep when I was too naive professionally to realize what I was getting into. (I had been Haup's lab assistant.) Though it was my area of specialization, I knew little about sleep on a native basis, having been an all-out insomniac since childhood.

After giving them my empty report, I heard myself revealing that in the past year, without the two of them to pal around with, I had done some re-evaluating. "I've about decided to chuck it. Quit Depsweth. Give up everything."

"You could do worse, old boy," Haup said.

I started on; my mouth worked—but no words came. For I was stunned. Had I expected Haup to argue with me, try to convince me to push on with my research? Did I want Fancy to get down on her knees and plead with me not to give it up? (I didn't rule out getting some of that from her later.) Haup's obvious comfort with my chucking things made me wonder how highly he had regarded my work— and led me to conclude that evidently he had all along felt it was of small consequence. And was there something in his reaction suggesting he had even felt my decision was inevitable? Was he surprised I had stuck with it as long as I had—and was he disappointed in me for so doggedly hanging on to something so fundamentally futile?

Frankly, I wanted Haup to question my reasoning, to examine the steps by which I had arrived at my decision—at least a half-hearted, "Let us think this thing through, old fellow, before you do something rash." But they just sat there gazing at me.

"In my re-evaluating," I said, "I have . . . how shall I put it? Well, I've taken to writing it all, and it is interesting how so much of it comes to . . . what's the word? Well, very little. Maybe the problem is merely the mood of my thinking, these days. Or the *way* I'm evaluating everything. Or the fact that in putting it all in words, which I've never thought about, actually, having been always more interested in pure research—in *things,* as you know, rather than words—makes everything seem so . . . pointless.

"Maybe deliberately pointless." Why did I say that? How would Haup and Fancy take it if I told them, all at once, how much I had changed in their absence? "I have changed a great deal," I said softly. Too softly: they didn't hear. "For instance," I said louder, "I'll write about this." I laughed. I could already feel myself writing this conversation. I could see my left hand resting on the page while my right hand guided the pen, the forefinger or thumb of my left hand reaching over now and then to lightly stroke the other hand or thump it, or take away the pen and start writing, for I am ambidextrous. "I'll write all this." I looked around the room. "It seems strange to speak out loud of it. You're the first I've told."

"When other know . . . ." Fancy began. I caught little of it. Something about conscious self, or self versus consciousness—did she say self-conversus? A subtle point, it slipped right by. Fancy was capable of exquisite subtlety, and in the past I had regularly seen Haup (and Ludy, before Haup) deliberately misunderstand her, or at least it seemed deliberate. I had often seen Haup interrupt Fancy's development of a complex point by ramming his hand up her skirt, so jolting all three of us that Fancy's idea would be completely lost.

But this time Haup followed Fancy's point. "Excellent!" he exclaimed. "Next time you come out bring what you write about this!"

"No. I don't want anyone to read it. Anyway, no one could. It's in code."

They shook their heads. Fancy said that their reading it wasn't the idea.

"We don't want to read it," Haup said. "I'm sure it's just as boring as you claim. But like she says, just bring the damned thing out—the pages and"—his hand stirred big circles.

"Words," Fancy said.

"Words." He pounded the nearest crate. "Bring it out and set it here. We'll involve it in our research."

"I don't understand."

Haup sighed, downed his drink, and as Fancy started to speak, stuck his glass in her hand. "Pipe down. He don't like your idea. He's afraid we'll crack his code and see what he's saying about us—eh, Sherwin?"

Fancy replenished our drinks and turned the conversation to sleep in Africa, for she regretted my decision to abandon my research, just as I thought she might, and I admit that as I listened to her I felt a flicker or two of my old naive enthusiasm for my specialty.

She scooted closer to Utowoga on the sofa, took her long, black hand in hers, and with a finger began drawing circles in the pale satiny palm as she slowly, carefully asked Utowoga to tell her new friend, the Sleep Man, about gurry really any go—if I heard her correctly.

Utowoga began and my first reaction was one of suspicion: she was a fake, and she and Haup were cranking up a hoax. For what she came out with wasn't language but what some Mo Town mama would come forth with if she were to "talk African." Something like "Do you duly deby the revel so blow, the rue, the pook, the rudely who blue? No, the rue'll blummy unglue. It's rob, bobble, and rooping reepy deep. Ruppa re-dop deglibby, deglibby, debow. . . ."

But spellbinding. Not only was she Utowoga the Snake Girl, she was Utowoga the songbird of dainty bebop, her voice twittery and amazingly wee. Within that gleaming powerhouse of feminine muscularity chirped the most delicate and sweetest of cuckoos.

Haup sat on the other side of her and stroked her arm as she twittered, booped, and burbled along, her eyes half-closed, looking dreamily from one of us to the other, even gazing down at the dogs who, lifting their thick heads, listened closely.

When she finished, we sat motionless, watching her words wing off to Africa. The wind surged through the trees and the old house groaned. The dogs jerked their heads in the direction of the sound, and one of them whined deep in his throat.

Utowoga went out back and I heard an engine cough. "The generator," Fancy said, sorting through her slides and arranging them on a carton by the projector. There was more coughing, a frazzled spewing, then the motor caught. "Too fast!" Fancy called, and the generator slowed to a steady chug. Utowoga returned and pulled the blinds, though it was hardly necessary; darkness was closing in.

More drinks all round. Then Fancy switched on the projector and upon the blank wall, in the molten browns and reds of Africa, Haup appeared, deep in conference with half a dozen black men. They were naked, drunk, and down on the ground. On his knees in the middle of them, Haup, apparently digging a hole with his hands, grinned at the camera. In another, Haup, soberer, stood barefooted and with his pants rolled up to his knees, among some black men and women done out in chaps, top hats, vests, short flapperish skirts, and gold lamé jumpsuits. Next, Haup's companion was a white man with a rifle slung over his shoulder and sporting a walrus mustache and glinting spectacles. Jennings Blore, Fancy said, a hunting guide. Haup, too, wore bright, round spectacles. Beside the two men squatted the remains of a Land Rover, smashed nearly beyond recognition, its headlamp sockets gray holes. The Rover had been ravaged by adolescent rhinos. Next, Haup, Jennings Blore, and two white men and three white women, held up the ears of a fallen elephant.

There followed dozens of safari shots. Haup was in all of them, though never with a gun, and never with the least expression of dismay, alarm, or amazement at the carnage in the midst of which he stood literally kneedeep. Rather, he seemed as contented as the ladies and gentlemen who were doing the shooting. But that isn't quite accurate. For the ladies' and gentlemen's expressions had a certain petulance, as though they were still waiting like fretful children for their fun to make them as happy as they deserved to be.

"What on earth are you doing, Haup?" I said when Fancy flicked a slide in which Haup appeared to be kissing the nose of a large, black-maned lion.

Fancy explained that Haup had clamped the lion's mouth and, with his own mouth over the nostrils, was drawing the lion's breath into his lungs.

"Oh," I said. In the dark they stared at me. The time, we knew, had come, and we waited for me to go on. Fancy switched on a little lamp; that might help. It did. "Would you think I was prying if I asked why you were doing that?"

Haup paced back and forth, lecturing loudly and, at first, uninterruptably. Then his big hands started flapping, trying to wave away the silence which closed in each time he faltered. Fancy and sometimes Utowoga darted in the word or phrase he needed, though when they did he scowled at them.

I must admit I found it difficult to follow. Indeed, I found it impossible to listen. Not because I let his disdain of my own work prevent my appreciation of his, though certainly many Depsweth scholars could barely tolerate Haup. For years they had been not only puzzled but appalled, frustrated, even in a few cases driven mad, by Haup's building right before their eyes an international reputation on dabbling research and woolgathering publication as fatuous as that of any random boozer sloughing through the marshlands of What-if, while their own diligent labors went unnoticed and unappreciated.

Forgive me, Haup, you old fraud, I whispered lower than a whisper (one of the dogs cocked an eye at me) as I wondered why I was here. Did I make myself sit through all this—

Utowoga, the slides, the old man (I watched as his hands flapped and flailed like a palsied person's trying to applaud his own lecture as it chased its tail)—just so I wouldn't be alone? No. I was then and remain today a scientist involved in vaguely meaningful work. And I am in a sense interested in someday actually understanding the work to which Haup gave himself so completely that it consumed him, though of course. I know that if it eluded me when these events took place, it surely will in the future. I wish I had forced myself to listen more closely, even though from the first word it was obvious rubbish. Why didn't I? After all, we often must sift through tons of debris to find one tiny clue, even though as often as not that clue will point in the wrong direction.

The fact is I didn't listen because I dozed off. Dozed isn't the right word. For as long as I can remember I have gone into a sort of daze as soon as Haup begins one of his lectures, tirades, or rants. This started years ago when I would drift off in Biology 202 while Prof. Louis Haup lectured me and 100-odd other sophomores. At the time, I thought I was merely taking a snooze. But, as I gradually realized, my snooze wasn't my own doing. Instead of exercising my prerogative as a sophomore to seize the escape and wonderful freedom of a catnap, I had innocently yielded to Haup my mind, my will, my very soul.

I soon realized I was going under not only when Haup spoke but when others did too. In panic I assumed they all wanted to gain control of my mind, will, etc. It was a major crisis, but I endured it with the sophomore's steady plodding fortitude, for even when things are at the very best that period of one's life is an epoch of continual travail.

Young scientist that I was, I "observed" what I was undergoing. I became intrigued by the seemingly banal but in fact incomprehensible phenomenon of sleep—incomprehensible especially to an insomniac. But during this period I became aware that I was losing, on occasions, several hours at a stretch. When I would look back, trying to determine if I had perhaps slept those hours away, I could invariably reconstruct everything that happened in the lapse. Which meant I hadn't truly slept. Which next led me to wonder if I had in a sense slept in that moment when I couldn't recall what had happened . . . and so on. But surely I was sleeping at least a few minutes a day without being aware: catnaps that apparently passed unnoticed by those in the same room with me. I became convinced that I slept only at those moments during which it was most crucial that I remain keenly alert.

The next day I told Ludy about my night with Fancy and Haup. I opposed Ludy's theory that Haup's mind was gone or so riddled that he had gotten lost in himself. But I admitted Haup seemed even more incoherent than he had been before the African expedition. "You should have realized that the minute you saw him," Ludy said. "In Africa the old fool probably suffered a stroke. Or a nervous fit. Or a series of intermittent strokes and fits. . . ."

"Or, overnight, senility had like a great stinkhorn shot up inside him."

"He's definitely over the hill," Ludy said.

Across a wide yellow plain (Africa) I saw a sunset, and I put Haup out there, facing it. But instead of trudging over the hill and into the sunset, Haup stopped, turned, and stood with his arms at ten till four and his head crooked on his neck in classic scarecrow fashion. "No," I told Ludy, "I'm afraid we'll see something from this African expedition. Indeed, there's no doubt of it."

For Fancy could put together something from all the debris in those crates and trunks. And even seven-eights done for and one-eighth mad, Haup could spin something out of nothing.

As Haup talked that night he had dived into one trunk

after another, pulling out bundles of slides and strings of shell and tooth, beads and pretty rocks. And animal hides painted with stick-people running with their hands over their heads, while simpering fish, or phalli with dorsal fins, soared after them. In others the little people stood in circles around dancing lions, elephants, and hippos. Haup pulled out gourd rattles which he shook, grinning at me, and animal skulls, plenty of animal skulls, and little red and purple wads which, Fancy showed me by stretching one between her fingers, were lizard masks. Haup kept piling the stuff on Fancy's lap as if she should on the spot whip it all into something he could sign his name to and wave in the face of Science.

"But you wouldn't deny that Haup is done for?" Ludy whispered. We were sitting beside our frogpond in the greenhouse lab which we shared with O'Hanrahan and Green, our enemies.

"Haup is done for, yes and no," I said. "He's a mere flapping fake, a caricature of the astonishing scientist he once was. I tried not to show my dismay, my chagrin, but I could have broken down in tears or stuck out my tongue, jabbed my thumbs in my ears and wagged my hands, and Haup wouldn't have noticed. He was in Africa again, Ludy—or that dark, lofty place . . . I think of the old Victorian house where he used to live on Wurvell Hill overlooking Depsweth—that place where he used to spend so much time roaming around— lost or not, who knows?—that place where Africa was a small matter, occupying only one corner of the attic.

"No, my dear fellow, Haup is no worse than he has always been. Only less cautious. That's it—he's no longer *wary*. He's convinced he has at last everything he needs. Leaning heavily on Fancy"—here Ludy ground his teeth, squeezed his eyes shut, and furrowed his forehead with ridges—"depending especially on Fancy for her clear-headed prose, her organizational tenacity, her splendid Puritanical three-by-five card cross reference filing skills, Haup will patch something together from all his African junk. Then, oh then, the

Haup of years gone by, Haup the Mighty, Haup the Terrible, will lock jaws with the scientific, anthropological, anthropomodular world, and shake it back and forth, shake it oh most violently, and prove that which the world not only can do very well without, but which the world would indeed much prefer doing without; that which, once Haup has relentlessly, mercilessly proven, the world will do its best to deny, howling at Haup to take it back, take it all back—back to Africa, for God's sake, where it belongs, dig a hole and stick it in the ground with some bones and hair, and give it a word or two of ceremony, and a shake, a squat and a hopabout of ritual, and let it stay down in the great deep earth where it belongs. . . ." My voice carried to the far end of the greenhouse.

"And if Haup doesn't take it back to Africa, which of course he won't, for you know even better than I that he isn't one to back off, there is a chance . . . Ludy, get this— there is a chance, I do believe, that the scientific world will rally and send forth a champion to do battle with Haup." I paused to let that find its mark. "Someone younger, though not necessarily actually young, but someone not yet completely established in his field, though well-trained. And a popinjay."

I leaned down and again spoke in a whisper. "Above all he must be a popinjay who, moreover, *knows* he is a popinjay and cannot live with the fact. Who must somehow redeem himself, save himself from the failure which, though it is looming hugely before him, it will take him a lifetime to fully attain. This popinjay will see instantly that by attacking Haup he can enter onto that vast battlefield, that wide gray plane where the Truly Great sit their mounts like distant thunderheads, the only sound the swish of Time and the murmurous far-off adulation of generations, and the occasional clip-clop of interlopers riding asses and wielding switches with which they deliver fearsome blows to the stirrups of the great.

"This champion popinjay will prove that Haup's latest work is bunk, that Haup is bluffing along on the reputation of his past work. This tinhorn, this volunteer popinjay, will go deeper—he wlll need to go farther; he will need, in fact, to go much *too* deep—by proving that Haup has at last pushed matters too far, himself included, even to the point that he has ceased haunting the edge where he had teetered throughout the 1960's, ceased hanging *over* the edge as he had through the 1970's, and has gone irretrievably *all the way over*—and *down*."

Ludy stared across the frogpond with the fixed, furious gaze with which he awaited attacks by O'Hanrahan and Green's Luftwaffe.

"Of course," I said, "there's the possibility that Haup won't get anything of his African adventure put together, since so much depends on Fancy."

"What do you mean?" Ludy quickly said.

"I simply mean there's an excellent chance that most of what Haup said that night not only I but Fancy was hearing for the first time. Quite possibly he hadn't given her the least notion why he was dragging her off to Africa, or what he wanted, other than to drink palm wine by the caskful and buy a marriage to a tribal princess.

"And there's the sad fact that . . . well, Fancy has suffered from her life with Haup."

Ludy sprang to his feet. "What has he done to her?"

"Well. . . ."

"Damnit, Goody, I thought you said she looked okay."

"She does look okay. But . . . it's not easy to explain."

Indeed.

As Haup has lectured on and on, I gazed at Fancy. I was looking for a clue to how she felt about Haup's condition, about his researches, his bunk and general huffa-chuffa. But she was quite imperturbable. Wonderfully imperturbable! She seemed to positively dote on his lunacies, his gasping lapses, his inarticulate flapping spasms. Her voice caressed him as she slipped in the right word when he floundered.

Poor girl. She was still lovely, or almost lovely, despite her thinness and the dull, fagged weariness beneath her smile. (How could I tell Ludy that?) Her gingham dress was tattered and faded, and her tennies were so worn her toes were sticking out. Haup had locked her in the role of Young Mother Hubbard. How cruel, for that was the same role in which she had got locked with Ludy.

Haup met Fancy at O'Hanrahan and Green's Christmas party, an annual affair for faculty and spouses. I usually took my current lab assistant. (My wife long ago withdrew from appearing at these and other such fetes, not sharing my curiosity in my colleagues' vagaries.) But Ludy refused to go with me; he suspected that O'Hanrahan and Green were giving the party to draw him and me away from our lab. So while Ludy stood guard, I took Fancy to the party, after we deposited the Nagel children at the home of another lab assistant and his wife.

So I was on hand to witness the great moment—the tragic, the obscene moment, when Haup and Fancy met. In O'Hanrahan and Green's so-called "game room" she was looking at a painting titled "Skyscape," the sun spewing forth a turmoil of crows across the sky (or most people would have assumed they were birds). Haup came up to Fancy, they chatted, then Haup slid his long arm around his waist (I held my breath) and told her he was Louis Haup. She smiled, said she already knew, and let him turn her on.

That should have been that; at most, an exhausting weekend. But apparently Fancy liked what Haup had to offer— and much preferred it over Ludy and the children, the lab, and the war with O'Hanrahan and Green.

As my lab assistant, Ludwig "Ludy" Nagel's future at Depsweth was assured, so long as he kept his large rectangular nose to the grindstone and his bony shoulder to the

wheel. He had distinguished himself with a brilliant under-
graduate career in biology; his area was amphibians, and at
Depsweth his specialization had become aerial combat with
O'Hanrahan and Green whom we suspected of deliberately
letting their hybrid bats raid our pond.

Ludy developed beautifully complicated bat traps, but
they all failed. It was taking us a long time to realize that we
were underestimating the intelligence of those bats. The
failure, time and again, of Ludy's traps and defense systems,
threatened to ruin his health, mental grip, and professional
productiveness. The same weekend that Haup stole Fancy, a
short circuit electrocuted thirty young male frogs which
Ludy had wired for a sleep run. Then his latest bat trap
backfired miserably and tragically: twenty-two frogs were
asphyxiated and another half dozen were left hunkering at
the edge of the pond, their heads lowly nodding as if they
were finally realizing just how enormously Ludy had betrayed
them. Or so it seemed to Ludy. Actually, they were suffering
cardio-vascular collapse and brain damage. But their mute
accusation was too much for Ludy, along with his self-
reproach for Fancy's infidelity: he put all the blame upon
himself. He removed his thick-lensed glasses, rolled his eyes
back into his head, and began quaking in a spasm similar to
the final throes of the gassed frogs.

I led him from the lab and drove him to my place where
he thrashed about, clawing runnels of plaster and butting
holes in the walls with his massive Bohemian forehead,
thoroughly terrifying my wife and our dog Bobo.

Fancy went to their home, after her weekend with Haup,
to pack a suitcase and tell Ludy she was leaving him "at least
for the time being, for I must experience this opportunity
with Louis"—her words to me when she phoned to ask where
Ludy was and what he had done with the children. I told her
the children were with Mrs. Bell (my wife's Sunday School
teacher), and I assured Fancy that I would pass her message
on to Ludy when I was confident he could endure hearing it.

She insisted on coming by, driving Haup's old Jeep, and I took her behind the house and gave her a peek through the window into the room where Ludy lay balled up in a corner, naked, bony, and needing a shave.

He recovered and was back in the lab in a week. But that first day he went about mumbling out the corner of his mouth. Was it bitterness? Suppressed rage? Was he telling off the frogs? Nothing of the sort! It was a manly version of the clucking of a mother hen. How he loved those frogs! And how they loved him! And how O'Hanrahan and Green hated him! (Me they feared.) For O'Hanrahan and Green knew that Ludy would someday get those great hybrid brutes of theirs, with their two-foot wingspans and heads big as tomcats'. But O'Hanrahan and Green needn't have worried. True, Ludy's hatred for the bats had become something really special as it became entangled with his hatred of Haup—and a cold, patient hatred of Science. But I doubted that Ludy would ever succeed in striking those bats the deathblow they so richly deserved.

Perhaps I misjudged Ludy, that part of him which wasn't directly connected with frogs. Thoroughly dedicated, he lived frogs, walked and talked frogs, slept frogs, breathed, ate, and dreamed frogs. But Ludy was a man, and at the end of each day (I should say in the Pre-Haup days) he left the lab and cut across campus, climbed the wall behind Huickerman Hall, and ran downhill to his other half.

I was never at Ludy and Fancy's place on Happy Lane when the little apartment wasn't insufferably hot. From the steam-filled kitchen came the continuous blup-blup of a thick bean soup which they ate day in and day out. Surrounded by babies, which Fancy dressed in green jumpsuits, half of them shaking ther chubby fists at the other half and, red-faced and big-eyed, holding forth at the tops of their lungs, Ludy sat in his big chair in the middle of it all, sweating in his undershirt and baggy shorts, his forehead gleaming, his spectacles steamed over, drinking beer and lecturing on the frog. He contended that I would never penetrate the sleep of this species unless I knew the total frog, from tip to tip, even though I had explained to him a dozen times that the research for which I had hired him was aimed at providing a footnote, at most, in the larger study of sleep. This baffled him. He viewed my unwillingness to dedicate my life exclusively to the sleep of frogs as a grave misuse of my science. From that he would shift to another favorite theme: the bone-headedness of administrators and certain faculty members who not only install bats and frogs in the same lab, but attempt to pursue research under such conditions. Fancy would interject to inquire whether Ludy thought it was wise to shoot off his large mouth so critically of certain faculty members, though of course Ludy was not criticizing me but those irresponsible madhatters, O'Hanrahan and Green. Ludy would throw an empty beer can at Fancy and urge her to shut her yap.

From that high point they would fly into one of their wonderful exchanges, mercilessly itemizing the many problems currently sensitive in their life together. They rattled through this as if it were a script, though each time there were interesting differences, and they would even swap roles in the accusations and responses. First, Fancy might explain how Ludy had ruined their life with boredom, to which Ludy would shrug and reply, palms up, that he was what he was, and that Fancy should give serious thought to going home to her mother—there was the door, take half the kids. Thirty minutes later they might flare up again, only this time Ludy would attempt to open Fancy's eyes to how utterly she had lost her enthusiasm for life. Fancy would reply that she was what she was, and that Ludy should try finding another woman who would be willing to get in bed with him every night. At this point one of them might go to the door. All the little children would fall silent, giving the moment the full drama it deserved. Then Fancy or Ludy would announce he/she was leaving—and this time for good! He/She would storm out the door, amid a caterwauling of sincere grief from the children, and stand on the back porch for five or ten minutes before coming back in, sitting down, and taking two or three euphoric babies onto his/her lap.

My visits with Ludy and Fancy would last quite late, especially on weekends, and winters we would top off the evening by all of us bundling up, including those of the children who were still awake, and marching down the middle of the deserted street to the end of Happy Lane to the little park with its frozen lake, where Ludy, Fancy, and I would skate, and the children would scoot around on the ice. Morning often found us back at their apartment in the kitchen having big bowlfuls of soup. Then Ludy and I would hike across the campus to the lab for a look at the colony, and more than once I bade him good-day there, leaving him to doze under the young willow by the pond and his beloved frogs.

What a change for Fancy was her life with Haup, how exhilarating, challenging, and how soon it must have become clear to her what dangers—and what exciting possibilities!— were involved. For not only did he want her for herself, he wanted more. He was keen on "researching" her! And Fancy grew keen on being researched! They became a project, days and nights of research, all very intense. Fancy loved it. She was bright and she was earnest about Haup's work (and her own work, too, which had been forgotten in recent years, always taking backseat to Ludy's frogs and all those babies). She was utterly caught up by Haup and his research with her, with the "exploration" of what I once heard her soberly refer to as "the uncharted plains and high plateaus of my interior." I could hardly keep from coming right out and asking what they were up to.

Instead, I waited, watched, and after she moved out of the little place on Happy Lane and into Haup's big house on Wurvell Hill, it was all I could do to prevent Ludy from dying of grief one day and, the next, from killing Haup. I kept close watch on Haup and Fancy. (I did this in part for Ludy's sake, and I reported back to him. Sometimes he came with me, waiting in the car and, sometimes, at night, sneaking up to the house and peering in the windows.)

I was the first to realize how utterly Fancy had handed herself over to Haup—body, soul, and complete secretarial services, for when they weren't "exploring" Fancy, Haup kept her hopping with other projects. Now and then he let me take a look at what they were producing. He claimed they were a team, but it was obvious that only a small part, if any, of this new work was his. All in Haup's name, Fancy was doing a tremendous amount of work, and not only was it good, it was so brilliant I got monolithic headaches from reading it. But what exactly were they "researching"?

On the surface it was perfectly customary, perfectly dreary. As Haup's sweetheart, Fancy was his little circus, tritty-trotting back and forth for him, and, when that bored him, going at it on a treadmill which Haup cranked faster and faster. One imagines the interludes, Fancy sprawled on the floor, panting, blinking at the ceiling, her face shiny with sweat, while Haup paces about, waiting, watching her . . . and seeing the glint of yet another face surfacing, sleek and slow, to slip itself into Fancy's mask. For it had led to that.

With Haup, and at first only with and for Haup, Fancy could "change," that is, become someone (or something; it wasn't exactly a person, sometimes) completely different from what she had been the moment before, completely unexpected and unprecedented.

How exciting all that must have been for both of them, but especially for Fancy. So excited by him, so stimulated, inspired, so enflamed by Haup!—the great and famous Louis Haup himself!

She went at it hard and fast, changing continually, at first on a daily basis, but then more often. Hourly! And still more often until she was competing with the person she had just

that moment become, and always trying to outdo herself,
while Haup watched every move, every gesture, urging her
on, that great wide mouth of his hanging open. She gave him
everything, fed him the unborn generations which were
snugly tucked away, awaiting their life, inside that beautiful
woman who only a few months ago stood gazing out a little
hole rubbed in a steamed-over window in the apartment on
Happy Lane.

One day Fancy and Haup found by accident that, as person after person flickered through her, there were moments,
half-seconds at the beginning, when her face and eyes, everything, turned to wood—that was how Haup had put it, meaning, I assumed, that she went blank. While he told me this,
leaning forward and whispering loudly, Fancy who was doing
some work for him at the other end of the room (typing; she
had been at it all afternoon) turned to reach for a stack of
file cards, and I saw on her face the very look Haup spoke of.
But I thought it was just the light. Or her expression—the
stern look a person gets when life seems for a while to be a
small, dull proposition. Or even that the two of them were
playing a trick on me. For when Fancy turned to reach for
the file cards, it wasn't her own lovely face I saw but something simian, obscene, a face carved from a coconut.

As I stared at Fancy, sitting with Utowoga on the sofa
in that wretched farm house in the middle of the woods,
Fancy Nagel's face is again her own, though pale and thin,
drawn by an exhaustion of which, because she is still young,
she probably isn't even aware. It occurs to me that, though
she doesn't know it yet, and though she would bravely deny
it, she is done for. When they are at last finished, done for,
and down in the dust, there is none so utterly finished as the
valiant. And Fancy, this splendid, gentle little Fancy, was
indeed valiant. She not only endured the last two years of
Haup's life, years beyond doubt the most harrowing and
ridiculous of a lifetime of harrowing, ridiculous years, but she
truly dedicated herself, gave herself with the sublime and out-

rageous ease of the faithful. And all for "Science"? To "know"? Yes, and worse—to capture things that cannot happen, things that simply cannot, must not, be.

*

Utowoga, after yawning as widely as a lion, and after peeling the bat off her face and tossing it into a trunk, tottered off to bed. Haup went in with her.

I joined Fancy on the moundlike sofa and spoke of Ludy and the children. "They miss you so much," I said. "We *all* miss you."

"Dear Goody." She patted my hand, sighed, and said, "It's so hard to think of them—of him and all of them. They're so far in the past, it seems."

Her tone changed and she began a loud and rapid-fire account of her negotiations with a certain tribe (the Monotoneys, I think she said) who were excellent bearers for flatland travel but refused to climb one step up a mountain, claiming that their backs would bend and break, and their heads roll off. While their neighbors, the cliff-dwelling Waukupies, were certain that they would sink straight into the ground if they weren't at all times tilting so far off the perpendicular that their shoulders brushed the mountainsides as they trudged along. . . .

Obviously Fancy was attempting to cover the sounds from the next room, the unmistakable rapturous babble of love-making. (I admit to wondering, even at his funeral, how Haup, a brass-faced scarecrow with an atrocious alcoholic halitosis, managed all his life to attract and hold such beautiful and intriguing women. Was he somehow a lover? Did he, before they knew what to expect, spring something on them that knocked them completely out of kilter and left them everafter vulnerable to him?)

"Oh, Fancy," I said low and had a try at her top button,

which was cutely hiding under the lace doily of her dress. Only interrupting herself with a surprised, "What?" she pushed my hand away and went on, ". . . no labor unions as such, though they will strike at the drop of a hat and are keen on work slowdowns. . . ." I tried again, sliding my other arm around her waist to hold her still. "Don't," she whispered.

"Please," I said, nuzzling my big nose into the doily, sniffing her special smell and the sharp scent of liniment. (I pictured Fancy giving Haup a rubdown, kneading his pale, flabby, old-man back. Or giving a voluptuous massage to Utowoga, a rippling, glowing black sea undulating under Fancy's hands. But I later learned the liniment was for the dogs. Fancy would lay the mastiffs out on the kitchen floor, stretched to their full, incredible length. They would grunt and groan, and look over at each other while Fancy, kneeling on the floor, worked them over.) Fancy's liniment smell was faintly tinged by curdled milk, rather vomity, and her own distinctive, rather high but wholesome scent of sweat and basic girl. Fancy was notorious for her refusal to use soap, perfume, or deodorant. She scoured herself with pumice. I marveled at how she would shine pinkly for days after one of her fierce baths. Others marveled, too, and found equally marvelous the odor which followed the fading of the glow from her cheeks. As one wag put it, "Fancy goes from pink to stink."

She turned her face away, straining, and I kissed her neck, then licked it, and when she put her hand up to push my face away I gave it a nip. I moved my arm up from her waist and, digging my fingers into her tightly braided hair, turned her so we were nose to nose. "Please," I said. "I love you. I always have—with all my heart. This is no life for you. He's a lunatic and dangerous. Give me a kiss. No tongue, just a kiss. . . ."

Her eyes gray and lucid, calm and canny as a soldier boy's, Fancy looked into me and refused to either kiss or answer, her head straining so hard I was afraid I'd pull out her hair.

I stood up as Haup's thumping footsteps came from the other room. And, supporting my theory that it was his treasure of love that bound women to him, as he entered, lighting a cigar, Utowoga's moaning continued in the bedroom, not as loudly as before but as if she were luxuriating in a mortal wound.

Fancy's face was red. Pouting, her eyes bright, she wiped her neck with the back of her hand, and gave a pat to her hair.

Haup told a rather lurid story of how Fancy, who had been the only one of the expedition who could make heads or tails out of the dialects, had to sit all day haggling with a tribe of nudists. "Some are and some aren't," Haup said, "and these fellows were. They wanted Fancy to see what enormous brutes they were!" He laughed uproariously. "They were true whoppers, weren't they, Fancy? I mean"— with both hands he measured what he considered a true whopper. "Remarkable specimens."

Through this, Fancy undid one of her braids, twisted it tighter, and nailed it to her skull with a dozen bobby pins.

Haup picked up the thread of his lecture, and before I could put up any defense against hearing, he said the "real" reason he was living out here was "better access."

"Surely you're joking," I said.

He asked if I had noticed there were windows facing all directions. I answered that I had somehow overlooked this fact. He smiled. "But you don't know what you're looking for, do you? Or, what's looking for you."

The sinister ring of this, and the sinister manner in which Haup said it, struck home. "I would rather not go into. . . ."

Too late! He had me. I could feel it even before he tested me (or that's what I thought he was doing) by looking away and chuckling, puffing his cigar, leaning down and exaggeratedly gawking at Fancy's breasts, and, without speaking a word, commanding me to look at them also.

I wanted to refuse, but I looked. Haup unbuttoned the dress and Fancy herself opened it. Her breasts were beautiful. I wanted to weep, they were so beautiful. But then Haup told me to look closer and I obeyed, leaning down, and I saw beneath the soft translucent skin a scene of turmoil—tumbling, struggling men and women, and hairless beasts, and babies squirting into the air out of the writhing bodies. Haup explained that this was nothing new, that I had seen all this before, and I automatically agreed (though if I had seen it before, I had no idea where), "But now," Haup said, "you'll see more than what you already know."

"Yes," I said, ready in spite of myself, admitting that I had known all along that it was leading to this, riding the surge in volume from Utowoga who had struck a hard, driving rhythm which, the small, irrelevant part of me capable of stepping back, doubted would ease her into sleep.

The night at Haup's became a blur. I had, of course, expected that it would, even before I went out to his place. I see Haup towering over with his shirt off. (Where is Fancy?) Haup lifts his arms and flexes his biceps, his arms and chest thick with muscle. The scarecrow has leaked his straw and he has stuffed sausages and snakes up his pants legs. And his cheeks and nose are bulging. (So Haup's face peeled not from continuous sunburns, as I once thought, or from some skin condition which he ignored or for which there was no cure: his skin peeled because it had been stretched to splitting.) Then he begins cranking. First one arm, at the elbow, then the other, the forearm and fist turning all the way around (how does he do that?), the biceps squirming and rippling.

Fancy is curled up at one end of the sofa. I sit at the other end with Haup standing over me. I rise and start for the door, but Haup blocks my way. We stand chest to chest. There is a great deal of shouting, all in all a drunken rout, shameful, apologies are called for all around. . . .

Were we arguing about Fancy? Did Haup question my honor?

Something to do with his work. Africa. A lecture of his which I had refused on principle to listen to. We perhaps even grappled, tried to pull each other off balance, shoved each other. (I am quite large and heavy, but Haup surprised me with his strength.) I see his mouth opening wide, not to speak but to show me a tooth, or his throat, and as I step nearer to look he tries to burn me with his cigar.

We stand side by side with our arms across each other's shoulders, and watch Fancy sleeping. Her face, arms, and legs are pale and smooth.

On the porch Haup and I listen to the steady chirping of a bird deep in the woods. Like an elaborate sigh, wide enters the woods, then stops abruptly and crouches. On the porch Haup tells me everything. I nod earnestly. What he is saying means the end of him. Just as well. He should have stopped his work years ago. He should have died. At any rate from here on he should live in complete reclusion, seeing no one, corresponding with no one, allowing absolutely no insights into his work and, especially, the person behind it. Let the world sit down with his work and if it needs a "Louis Haup" let it invent one. Perhaps I told him this.

Were we waiting for something? The whole business was of course leading up to my seeing in the vague dawn light something coming out of the woods into the clearing. Haup might even have brought an animal back with him, dragged it through customs in a big wicker hamper, awing the inspectors with the fact that he was Haup—Louis Haup! World-famous scientist!—whose stinking crates were filled with bones and hides and general anthropological metamorphological materiel which would only dismay and disorient the officials if they should poke their noses into it. . . .

The last I recall of that night is not something that "happened," but rather a mood that fills me: the feeling that *I* am what is being seen. Not that I am that which is . . . going forth, but rather, as I stand there naked, I am that which is . . . coming back. And, always at this point, when I try to remember, try to push through that cold mist, which is how it seems to me now, I break away from myself, away from thought, memory, and understanding, and I push physically through the air around me, into contact with the things surrounding me, and I laugh, I talk loudly, I make all the appropriate sounds.

And when word came, that snowy afternoon, to all of us in Hofmockel's that Professor Louis Haup had got shot out of a tree after raping a fellow prof's wife four times, I nearly strangled. I was choking back what I was afraid might be wild laughter—and I definitely didn't want to let those men see me laughing about Haup's death. While just as likely what I was suppressing was an explosion of tears. I didn't know in what form the upsurging I felt would come forth. I had never felt anything like it in my life. It was an incredible exhilaration—combined with grief. Or maybe the exhilaration was grief itself, in its purest form. It bubbled inside me, forcing its way up my throat, and I held it back by hyperventilating as I forced my way toward the door of Hofmockel's, the details of the deputy sheriff's account of Haup's death ringing in my ears and blurring my own sense of how it happened. Then I was at last out into the cold air, stumbling and skidding down the sidewalk.

I drove north of town into the storm, reaching out my window and scraping ice off the windshield, but even with the windshield clear I could hardly see. I turned off the highway onto a farm road, though I was only guessing that it was the right one, from my vague memory of Fancy's map. Soon I was deep in the woods, my car burrowing down a snow-clogged trail. I got out and walked ahead. All I saw was the blue darkness of the woods filling with snow. Then I heard dogs howling.

Haup's dogs! The sound vanished on the wind, and though I stood waiting five, ten minutes, maybe longer, I didn't hear it again. I set off in the direction from which I thought the howling came; I didn't go far before I got stuck trying to push through a drift. Buried under the snow was a barbed-wire fence—the same one, I was certain, that bordered the clearing around Haup's house! But there was no clearing. The fence zigzagged through the woods.

I drove backwards for miles before I could turn my car around, and it wasn't until morning, and the end of the storm, that I found the highway and headed home.

*

For two weeks search parties drove up and down country roads and trails, and trekked into the woods, but we didn't find Haup's place. The woods are so vast there has been increasing doubt whether we were even looking in the right general area: all we had to go on was my memory. We hoped that Fancy and Utowoga might hike out and find the town, but we have concluded that they have no better idea of where we are than we have of where they are. And though Fancy made the map which I used (and lost) that afternoon, the map was incorrect: I had found them quite by accident.

Haup was eulogized as one of the modern greats in his field, the dubious circumstances of his death being left to float in abeyance to preserve the dignity of his memory, Depsweth, and Science. Professor Peter Bluffeau, Depsweth trigonometer, has been charged with Haup's murder, though it is well known that the prosecution's case is flimsy. For one, Bluffeau has an alibi: Ludy Nagel will swear that Bluffeau was with him in the greenhouse lab the night of Haup's death. The weakness in this alibi is Ludy's credibility: if he is pressed in cross examination, he might have a nervous collapse on the spot; on the other hand, since Haup's death

Ludy is capable of unimaginable euphorias: on the stand, he just might burst into song.

There is another weakness in the prosecution's case: Peter Bluffeau's frailty. A small, delicate man, could Bluffeau draw a bow far enough to shoot an arrow with sufficient force to penetrate Haup's skull, which, Haup's autopsy disclosed, was abnormally thick?

More likely, everyone at Depsweth agrees, Myra Bluffeau herself shot Haup, though her motive is open to speculation:

1. She was defending herself: it was a case of attempted (successful?) rape.
2. Myra shot Haup in anger following a lovers' quarrel. (Though no one believes Myra and Haup were lovers.)

Another theory is circulating: Haup was killed by one of the multitude who have collected grudges, grievances, and pure and potent hatreds against Haup. This opens the matter to such a large, indeed universal, scope that silence reigns wherever this theory is brought up; it would seem that each of us, from deep in his heart, shot an arrow into Louis Haup's head.

There is still hope that I might someday locate Fancy Nagel and Utowoga, for while spending so much time in the woods with the search parties, I found myself responding to what is awakened in men and satisfied by hunting. I derive increasing pleasure from moving through the forest, searching for those women, and it is hard to describe the thrill I feel when I surprise a deer or some other animal—once a bear; we were about the same size and when it saw me there was a hesitation during which we wondered who should flee; with a grunt and something very much like a shrug, the bear deferred, perhaps because he was the animal, and ambled off. At first my heart beats hard, my breath comes fast; then I am filled with stillness as I stand watching the animal as it grazes or picks up nuts or, as in the case of the bear, scratches the back of its neck languorously and loudly with a hindfoot. Sometimes I move even closer, hardly aware that my feet are moving, as if I am gliding. Once I came so close to a deer I could have touched it. When it turned and suddenly saw me standing beside it, it exploded with a bound that sent it soaring the opposite direction—straight against the trunk of a large tree, knocking the deer down. It struggled frantically, its hooves and legs making a blur while its large eyes stared straight into mine, as if concentrating mightily, willing me not to move until it got to its feet, which it did, making a loud wet gasp of relief, and ran off.

One day I became aware that I was being stalked. Perhaps he saw my coat as I passed over a ridge, and from where he stood it suggested a deer, or more likely a bear, for my coat is dark. My pulse raced and I felt an excitement which seemed to bloat me, then abruptly ceased, leaving me cold and immensely calm. It was quite early in the morning and the woods were thick with mist. The ground along the ridge was hard; I left no tracks. Of course if there had been footprints, and if the man were smart enough to actually see them, he would have known what he was stalking along a wide trail left through the wet underbrush was a man.

The risk of his coming close enough, and being stupid enough, to take a shot created inside me—or inside the visceral excitement which I felt when I was on the trail of an animal—a steady intense tightening. On its surface, this was fear. But beneath fear and anger, it was the pleasing, immensely full sense of concentrated readiness.

It inspired me to begin a bend to my left, a turning that was gradual at first but which became tighter. The hunter didn't notice, or if he did it didn't matter, for he was so eager to close in for a shot. I easily circled back, picked up the wide path the two of us left through the brush, and came up behind him.

He was most ordinary. He was a man. He wore a black woolly cap and a tan hunting jacket, green trousers, and boots. Carrying his rifle at port, he walked leaning forward. He disappeared into a dense thicket.

I followed him in, then paused, hearing him thrashing his way through. He wouldn't hear me; his struggling made the path through the thicket so wide I had easier, quieter going than he. I closed the distance between us. He paused; the woods were perfectly still. Perhaps he sensed that he was very close to his bear. He went a little farther, and this time when he stopped I took a step nearer and, though I didn't actually touch him, he became aware that his bear was directly behind him.

With a roar I grabbed him. He dropped his rifle, gave an odd piping cry, and trembled. I shook him back and forth, his feet off the ground, then I burrowed my face between his collar and cap, and blew a loud trumpet blast on his neck.

I lowered him to the ground. He lay with his mouth open, breath fluttering his lips as if he were trying to snore. I went off a short distance. He woke carefully, opening first one eye, then the other. Then he cautiously lifted his head and looked around. He jumped up, grabbed his rifle, and ran. I roared, most convincingly, I thought; I'm sure it convinced him, hearing it as he did above the noise of his running, his panting breath and pounding heart, certain that even if the bear wasn't at the moment breathing down his neck, it was not far behind.

CHUMS

He didn't try to escape but turned his back on the schoolyard, that wide, rolling prairie with clumps of brush and, far
off, the brick maze where every morning we found things left
the night before by roving gangs, strange, horrible things
which were beyond our imaginations, though some of us, inspired by the strange needs of innocence, kept them and
speculated on their uses, their meanings, with results that
were invariably exciting, invariably terrifying.

The boys surrounded him, shoved him around, tripped
him, kicked him—he didn't try to defend himself. He was incredibly thin, a stick with a pale narrow face and sharp nose.
I don't know why the gang had suddenly noticed him, why
they singled him out. It's doubtful that he had done anything
to provoke them, but the gangs that roamed the schoolyard
and who in later years roamed the streets, occasionally returning nights to attack the school building for old time's
sake and perform depravities in the brick maze—these gangs
didn't require provocation. Straightforwardly vicious, they
existed in a state of obliviousness: everything they did, every
gesture, had a bland gracefulness, a stonelike superiority.

They got him down, took turns kicking him, then they
stood him up and a boy on each side socked him back and
forth good and fast—so fast his face blurred. The gang
cheered, and I admit it outdid anything I had ever seen them
do. The way his head twanged back and forth, faster and
faster!—it was fascinating.

The cheering distracted one of the boys punching him; he broke the rhythm and the victim, propelled by the force of the last punch, stumbled to the edge of the tight circle, somehow through them . . . and farther. He was running!

In disbelief we watched as he ran very slowly, barely lifting his legs, leaning forward very far as if that might make him go faster, and his running became a spectacle in itself. Stunned, the gang let him reach the school building and turn the corner.

"Come on," someone called, and they trotted to the building. The gang rounded the corner, came back, stood with their hands on their hips, looking at each other. Their fine little victim, the thin, narrow-faced boy, had disappeared. They even boosted someone up to look in a window, but he wasn't inside.

"We have not got him," one of them said and the others turned and looked at him as he said slowly and blankly again, "We have not got him." They walked off a ways and immediately forgot about the narrow-faced boy. Such a disappearance would keep me and the other secretive youths like me entertained, dazed, and content for weeks; we would be lost and tantalized in it, our parents would think we were sick or in love or in trouble with the cops. A disappearance would keep us going, for we loved the impossibility, we couldn't resist it; I would even go so far as to say we lived for it.

But the gang, of course, immediately forgot the victim had ever existed. They wandered off and soon they could be seen, far off, swarming across the prairie in running combat with another gang.

I went again to the corner of the building and stood with my nose to the corner, my left eye staring down the endless south wall of the building, and my right eye looking down the east wall. And I discovered the gang's victim was still there! In his extreme thinness he had become the corner, his narrow face and sharp nose becoming part of the sheer line of the corner. I stared into his eyes and whispered, "I see you."

The corner moved where his mouth was: "Don't tell."

"Yes. I'll tell them," I said. "Unless you give me something."

The corner closed as he closed his eyes and I could see the corner straining around him as he tried to disappear totally. But he couldn't. He opened his eyes. "All right," he said. "What'll you give me?"

"I don't have anything. I'll let you hit me."

"Fuck that. I want something to show. Something I can think about."

"I'll show you my place."

"I don't want to see your place. I *want* something."

"It's not where I live. It's my special place."

"Is it a club?"

"It's better than that. Something is there. In it."

"What?"

The corner wobbled as he shook his head.

"Is it a gang?" I said.

"It's like a person," he whispered.

He had me. I asked more questions, but he wouldn't tell me anything more. I stood between the corner and the playground, and he emerged from the corner, though by now the gang was at least half a mile away, beyond the brick maze: clouds of dust rose above them, for they had apparently won the battle with the rival gang and were now stomping them.

He stood close to me, looking at me with his severe, narrow face. He expected me to ask how he had done that with the corner, but I refused to ask. He turned and started off. I followed, calling, "When?"

He went faster, and I ran to keep up. "When?" I yelled. "When, goddamn you?"

Now he was running across the playground as before, not moving his arms or shoulders but leaning rigidly forward from the waist, his legs not bending at the knees but stiffly swinging like scissors—but he was running very fast, and I realized he had earlier run slowly to deceive the gang, sly fellow. He outran me easily. I stopped and as he topped a hill he called over his shoulder, "After school," and disappeared.

I spotted him after school in the crowd pouring from the building. He was hurrying, trying to lose himself among the other boys and girls. But I was right behind him. I reached out and grabbed his neck. I swung him around and smiled in his face. "Remember me?"

His eyes were enormous and yellow, with great wide whites. The yellow was unlike anything I had ever seen—yellow like a cat's, maybe, but deep and far like plains.

I turned away, angry, for he was grinning at me; he knew his eyes had surprised me. His grin took the corners of his mouth up sharply, making his mouth a quaint V under the V of his nose.

"I want to see that thing," I said.

"Sure," he said. "Let go." I let go his neck and we walked on. "Nice day," he said. "My name is Bob. Where do you live? Do you have a dog?" He smiled slyly as we crossed a street. The crowd of children was thinning; in another block they had scattered completely; he and I were alone. "This way," he said, and we turned down a street with few houses, and those the dark, run-down sort, some with boarded windows, ruined trees leaning into each other. Several blocks on, the street gave way to a dirt road, overgrown and untraveled.

"Do you live down here?" I said.

He jerked his hand, thumb up, over his shoulder: beyond empty fields with brush and thickets hulking larger and larger in the shadows of late afternoon, were hills, and beyond the hills a water tower hid in a clump of trees and low bushes.

At the end of the road was a cemetery. He went up the path and under the iron arch that said *Bethel* in leafy iron letters. He looked back at me.

We followed a grass-covered lane through tombstones; statues of angels here and there looked off as if frozen stiff in the middle of doing something they started long ago. We topped a hill; the cemetery went on for miles, and I saw the first of the square stone houses. Not far ahead was a big one, a mausoleum as large as an apartment house, with barred windows set high in the walls, almost to the slate roof.

He turned off the lane and went straight to the mausoleum. He turned very slowly and smiled his V smile, his big yellow eyes looking right at me. "Here we are."

Still looking at me, he reached out the other direction, took the handle of the big iron door, and it opened smoothly. "It's in there," he said.

"What is?"

"The thing."

I shook my head.

"You can stand here and see it," he said. He stepped inside. I waited, then went to the door and looked into the long, empty room. Gray, distant light spilled down from the high windows. He stood half-way down the room, gripping the handle of one of the square steel doors that lined the walls. "*Don't,*" I whispered, but he opened it, staring at me, and reached inside. There was a screech, then a grumble of rollers as he pulled out a casket—it was huge. And all the while he was looking at me, his face locked in that V grin, his eyes big.

I backed out and pulled the door almost closed, until there was a crack just wide enough for my face. I glanced behind me—there was nothing but the tombstones, the angels, the sky going away to night. I put my face to the crack in the door.

He lifted the casket lid, his head jerked my way and, grinning, he stepped up onto the side of the casket and unbuckled his belt and unzipped his pants. "*Don't,*" I whispered. He grinned, dropped his pants. He didn't wear underwear. He put his arms out straight and swayed his hips. He kicked up his right foot, then his left, and clasping his hands behind his head, squatted down, his knees wide apart. Then he hopped down into the casket, reached down, and hooked

big legs, bent at the knees, over the sides of the casket. He
knelt, staring down seriously.

"*What are you doing?*" I whispered.

He ignored me.

I opened the door and tiptoed down the room. Just as I
was about there, the legs slowly lifted straight up.

"Oh," I said and stood there.

After a while he stood and, hands on his hips, stepped
up on the side of the casket again. The legs in the casket remained lifted in a big V, and he nodded toward them and
said, "Want a turn with Rosie?"

I didn't answer.

He laughed and tumbled into the casket, banged down
onto his knees, and lunged forward. "Uh!" I heard.

The light dimmed, the walls dissolving. "What time is it?"
he called over his shoulder. I looked at my Mickey Mouse
and told him. He bounced around in the casket, then jumped
up and the legs lowered. He climbed out, closed the casket,
and pushed it on its rollers back into place and shut the steel
door. "It's cold in here," he said, quickly putting on his
pants.

We carefully shut the mausoleum door, not banging it,
and ran up the lane to the cemetery gate. At the road we cut
across empty fields toward the water tower looming above
the low houses. His house wasn't as bad as some of the
others. He asked if I wanted to come in. I said no.

He waved and went in. I started off, then came back and
looked in a window. He was in there with his family—a
mother, a father, a sister and a little brother. They had joined
hands and were dancing around the dinner table. I heard
them laughing. Then he saw me looking in, and as he danced
by he squinted his yellow eyes and stuck out his tongue.

I backed away and turned to the darkness to find my way
home.

FABLE

~~~~~~

Babs was leading-in her *Girl in the Bikini* when the studio exploded, all the atoms becoming white balloons and crying *wah wah wah* like oboes. Far away she heard herself talking, but Ralph the director was squinting at her which meant everyone out there in Sun and Fun Land was also squinting, while Mr. Crowell the anchorman frowned.

The film clip began and in the monitor Babs watched herself, in her orange lamé bikini and golden skin, interviewing a Canoga Park resident who had a sure way to protect his roses. "The aphid goes right in there," he said, and Vince Fong did a marvelous close-up. The Canoga Park man pried off the roof with his thumbnail and the folks saw a tiny maze. "The door shuts behind him automatic."

Babs unpinned her mike and left the news desk. *What?* Randolph said silently. Babs answered *Sickish* and, as if demonstrating a halo, radiating both hands from her head to the size of a pumpkin.

In the dressing room she lay down and through the top of her head something smooth and stunning like cold honey came into her. It numbly occurred to her someone was drilling a hole in her head. Closing her eyes, she floated suspended over an unbelievably deep tide pool of bright water.

"Gee, doll, what's wrong?" Randolph said. Connie the receptionist was standing there too.

Babs sat up and looked around. It was the same dressing room, but the chairs, the table and its dirty mirror were exceedingly distinct; unnoticed by anyone but Babs, everything was subtly intensifying. She glanced at the grainy yellow wall and felt she could easily slice her hand into it like sand.

She stood in one smooth movement which she didn't feel and heard herself tell Randolph not to worry. Just a bad headache. She kissed Connie's cheek and was out of the dressing room and gliding down the corridor. Randolph called, "Go straight home, honey. I'll phone Arnold and tell him you're on your way. Okay?"

"On my way." She dropped the words and they sank.

She woke turning onto Van Nuys—she hit the brakes when a boy bobbed in front of the car and, laughing, leaned over and slapped the hood, making a hollow *thoon*. She woke again at night, pulled off a freeway in the foothills. Below, the misted city lights spread like stars under a veil. She took a deep breath which became the murmur of wind moving down the hill. Slowly Babs looked over her shoulder and stared into a huge ear-shaped frond.

"Ha!" Arnold stood with his hands on his hips. "Just driving around. For two days. And I'm supposed to believe that?" He turned and socked Babs' panda, sending it sprawling in a corner by the sofa. "Tell the truth, Babs. Was it Pete or that black cat Lucius? Or was it old Randolph the Rat again?" He bent down. "That's it, isn't it? You promised you'd never see that guy outside the studio and now two whole days." Babs smiled glassily.

Arnold paced up and down. "I guess you know I missed two days of classes looking for you. And I missed a Prophets 204 exam." He began wringing his hands. "And you come floating in like a kid on a rubber raft. Don't you have *anything* to say for yourself?" She just sat there. "Okay, Babs. If that's the way you want it, that's the way you'll get it." He

kicked off his tennies and shucked off his jeans. He grabbed
her hair, jerked her head back, and grinded his face in hers,
jabbing his tongue into her mouth.

Arnold carried her into the bedroom and undressed her.
He spread her out like a big doll, then jumped up on the bed
and stood over her. "I'm still the champ. Huh, Babs? Aren't
I?" She smiled up. "Aw cut it out, Babs." Hunkering down,
he cupped her face and with his thumbs pulled the skin tight,
stretching off the smile. "Stop it!" She blinked. He lifted his
thumbs and the smiled plinked back on. "All right," he said,
gritting his teeth. He made love to her, chanting in her ear,
"That's me. That's me. That's me."

Then he stopped. "Jesus Christ," he whispered. He
jumped out of bed, ran into the bathroom, and came back
with her mirror. He held it in front of her face, his hands
shaking. Babs took the mirror and Arnold parted her hair.
In the mirror Babs saw a pink nub sticking out the top of her
head.

Babs wore a bouffant, but it showed in other ways.
Randolph called her over after he'd looked at the latest
Girl in the Bikini clip. "Okay. What's wrong, sugar buns?
Is that bum Arnold showing you Turd City? Give me the
word, I'll go over and unwind him all the way, okay?"

Everyone was extra cheery and very gentle, but of course
it didn't help. When Arnold picked her up at the studio,
missing more classes, Babs got in and sat staring straight
ahead. "Aw, honey, come on," Arnold said. "It's not so bad.
I still love you. You know that." He took her home and
made love to her until they were paralyzed. She woke in the
night and went to the kitchen and fried bacon and eggs.
Arnold came out and when she looked at him his mouth was
hanging open. "Oh my God," he whispered. He took her
hand and led her to the bathroom.

Her nub had broken through the skin and was now a

bluish gray horn two inches long—Arnold measured it. He tapped it with the ruler and a cold vibration passed down though Babs like the moan of a gong across still water.

She wore a turban. And Vince Fong was right —Randolph wouldn't use the footage. "Look, honey," Randolph said and put his arms around her waist. "A bikini and a *turban?* I mean, Jesu Christu, you look like runner-up for Klutz of the Year." He patted her bottom, nuzzled her neck. "I love you," he whispered. "I love you like my sister, like my wife and mother too. More! I've never loved anyone the way I love you. I'd cut off both thumbs for you and my left nut which as you know happens to be my best one. But you must consider what we're up against in this business. See, the folks in Funny-land don't want *weirdness.* They have weirdness up to here. They want *beauty.* They crave it. So, Babs, doll, true heart lambkins honey-twat, you just *gotta* take off that ferking turban."

So Babs didn't go to the studio the next day and Arnold took her to a specialist. They were alone in the serene and spacious waiting room with runt palms and a running brook and pool with foot-long gold and black fish. "This guy's the best in L.A.," Arnold whispered. "He's a gland man. My uncle says this guy worked on King Faruk." After an hour's wait they were led by a beautiful nurse into the office. Behind a black marble desk he sat, an immense doctor with cookie crumbs in the corners of his mouth. When Arnold unwound Bab's turban, the doctor started laughing. He laughed so hard his big chromium swivel chair tilted and squirted out from under him, and he lay behind the desk whoo-hawing.

The next day Arnold took Babs to his favorite professor at divinity school. When Arnold undid the turban, Prof Flish's forehead pinched into a rigid eleven. "I've seen it before." Arnold let out a sigh of relief and nudged Babs. "Not this particular one," Prof Flish went on and with thumb and forefinger began massaging his black-ringed eyes. "But it's one of God's mysteries. Obviously. Another one. I've seen dozens, of course, which should be some consolation to the young lady." He looked at his watch.

"I . . ." Arnold began wringing his hands. "I don't know what we ought to do."

"You ought to wait and see," Prof Flish said. "Meanwhile, we maintain faith." He stared into Babs' eyes and she stared back. "Hi," he said. "Hi," Babs said. Then Prof Flish looked to Arnold and said, "Does she have faith?"

"She has some. Not a lot. I guess she sure could use some work on it."

Prof Flish nodded. "Now's the time." He slowly closed his eyes and his hand came up for another massage. "Young lady, you've got to see this through. I frankly don't envy you."

"But you can pray for her," Arnold said. "Won't you?"

"Sure. But look, let's be frank. My praying for her won't change the course of this, and that's what you're after." He glanced at Babs' horn and shook his head. "No, this will have to go the route, whatever that might be. Any and all prayers will have to be not for *it*, but for her, so she can bear up. But she appears to be the sort who can. How old is she?"

"Twenty-one," Arnold said.

"Good. The younger they are, the more resilient they are." He looked at his watch and the hand irresistibly, as if beckoned by a lover's glance, came up to his eyes. He stood with his hand to his eyes and, rubbing them, said, "I'll of course keep this to myself." He extended his right hand and Arnold shook it. "Bring her back in a week and let me take another look." Arnold thank-you'd, pushing Babs ahead of him toward the door, and when Prof Flish peeked through his fingers, Arnold bowed.

As they crossed the parking lot Arnold said, "I don't know about you but that makes me feel a lot better. You're young and resilient, Babs. You've got to keep that in mind.

So we'll just wait and see."

"I'm going home," Babs said.

"You bet, doll." Arnold put his arm around her and gave her a hug.

"I mean home. To Mother and Daddy," and Arnold didn't argue. After dinner he took her to bed early and around midnight Babs vowed Arnold was still the champ and always would be. The next morning Babs packed her suitcase, tucked her panda into a plastic bag, and put on a red straw hat with a high crown. At the bus station Arnold kissed her good-bye a dozen times and, running alongside as the bus pulled away, he kissed the palm of his hand and slapped the thick window by her head.

Her mother and father sat at the kitchen table, ready. She took off the hat. Her mother blinked. Her father reached for a cigar.

"How did you do it?" her mother said.

"I didn't do it, Mother. It just happened."

"No, Babs. Something like that doesn't just happen."

"Hold on," her father said and struck a match. They waited as he lit his cigar. "The main thing isn't how it got there. The main thing is, it's there."

Her mother shook her head through this from the first word. "You're all wet. If we know what Babs did to get it there, she can undo what she did and be rid of it."

He shrugged his eyebrows. "Worth a try." He turned to Babs. "Okay, sweetheart. Tell us what you done."

"I didn't do anything."

"That preacher still dating you?"

"He's not a preacher yet, Daddy: He's studying for the ministry."

"Reverend Birdsong didn't study any," he said. "He just read the Bible and started preaching. Why does this young fellow think he has to go to college to be a preacher? And in

Los Angeles. That don't seem like the right place to be a preacher, if you ask me."

"Maybe *he* did something," her mother said.

Her father nodded. "Could be." He looked at Babs. "Well? What'd he do?"

"Nothing, Daddy."

Her mother said, "Babs, does he love you?"

"I don't know, Mother. I guess he does."

"Does he say he loves you?"

"Yes."

"Is he going to marry you?"

She sighed. "I don't know."

"Does he ever talk about it?"

"No."

"That's not a good sign. Babs."

"I know, Mother. But I don't know if I want to get married. Especially now."

"Good point," her father said.

They looked at him. He stuck his cigar in his mouth and turned away.

"Babs," her mother said. "You can stay here. This is your home."

"There'll always be a place here for you, sweetheart," her father said.

Your friends ask about you all the time. Charline Meyers had another baby. Her fourth in four years."

Her father said, "Peter Hooper got killed. Logging truck ran over his Volkswagen. They couldn't get him out, worked on it two days. Finally had to bury the whole car."

"Eunice Kilsey divorced Ernest Hope and married Rusty Dodge," her mother said.

"Did Ernest re-marry?"

"No, but he left town."

Her father suddenly said, "Pierre Dupree is still in town."

"Why, yes he is," her mother said. "I saw him the other day driving one of those cars."

"Does he still have all those old cars?" Babs said.

"He races them at the fairgrounds and all over the state, don't he, Daddy?"

"Yes, and he works at the Ford garage. He's the best they have. Best in town, for that matter. He's the only man in town I'll let lay a hand on my car."

"Pierre Dupree was always such a nice boy," her mother said. "Wasn't he, Babs?"

"Pierre was wild," Babs said. "Very wild."

"Some start out wild and then level out," her mother said. "I'd say Pierre has leveled out pretty good. Wouldn't you say so, Daddy?"

He nodded thoughtfully. "Yes. I'd say that."

"Tomorrow I'll call Bertha Quigley," her mother said. "She's still the bookkeeper at the Ford garage. Bertha can pass the word on that you're in town."

"Mother, I don't want . . . ."

Her mother shook her head. "You are not going to sit in this house and sulk your life away. In this house nobody sulks. Isn't that right, Daddy?"

"That's a fact," and getting up, he went out the back door and headed for the store.

"Hi." Pierre Dupree walked right over and took off Babs' red straw hat. "It's not bone," he reported. "That's an actual horn, like a deer's."

She rigidly stared at his overalls which were faded and grease-stained, though he smelled of soap and after-shave. Babs' mother, sitting at the other end of the sofa, looked straight at the wall. Babs' father puffed his cigar and watched Pierre closely.

"Gosh, I don't know," Pierre said. "I've never seen anything like it."

"Nobody has," her father said.

"Babs," Pierre said, "I've got an idea. If you're willing."

He went outside and they heard him rattling around in a tool box in his pick-up. When he came back they went into the kitchen and Babs' mother spread a sheet on the table. Babs climbed up onto it, lay on her back, and Pierre walked around the table. He leaned over her, his face, upside-down, a narrow rather nice face though somewhat unfocused as if no matter where he seemed to be, in reality he was always off somewhere taking apart a carburetor or blasting through a turn onto a straightaway. "Close your eyes." She felt him part her hair. "Okay. Here we go."

A cold chime washed through Babs and opened an enormous mouth of sky. A white owl with round yellow eyes watched her fall.

Babs was on the floor and Pierre Dupree was on his knees beside her, his face drawn with the sincerest, most tragic expression Babs had ever seen and which she instantly recognized as the agonized and saintly look of a man in love. Pierre laid down the saw and put his hands on her shoulders. "Oh Babs," he whispered. "I'm so sorry, honey. I'll never do that again. Never, never, never . . ."

And he was good for his word, even when two weeks later glossy cat whiskers sprouted from her cheeks and Babs and her mother and father wanted to snip them off. Pierre refused, his hard arms crossed on his chest, and shaking his head. "No way, you people. No way."

"But I don't like it," Babs sobbed, for now that Pierre loved her and came to her every day, she could cry. As soon as his pick-up came down the street, Babs' eyes filled with tears, and by the time Pierre reached the porch she was crying. He held her and said, "Yes, honey. Oh yes, yes, yes . . ." Then they sat down and talked about cars.

He left her on weekends and went to Pasco or Ellensburg or Wenatchee, pulling the trailer and "Tony the Tiger," his striped Buick, or the big white-washed Chrysler, "Morbid Dick." One weekend he didn't race, and he and Babs were married in a small service in her parents' living room.

He moved her to his place, a house in the woods off the Yakima road. Out front a dozen mangled junkers with numbers painted on their sides finished before a crowd of sunflowers who strained to look through the windshields. Mornings Pierre left for work before sun-up, and Babs worked around the house and watched t.v. Now and then her mother visited. Then one weekend Pierre went to a race and didn't come home.

Monday Babs sat by the window and looked up the road. As afternoon sank, the road narrowed to a crack. She lay awake all night listening to the woods and at dawn she went to the door. Gray filled the clearing like a pool and as the junkers emerged Babs realized one of them, a huge green Nash, number 69, was apart from the rest, set by coincidence and that last tow-job in a place of prominence: all the others, with that profound silence of which only steel and stone are capable, and the monolithic reverence innate in dense things, were nosed down to the Nash.

Wednesday she packed a suitcase and stood on the front porch wearing the blue sombrero she was married in but which was already too small in the crown. When afternoon gave way and the woods took the road and edged in on the clearing, Babs went back inside. She lay in the dark, waiting. When she went to the bathroom she didn't turn on the light, but in spite of herself looked in the mirror and saw the smooth black glint. In bed she lay listening to an insect burrowing deep in the house. She admired the bug's determination—wonderful bug, and amazingly strong, for its grinding burr grew louder and louder until Babs woke, realizing it wasn't an insect but a car approaching!

She ran to the door and switched on the porch light as the pick-up towing the white Chrysler pulled off the road. As it swung up in front of the house, the truck door on the passenger's side popped open and a huge black-taped baseball, the tape-ends loose and flopping, bounced through the dust and rolled into the grass—a base hit! The truck stopped and Pierre got out carrying a gunny sack and a cardboard suitcase speckled like a bird's egg. "Hi, honey," he said. He put the sack and suitcase on the porch and walked into the tall grass. He bent down and spoke low. The lumpy shadows stirred, and Pierre helped a man to his feet.

They came into the porch light. The man wore a blue suede jacket so old and tattered and dirty it was no longer "blue suede," and jeans, cowboy boots, and a black knit cap.

Babs backed into the darkness of the living room. But in the doorway the man stopped, raised his head like a dog sniffing, and looked straight at her. "Jesus," he said in a thick, mucked voice and fell on his face. Pierre carried him into the spare room and Babs heard them back there mumbling and laughing as Pierre set up a cot for him.

While Babs was hanging the wash she saw him peeing out the window of the spare room. He stood with his eyes closed, his face all downbent lines, abstractions cut by shabby luck and the cryptic logic of the wind. From this distance his mouth was hidden within the lines, and his eyelids were flat as coins. "How's he doing?" Pierre said when he came home from work.

Babs didn't answer, for she still wasn't speaking to Pierre. But as if their guest had heard all the way back there and with the door closed, he yelled, "A beer! Great Christ, a beer!"

The gunny sack Pierre had carried in last night was full of cans of beer which now crowded the refrigerator. Pierre got two and went back to the spare room. Five minutes later Pierre came out for more. Then they both came down the hall and for a moment Babs thought the man was leaving, for he wore his coat, zipped up to his throat, and his cap. But he was barefooted.

With his eyes open his face had some shape, though there remained the indistinctness of those almost-faces in the bark of trees. Pierre said, "This is Babs."

"Ah hah. Exactly who I thought it was."

"Honey, this is Wayne Bear."

Wayne Bear crushed his beer can, threw it at the waste-basket, missed. "The full and official name—" He belched solidly. "—Wayne Cutting Bear, Esquire. Need a beer."

Pierre got one, and as Wayne sucked the foam off the top and tilted up the can, Pierre nodded toward the door. Babs followed him out and they walked down the lawn. "I know you don't like this guy, honey, but he . . ." He glanced toward the house and whispered, "He's going to help me."

"How?"

"With the cars." He watched her out the corner of his eye. "All I have to do is buy the beer and a bottle of V.O. now and then. And he wants a car when he's done."

"Why doesn't he stay in town?"

"Well, he's kind of broke. And out here is better because he likes to be close to what he's doing."

She looked into the woods, watching from its darkness and listening to every word. "I don't want him here."

Pierre turned and put his hands on her shoulders. "He'll help me out and then he'll take off, soon as he's finished."

"Everything will change," Babs said.

"Don't think about things changing, honey." He shrugged gently. "If things hadn't changed, you wouldn't have left L.A. and you wouldn't be with me now out here"—he made a sweeping gesture as if inviting her to the woods. "And you trust me. Don't you?"

"Yes."

"So there you are. Okay?"

Babs lowered her head, her neck aching from the weight of the horn. "Okay," she said, staring down through her glossy cat whiskers.

When Pierre came home from work Wayne was on the

front porch drinking beer and reading comic books—the speckled suitcase was full of them. "What's he been doing?" Pierre asked Babs, pulling the curtain aside and peeking out.

"He just sits and drinks beer," Babs said. "Sometimes he goes for a little walk and talks to himself."

"Did he . . . try anything?" Pierre looked at her significantly.

"No, Pierre," Babs said impatiently. "He didn't try anything."

That weekend Pierre didn't go to the races, and the three of them watched football on t.v. and played Chinese checkers. "When is he going to start work?" Babs said Monday morning while Pierre was eating his breakfast.

"Can't rush him, honey," Pierre said. "He's got to get on his feet. He told me his last job took everything out of him, left him a little out of whack."

The next weekend Pierre went to the races at Pasco. When he came home Sunday night Babs and her panda were watching t.v. "Where's Wayne?" Pierre said.

"Who knows?" Babs said. "I suppose he's off somewhere trying to get on his feet."

Pierre went down the hall to the spare room and came back. "He's not there," he announced. He went through the house calling Wayne's name. He came back in. "Damnit. He just up and left."

"That's too bad," Babs told her panda. "Now who'll help poor Pierre?"

Pierre went grumbling out to the kitchen. "At least he didn't take the beer," he called.

"Isn't that wonderful?" she asked the bear. Its red glass eyes stared back with round clownish urgency.

The next morning Babs went with Pierre out to the pickup to see him off to work. They kissed and as Pierre reached for the door handle a low muffled sound like the rumbling of an owl became a smooth Eeeeooo that floated and echoed in itself, opening like ripples ringing wider and wider on the sky.

Wayne Cutting Bear climbed out of one of the old cars, his head down, not looking at them. Again he gave the call and waded through the grass to the porch, his face no longer cut with lines and creases but bloated smooth as if amazed or absurdly determined. His eyes were holes.

Wayne Cutting Bear sat in the far corner, his head and shoulders huge in shadows. Pierre slumped beside Babs, snoring. Slowly she got up and went to the kitchen. She was drinking a glass of water when she felt herself being watched. She turned to the window: in the clearing a fox posed with one paw lifted, its head turned and staring at her. It trotted through the grass and slipped into the woods. The chanting began, loud, with a rigid twanging mockery and ferocity.

He whispered to her, then ran to Pierre, then back to her and she was amazed he could find her in the dark, rushing up and stopping so close his lips brushed her ear. She shuddered at the wind of his breath as he whispered what sounded like *rugby rugby rugby* . . . .

Then he touched her arm, startling her, and as he took her to the bedroom where she and Pierre slept, Babs thought with sad amusement, So this is what they wanted.

He left her and in a moment returned with Pierre. Babs had switched on the overhead light; it glared down on the narrow room, the bed and dresser and yellow walls, crassly exposing this as the sad little place where people hide and sleep.

Wayne sat Pierre at the foot of the bed facing Babs at the head between the pillows. Then Wayne took off his cap.

His head was slick with grinning blue-green snakes. He unzipped the suede coat and took it off: his chest, stomach and arms to the wrists writhed with blue vines and twisting maroon intestines stretched tight over blurred creatures gazing out as they squeezed onward, and beyond, staring through the tangle, a bright-eyed fox watched a long lean jackrabbit spring skyward, ears back, eyes squinted and determined on flight, and at the bottom, carrying everything slowly but easily and inexorably, a turtle strained on its long journey, its right hind foot and precisely webbed and sharp-clawed toes extending into the pale flesh below Wayne's navel.

He climbed onto the bed and lifted his arms. He tilted his head back to the overhead light, a fat round face in the ceiling, and inhaled tremendously, as if he would never stop. He slowly waved his arms up and down at his sides and hummed. So gradually Babs was unaware of the change, the humming grew louder, his arms moved faster, the bed surging, the springs small insistent voices far away.

She jerked, her neck popping, for it had been rigid, as Wayne broke and bounced high, his arms as wide as the room, and the bed fell through with a crash.

He lay on his back, his arms and legs extended. When his glistening blue chest stopped heaving, he spoke in the language of the chant. Though his eyes were closed he lifted a hand and pointed at Babs' horn, and he pinched air as if seizing cottony dandelion seeds, then threw the empty handful at her. Babs cried, her head drooping under the weight of the horn, tears running down her whiskers and dripping in her lap.

Abruptly the window shrank—dawn. The gray world rushed up to the window and, looking in, shriveled the overhead light to a dot. Babs sighed—and Wayne Cutting Bear heard, or it was a coincidence, for at that moment he fell silent. When Babs looked out the window the old cars were rising from the grass, floating up like moony submarines, the big green Nash silently bumping a Ford that tried to pass.

The next day when Pierre came home from work he went

back and knocked on the door of the spare room. "I've got to talk to you," he called. There was a groan inside. Pierre went in, and Babs listened from the kitchen. Pierre did all the talking, and though he spoke too low for her to hear, she knew he was talking about her horn.

Pierre came out intent and energetic. "Hi, honey," he said. He kissed her and glanced at the horn. "Let's you and me go ahead and eat. Wayne doesn't feel too good."

Pierre talked about cars and the races, and several times he reached across and patted Babs. When they finished supper he helped her with the dishes and took her to bed. He made love to her and then while she lay with her eyes shut, he measured her horn.

He went and got Wayne.

Leaving, Pierre reached out and felt, up his arm and through his chest, the watery quiver of magnetism. She rose and Pierre slowly ascended after her. Then a mild pring, a pat of air like a thought, winking out, and as Babs slid away, Pierre bellied down a chute that took him banking back. Beside him slid the sleek side of what he at first thought was one of his cars. But it was a giant fish, its gray eye looking directly at him just before the fish shot forward, sucking Pierre after it as it whooshed straight down.

Pierre pushed his plate aside and Babs picked it up, scraped off the eggs, and went to the sink. Pierre got up and stood beside her. "Where did you go?"

She shook her head and a fine dust of plaster sprinkled the dishwater, for she rested her horn against the wall. "I'd rather not talk about it."

"Oh." Pierre picked up a cup she had put in the drying rack; soap bubbles slid along the bottom and disappeared when he blew into the cup. "Well, are you alone?"

"Almost."

"You mean he goes with you."

"No." She turned and looked at Pierre. "But he must be somewhere. And so are you."

"He's somewhere, all right. But it's not where I am. And I have a sneaky feeling where you are is where *he* is."

She looked at him and Pierre held his breath as he saw something of the same knowing, gray indifference he had seen in the eye of the fish, a calm, rather sad remoteness that was beyond questions, doing, and surprises.

He went to their bedroom. Wayne was still there, on the floor, an arm over his face. "Hey, Cutting Bear!"

"Shhh."

"You *done* something to her." He kicked him in the shoulder but not too hard. "Where do you go? Huh?"

Wayne looked up at him. "I been here all day. Me and Smiley and Buster played a couple hands of blackjack and I read some books . . . ."

"You know what I'm talking about," Pierre yelled. He squatted down and said low, "You're a damn flop on that horn—you've made it even bigger. And now you've done something to her personality."

"Horn?" He rubbed his face and squinted at Pierre. "Good buddy, I'd sure as shootin' appreciate a cigarette."

Pierre stood and crossed his arms on his chest. "I'm not letting her outa my sight. Next time I stay with her."

"Ah," Wayne said. He nodded as if he at last understood. "Neighbor, I hate to be a spoilsport, but doing what you just said is exactly how a man learns what he don't want to know. Let little what's-her-name have her fling. She comes back, don't she? But if you go after her"—he shook his head— "that's crowdin' the stage. It might be she don't want you there. That's her place, if you get the drift. So you just leave good enough alone, like the old boy said. You got it wonderful here and don't know it." He looked toward the window. "And while we're at it, good buddy, I wonder if you'd tell me where we are? I mean where exactly is this?"

Pierre kissed her and whispered in her ear, "Think about string all day."

"String?"

He ran out to the shed and came back with a spool of copper wire. "This is even better." He put it on the stove. "Look at it off and on. *Think* about it." He unlooped some and let it dangle across the oven door which, open a crack, was grinning at them.

"What's that for?" Wayne said that night when Pierre brought the wire into the bedroom.

Pierre had snipped off about eighteen inches and was looping one end around the little finger of his left hand. "No more damn hanky panky," Pierre said. "Not with my woman"—and he reached for Babs' hand.

"No," she said and jerked her hand away.

Pierre stared at her. "What? . . ."

Her eyes were half-closed and beneath the cat whiskers her lips were set in a thin implacable line.

"See there, old buddy?" Wayne said. "What'd I tell you?"

"Shut up." To Babs, "Look, honey. Have I ever lied to you?" She didn't answer. "Well, honey, it's the truth that I want whatever you want. But I've got to . . . *be* there. Because I've got to take care of things. Because I love you."

Again he saw in her eyes that indifference, the boredom of distance. But she extended her hand. Without hesitating, Pierre looped the wire around her finger. He smiled at her. But Babs watched him as sternly as before. With her free hand she reached through the maroon underbrush on Wayne Cutting Bear's chest and jabbed the fox over his heart. "Let's go."

And they went—Babs first, Pierre waiting to be sure. She

glanced over her shoulder at him, then did a chandelle.
Pierre's arm jerked out straight, stretching like rubber, his
finger pointing down the copper wire. She went faster, pulling steadily away. He opened his mouth and tried to call but
no words came. Gritting his teeth, he urged. *Wait.* She was
far away, a glass figurine sinking in a well.

Then she grew larger again and Pierre gained rapidly as
she slowed for her approach to L.A.

They swooped low over luminous buildings and houses
made of the smooth intricate cartilage of ears. They skimmed
lumpy trees like huge cauliflowers and, dipping, Babs floated
with Pierre down a long street. She nodded to him and
descended to the front lawn of a small pink house identical
to the others. Pierre unhooked the wire and followed Babs
inside.

The house was empty, shiny and slick. Pierre took a run
and skated across the front room, through a doorway and
from room to room. When he returned, Babs stood in the
middle of the living room. She took off her horn and handed
it to Pierre. *Thanks, honey,* he said. The horn was full of wet
sand, dead beetles, damp leaves, black stones. Pierre knocked
all this out on the floor and as he turned it up again and
looked into it, the ineluctable willingness of vertigo drew his
face into darkness. A glint of light deep inside grew swiftly
larger, spiraling up the horn. The horn shook in his hand
and, rocking the sky like jet planes, the horn erupted elk,
antelope, reindeer, bison, and moose, crashing straight up
through the roof, their eyes big with the amazement of
speed, their hooves churning a spume on the sky.

A mist of silence gently floated down. Holding his breath,
Pierre hooked the cooper wire to Babs' finger and his, and
they kissed, the moment stretching smoothly like a great
loop of taffy. A dying, only vaguer, an orgasm in his ankles,
curlicued up Pierre's legs, slipped up his hips, rippled along

his ribs and spiked in from his shoulders to his ears and Pierre heard far off the eternal gasp of water and air reaching into each other. Looking up through the hole in the roof, Pierre and Babs saw a wave as big as a storm cloud and rising still higher, in the gape under its crest the air as still as the air cupped in the pupil of an eye. Then the wave crashed down, filling the sky above L.A. with the bath of the universe.

Pierre clenched his eyes. End-over-ending, gone, crashing sound so loud he heard nothing but his small self inside wondering *Is it death? Is it everything?* and he was a ball then his arm jerking out straight he was an arrow. He opened his eyes but saw nothing. His little finger pulling all his weight throbbed as he went faster and faster losing his clothes first then his ears, face, losing everything but the finger by which she drew him on.

Wayne Cutting Bear woke. Big headache. Got up, mumbling, walked around the room trying to see. Stopped and, whimpering, held his head. "Poor Wayne," he said softly. "Poor little feller." With great difficulty and slowness he put on his clothes except for his boots which he couldn't find. "Screw it," he whispered. Got his speckled suitcase and went to the kitchen, found a gunny sack and filled it with beer from the refrigerator and, seeing eggs on a shelf, he cracked the shell of one and sucked it, looked out the window at the woods. He wondered where he was. Canada?

Went out the front door and saw a dozen junkers swimming in the sunlight. He waded through the high grass and lifted the hood of an old green Nash and looked in at the rusted, banged-up engine. He let the hood slam, put the suitcase and sack in the front seat, and got in. The sun shone through the dirty windshield and as he closed his eyes the light created, on the sky inside his eyelids, faces that curled into conches or spun into dense buds grinning down from the rosetted ceiling of the lobby of the Portland Y.M.C.A. As the little faces rattled down the sky, Wayne tried the ignition and the old Nash started right up. It pulled out of the tall grass and leaving the ring of cars it had consoled for years, drove down the narrow road to a highway which led eventually to a town and beyond, eventually, to a city which poured the noise of people and all the inestimable eagerness of their being into the man at the wheel who, while he drove, was drinking a Budweiser and reading an old issue of *Bible Stories Comix*.

PLENTY OF TIME

Teecy McTavish hurried through the snow, bent over, clutching Michael's buttonless fatigue jacket to her throat. Inside the science building she stomped her tennies, slung off her backpack, opened it, and plunged in—past books and notebooks, past a coyote skull, a jar of Boston baked beans, through broken pencils and an unrolled but unused ribbed condom (with a giggle of dismay Teecy wondered how it got there) and half a dozen photos of Michael and Lori—until she found some Kleenex. She stacked up four, carefully squared the corners, and blew her nose so hard she staggered.

She went down the corridor to the office directory and stared at the face reflected in the glass case, a shiny bright red face, Christmassy and delirious. She stood there shivering and dizzy but only vaguely aware of it. For a long moment she succeeded in forgetting where she was and why she was here. She started down the corridor.

All the classroom and office doors were closed and no lights shone beneath them. Of course not. What a dummy. It was almost 4 p.m. on Friday, the last day before Christmas break. At the last door on the left she read the office hours, then turned away. But she knocked, very softly, the sound murmuring down the hall to join the preoccupied sputtering of a radiator.

There was no response. What now? Trying to think was like squeezing some physical object out of her brain. That was the repulsive kind of thing she got when she tried to

think, the awful picture of something like a fish struggling
to get out of Teecy's brain tissue . . . .

She had told the girl at the clinic she wanted to see a
counsellor. "Why do you want to see one *now*?" the girl said.

Teecy had stared off, amazed this stranger could know,
just by looking at her, that it was too late for counsellors.
"Well," Teecy said with a sigh that ended with a quaver on
the verge of tears, "I've done something terrible and I think
I'm going to kill myself. I want to . . . ."

"No," the girl said quickly. "I mean now isn't a good
time to see a counsellor because everybody's gone. There
aren't even any patients in the beds. I'm just here to, you
know, answer the phone and answer questions." She tilted
her head to the side slightly and frown-smiled sympathetical-
ly. "I can give you some aspirins. I have a cold too. Isn't it
just awful?"

Teecy let her bring two aspirins and a little paper cup of
water, and on the girl's suggestion Teecy went to find one of
her professors, after ruling out phoning her parents as simply
out of the question, but Teecy refused to let the girl lock up
the clinic and go with her to find a professor. "You must
stay here," Teecy insisted. "Who knows?—someone might
come in even in worse shape than I am."

And here she stood, wondering why the girl at the clinic
thought professors, of all people, would be available when
everyone else had vanished, and with tears forcing up inside
her, Teecy wondered why she had trusted the girl.

Teecy was about to leave when she thought she heard a
sound inside the office. She put her ear to the door. She
knocked even more softly than before, and whispered, "Professor Whisint?"

No answer. Again she turned to leave. But this time there
was no mistaking the sound: the grumble and creak of a
swivel chair. "Professor Whisint? I'm Teecy McTavish? In

your 9 o'clock? Could I talk to you?"

Another creak of the chair.

What now? This trying to talk to a professor was a first
for Teecy. She hoped she might get through college without having to actually talk to one of them, for her instincts
had warned her that such things as Prof. Whisint's closed-
door policy on conferences were the sort of thing you could
expect. Though the closed-door policy wasn't such a bad
idea, on second thought—most things come out easier if there
isn't the distraction of speaking to a face and seeing what
shows on it while it listens. "Professor Whisint," Teecy told
the door, a dismal old brown scarred gouged thumbtack-
pocky door, "I got an A on my midterm and I got an . . . I
got a B on my lab. What do I have to get on my final to get
. . . to get . . .?"

She started crying. Her grade wasn't why she was here
at all. She wondered why half the time what she said came
out sounding so unlike what she intended or what people
expected, that she just might as well try Chinese—and the
other half of the time something came out that had absolutely nothing to do with what she was trying to say.

The door opened about three inches.

Through a sparkle of tears Teecy saw the face of Prof.
Whisint. Teecy believed the face was smiling.

Prof. Whisint backed away, the door opened wider, and
Teecy entered. The office was dark, lit only by a narrow
north window. Teecy sat in a straight-back chair by the desk.

After shutting the door Prof. Whisint sat in the swivel
chair, tilted it back, slowly crossed her legs, and, looking
levelly at Teecy, said, "What's wrong?"

Teecy cried harder. And that central deep part of her
which should have been more completely the real actual
Teecy McTavish than any other part but which had been the
most delirious and crazy and dangerous part of her through
everything that had happened in the last two weeks—that
central insane part told Teecy, "*This* is honest," and believing

it, even answering herself with, "So true, so true," she was
finally ready to hold nothing back, even if it meant admitting
the worst things imaginable. And that, given recent events
and the awfulness of her imagination these days, was saying
a lot.

In her 43 years Prof. Whisint had cried a rough sum of
four weeks, for all the standard reasons and on most of the
standard occasions. Before this Teecy knocked, Prof. Whisint
had been crying bitterly but dryly for no specific reason,
the chain of familiar grievances and offences slipping through
her fingers while she clicked off each nearly thoughtlessly,
including each in its proper place but thinking of the people,
events, faces, only in essence, in formula. Finished with that,
she cried because no one on the faculty and none of her
many students loved her or even gave a damn that she existed. She was simply "Whisint" to her so-called colleagues,
"Whisint" to her students (she had overheard them in lecture
halls and corridors), and even the department secretary called
her "Whisint" behind her back. She was also crying because
she was a beautiful woman—strikingly beautiful—but it had
made no difference in her life. Something as prominent, remarkable, and important as real beauty should make a difference, but it hadn't. If anything, it had startled people and
shied them away from her. Which brought her to her real reasons for crying: this dull office and this snowy dark December afternoon.

She let this feverish-faced waif have a good cry, this
Teecy. Where do they get these names? Whisint's theory was
that they leave their real names at registration and pick up
the Teecies and Womkies and Boopies and Woowoos and
Weewees.

When Teecy's crying subsided, she took a loud wet breath
and shook her head like a bullock. Whisint said, "If you score
an A on your final exam your semester grade will be an A.

But I haven't finished grading all of them yet, and yours is
one I haven't done. The official grades will be mailed out in
January."

She noticed Teecy wasn't listening. So she wasn't here for
the grades. Whisint would give 8 to 5 it's a broken heart. 5 to
4 it's pregnancy. Even money it's a broken-hearted pregnancy
parlay.

Whisint waited. Prodding and prying didn't speed them
up. If they want to talk, they'll talk. Sometimes they change
their minds at the last moment and decide they don't want to
open up. Which was just fine with Whisint. And sometimes
they spill half of it and suddenly see the solution to the
problem and clam up and, thanking Whisint profusely, dash
out.

Whisint wasn't particularly interested in having Teecy
open up, though Whisint wouldn't have minded consoling
her. In fact Whisint wouldn't mind taking this Teecy in her
arms, brushing back the long black wet hair from that fervid
brow, and kissing her. But the girl was obviously corrupt with
germs. Whisint wouldn't mind making love this afternoon. In
fact maybe that's what she has been obscurely wanting.
She contemplated spending the between-semesters break in
the arms of this Teecy. Six or seven years ago Whisint had a
rash of love affairs with some older students—Bradley
Murphy who still sent her Christmas and birthday cards,
Carol someone who drove a Porsche, and a hairy Vietnam
veteran whose name has slipped . . . .

And with it slipped away the notion of love with this
Teecy. Though a kiss on that soft wet mouth was tempting,
perhaps because of the risk of flu, pneumonia, eventual
death. Not often are there such stakes on one kiss! Why, just
sitting here in this office with her involved a certain amount
of risk. A kiss (this Teecy was probably so wired with fever,
love, and possible pregnancy, that five minutes later she
wouldn't know if it actually happened or if she imagined it)
a lingering kiss with a little tongue action . . . .

"I . . . ." Teecy said. She felt terrible. She was a bona fide dummy. Here she sat, in front of a woman who was her biology prof but who was actually a complete stranger. She couldn't have found a more complete stranger if she went out and searched for one.

This whole conversation, if it could be called that, this entire scene—the two of them sitting there staring at each other waiting for Teecy to speak—became very strange and unreal. It was the kind of situation Teecy distinctly hated and daydreamed of, Unthinkable Ultimate Worsts, such as being tied down while her English prof poured Shakespeare into her ear. "I don't know," Teecy said.

Whisint leaned back and lit a cigarette. That helped. Teecy loved to watch women smoke. Whisint offered her a cigarette.

"Oh." Teecy laughed (and marveled that it came out laughter!). "I don't smoke." She giggled. "Thanks."

Whisint stared at her. Teecy sharply stopped giggling.

This woman *hates* me, flashed through Teecy's mind. My God, I have walked into a lion's den.

Utterly helpless and forlorn and again awed by her stupidity, Teecy looked down at her lap where she was cupping Kleenexes in her hands like a snowball. "Well," she heard herself say and realized she was trying to get out of here. She waited, and "I guess I better be going," came out. Brilliant! "I'm sorry I . . . . You know. I just . . . well." Leaning forward to rise, she said, "This has helped a lot."

"What has?"

The voice was so direct, so controlled, so severe. It put Teecy back in her chair and made her sit straight, and to her face came her alert-intelligent expression which was for taking lecture notes and listening to the occasional intelligent conversation.

"This," Teecy answered, lifting the snowball of Kleenex and vaguely gesturing toward a bookcase. She stuffed the Kleenex into her pocket.

Whisint lifted the cigarette to her lips and Teecy watched her thin sharp lips take the tip, the cheeks suck in slightly, the slow exhalation of smoke from Whisint's nostrils and mouth.

"Yes, I think I'd like a cigarette. If you don't mind."

Whisint expressionlessly offered the pack. Teecy had trouble getting one out. But Whisint smiled. Whisint struck a match and again Teecy leaned forward, more deliberately now, and this Teecy, this 18-/19-year-old child, Teecy, lifted her hand to Whisint's, and after the cigarette was lit (with too many puffs, enclosing Teecy and Whisint in a great egg of smoke), Teecy blew out the match and for two, three seconds, as if forgetfully, continued touching the hand, holding it there.

At the library Teecy found Lori and Michael down in the stacks. She walked up to them, "Hi" already in her mouth and her lips parting to speak. She was standing beside them, when Michael and Lori kissed.

Not just a peck on the cheek but a long kiss on the mouth, and they put their arms around each other.

Teecy's face was burning. She was holding her breath—she was standing so close she was afraid they would hear her breathing.

"You're wondering why they didn't see me," Teecy told Whisint. "Or why they didn't know I was there—you know, *feel* that I was there because I was that close. But they were turned to the side and . . . well, they just didn't see me. And after they started kissing, their eyes were closed . . . ."

Teecy looked away, shaking her head slowly. "But I really don't know why they didn't see me. I started worrying about that almost immediately.

"But they *didn't* see me. I was sure of it. I started thinking they saw me, or that they had even waited until I came around the corner and then . . . . No."

Teecy heard the rustle of Michael's jacket as he moved his arms, holding Lori, and Lori gave a little sigh-grunt, and Teecy could hear their breathing and the long sighs, and the sounds as they moved their lips, and the sounds inside their mouths . . .

It was terrible. But Teecy was standing so close she was afraid to move. Her tennies would make one of those little squeaks and Michael and Lori would look up and see her . . . . Oh God, she couldn't stand that. But what if they opened their eyes and saw her standing there watching them?

She lifted one foot at a time and slipped off her tennies. Then she tiptoed away, looking over her shoulder, praying they wouldn't open their eyes.

She went upstairs to the study hall. She was so embarrassed, so ashamed. It was a combination of the strangest and worst and most confusing thing that had ever happened in her life.

She felt that she had been betrayed. But as she sat there staring at the clock she started feeling guilty! They betrayed her, but she felt guilty!

Thirty minutes went by. What were they doing? Teecy's imagination was *terrible.*

When she couldn't stand it any longer she left her backpack at the desk in the study hall (her paperback *Othello* got ripped off) and went down into the stacks, and now she was ready, walking hard and loud, thudding her heels on the floor and squeaking her tennies for all they were worth, and whistling under her breath and humming. When she got there, Michael and Lori were sitting at opposite ends of the aisle, studying at two of those little carrel desks. They didn't look up. They were studying so hard they didn't hear Teecy coming.

She stood there, waiting. But they just kept staring into their books.

Teecy didn't mention the incident—and she was thankful Lori and Michael didn't bring it up. So in a way it never happened.

But there was the suspicion, Teecy's being thankful that they didn't bring it up—as if they *could* have brought it up because they had been aware she was watching them, and that, furthermore, maybe they kissed on purpose, for her sake—to *show* her. Oh, the awfulness of paranoia. It's just as bad on its one side as on its other. It would be so nice if, once you decide you're just being paranoid, it would ease up. But finding paranoia in your heart is like discovering a lump in your breast—just knowing it's there won't make it go away, in fact discovering it is the beginning of the worst part.

Teecy locked herself on the official position that Lori and Michael kissed accidentally.

Okay, that's the wrong word. But the idea was that Lori and Michael kissed without intending to, without planning to. That made sense. How can you undo something while it is happening? The best you can do is go sit at opposite ends of the aisle when you're done.

"That was so perfect, so . . . beautiful," Teecy said, smiling with her eyes almost closed. "Michael and Lori sitting there where they could still see each other and *be* with each other, but as *friends*."

Teecy stopped. She stared at Whisint in a rather blank way which led Whisint to guess that she was wondering how much of this Whisint was buying.

Whisint was buying very little of it. She found it credible that Teecy could feel as she did, there in the stacks, and feel as she did now. But where in Teecy was the native, wiser, older woman who corrects the girl, who sees through the foolishness the pitiful naivete of Teecy's hoping, then believing, then dedicating herself to such an impossible and, frankly, stupid ideal?

At this point Whisint could speak, representing wisdom, presenting skepticism, rude reality. She didn't. Though she knew she must, and would, undoubtedly, in her role as teacher—and "sister," as they say these days. She would explain to Teecy the error of her thinking, examine with her the misconceptions lurking in Teecy's hopes for a special kind of friendship, a special kind of love.

Teecy launched her campaign to give Lori and Michael (and herself, too) a stronger grip on their friendship, without coming right out and talking about the threat to it.

That was the hard part, to reach Lori and Michael without hitting them over the head with the fact that she knew what happened down there in the stacks. Teecy had to be clear but subtle.

Whisint pictured this intense trio sitting head to head in the small living room of the apartment the three of them moved into on Teecy's insistence. Whisint's Michael is an abundantly broad-shouldered, clear-eyed, wrinkle-browed freshman/sophomore with bushy curly hair, with clear, steady, rather large eyes which seem to become even larger, even clearer and steadier, as he struggles into words. Maybe he speaks rather slowly, but not because he is slow-witted.

Whisint's Lori is, at first glance, her name—a "cute" one who could have married any boy in her graduating class in high school, they all were in love with her. But in fact she is powerfully intelligent, ambitious (premed), ferociously competitive, and deadly serious. She doesn't suffer fools and doesn't have time for other girls generally. When she is compelled to have dealings with them she tends to take sarcastic advantage of them, quite deftly doing damage which they don't realize they've suffered or fully appreciate and actually feel until later. She is walking, talking proof that in all the respects that count most in the world of human affairs, a woman can be just as big a son of a bitch as any man—if there was ever any doubt. Whisint's Lori is like so many girls in Whisint's classes. They remind her of herself when she was their age—beautiful, bright, capable of great cruelty, and, surprisingly, even greater love.

Anyway (this was taking forever, and Teecy thought Whisint was showing signs of impatience, and it was getting late and the office was now quite dark) just when Teecy thought she had come to grips with Michael and Lori, one afternoon she came home unexpectedly and found them . . . together, so to speak.

Teecy unlocked the door and walked in and she couldn't stop or hold her breath or pretend she wasn't there or didn't see them, though Lori and Michael—naked on the big table in the middle of the room as if they were some kind of exhibit, on the *table* for God's sake!—didn't see Teecy, *couldn't* see her, for their heads were at the other end, so to speak, and they froze (not really) and Teecy gazed spellbound at a perspective . . . prospect . . . vista . . . which she knew even as she stared at it wasn't all that unique though it was the first time she had taken it in. The perspective/prospect/vista had Lori on top, her tail in the air so that was all Teecy could see, Lori's tail and and her you know what, and there was Michael's penis, just as if Lori and Michael had arranged it all so that when Teecy stepped through the door she would see *exactly* what they were doing.

Teecy nearly fainted. Maybe she did, though not blacking out or dipping out of consciousness for even a second or two, but losing the feel of time as she stood there, not thinking, not worrying about whether Lori and Michael would crane their necks and look at her, but sinking into *Fucking*, not actually the word but the gestalt.

She moved backward. She would just back out into the hall. But the door had closed behind her. And she was dropping her books which she had been taking out of her backpack, intending to put them on the table which she had expected to find relatively bare, not in use, unoccupied . . . .

"Teecy?" Lori said low, in an almost little-girl voice. "Is that you?" Lori turned, her hair hanging down, and looked over her shoulder. Michael leaned up and looked around the other side of Lori at Teecy.

"Oh my God," Lori said and raised herself from Michael —and as she did, Teecy saw all of Michael's penis. She didn't see it accidentally, there was plenty of time to look away and she knew what was happening, but she watched as it came out of Lori.

Lori climbed off the table and stood between Michael and Teecy while he got off the table and stood behind her looking over Lori's shoulder at Teecy, his face flushed, his lips wet, his eyes steady with something that hadn't been there before, or maybe it had been there but Teecy hadn't related it to *this*.

Teecy stared dumbly at Lori's nakedness, her breasts very pale and densely *present* as if they were independent entities that came forth when there was going to be some sex, and which were caught out in the open if the sex was interrupted, and lingered in a state of dull confusion. And Teecy looked at Lori's stomach and her navel and her pubic hair which seemed especially curly. Apparently fucking kinked the little curls tighter and tighter.

Then followed a long session, after Lori and Michael put on their bathrobes—and later, after Teecy angrily told them to get dressed, for she hated the idea that beneath the robes they were still naked. The three of them went into the kitchen, and with Teecy doing all the talking the three of them circled around the table, moving from the refrigerator to the stove to the window to the sink as if going from base to base . . . . Then they sat at the table and talked all afternoon and into the night.

Michael and Lori would move out. It was the logical thing to do.

Teecy said no. That was out of the question.

So maybe she could move out, after she found a new place . . . .

No. And she told them the real reason there would be no

moving out by anyone. "We are friends," she said, frowning hard, "we are still friends," her voice sounding strange to her. She hoped it sounded strange to them, too, it might give her some advantage. She needed all the advantage she could get, for she wasn't a good arguer. She tended to cry. And once she started crying, everything she was arguing for starting slipping away and the people she was fighting always caught on and knew they could win just by waiting and letting Teecy lose control. They could get everything they wanted just by watching her cry and waiting for her to hand it all over.

But this time she didn't completely give in and let crying dissolve her face, voice, and mind to total uselessness. Teecy cried, but she kept talking through it—for five hours.

Looking back, she could hardly believe she held them there. Michael tried to leave after the first five minutes. "I feel like hell," he said. His hair was messed up and his face was no longer flushed and bloated and horny-looking, but very pale, he looked sick, like he was coming down with something. When he tried to walk out, Teecy dug both arms into his belt in back and shouted "No! No! No!" louder and louder.

Teecy made them talk about how their families had failed them a thousand times, in so many ways, each time worse than before, until it finally became clear that "family" no longer meant anything, if it had *ever* meant anything, except some people living under the same roof. Teecy knew all about Lori's and Michael's families, and she brought up every painful episode they had ever told her (and they had told each other *everything*) every terrible detail, and made them go over everything again, analyzing it and reanalyzing it. Then she made them talk about their past friendships and how those relationships had failed one by one, inevitably, because of their lack of real feeling and commitment and sincerity and desire for something better that could exist between people. And she made them talk about their futures and how they wanted to be careful and not go through life just throwing people and relationships and love on a bone heap—and how if they were going to be the true people in life—*true* people—that they believed they really could be and really wanted to be, it must start now, it must rise out of the ashes of this deep friendship the three of them shared and which Lori and Michael had nearly ruined.

Michael and Lori promised they would not make love again. Lori said she had felt stupid doing it, anyway, and Michael laughed and said he had felt stupid too. They admitted that they hadn't actually wanted or needed to make love: they had just suddenly found themselves there on the table doing it. In fact they had just started when Teecy came in. In fact they hadn't really got started when Teecy came in.

Teecy, Michael, and Lori went for a walk. The night was cold, the sky incredibly clear and the stars shining in that bold, indomitable way they do in December, which makes humans so aware of their own personal smallness and how short a lifetime is and how all we really have is each other, just for a while, friendship and love.

Blind. Babes in the woods. Whisint sighed. But she wasn't surprised that Teecy didn't attempt to understand *how* the three of them could have possibly agreed to stay together beyond this point.

For that level of thinking had ceased. The relationship formed its own personality, one in conflict with itself—and one so different from Teecy's, Lori's, and Michael's singly, that it could not only accept this development but accept its inherent strangeness as well—and the strangeness of accepting it, too! As for the "personality's" awareness of the implications for what lay ahead . . . .

Whisint could easily imagine the tension in the apartment, a tension radiating from Teecy. And of course the tension magnified and reproduced itself in Lori and Michael. Each of the three of them becomes constantly aware of where the other two are at every moment. Every movement becomes grotesquely magnified by its physicalness, every gesture having immense underlying significance in the rollicking implications lurking beneath the surface of the simple, innocent movement which carried it, making a mockery of the sanity of friendship, a mockery of the sanity of human ideals, a mockery of the finer love which men and women might strive for, a mockery of Teecy and the sanity which she felt being demolished when Michael slouches on the sofa with his legs stretched out, his body offering itself to Lori—when at breakfast, Lori leans over from the stove and salts Michael's eggs and, jerking the shaker up and down "accidentally" shakes salt into his lap—when at night after her bath Lori comes into the living room braless under her Snoopy T-shirt and her nipples are hard and staring at Michael . . . . Teecy bathes silently, for when she is in the tub, rubbing soap over her body, Michael is perhaps in the next room running his hands over Lori's body, and when Teecy finishes, as the water runs out of the tub, she hurriedly dries off, for Michael and Lori are maybe finishing off, too, desperately, furiously trying to finish before all the water rushes out of the tub. Two or three times a night Teecy wakes, wondering what woke her and doubting that Lori is in the other bed . . . what Teecy sees is a couple of pillows Lori put there. Teecy listens for sounds from Michael's room, then she gets out of bed and tiptoes across the room and leans over Lori's bed. Once as she leans over, Lori's eyes are shining up at her.

And of course there is that enormous world of time when Lori and Michael leave for classes. Teecy knows their schedules by heart, every minute of each day of the week, and she spends a tremendous amount of time and thought in checking to see that Michael and Lori are where they are supposed to be—all the while doing it without being *too* obvious to them that Teecy is constantly watching her . . . .

"I mean, constantly watching them," Teecy said.

Whisint caught that. She saw both possibilities: that Teecy felt Lori was the real threat to the friendship, and that Michael was the gullible male dupe and tool. And that perhaps Teecy saw Lori as a rival for Michael's love.

But there was another possibility, and that didn't slip past Whisint. She wondered if Teecy had been at the time aware of this possibility, and if she was perhaps vaguely aware of it now.

Then came "the final blow," as Teecy put it. Yesterday Lori told Teecy, while Michael sat across the room watching them, that she and Michael weren't staying in town over the Christmas break, as the three of them had planned to do. Lori and Michael were going to visit their parents.

"But it's worse than that," Teecy told Whisint. "They aren't just gong home, they're going together. They're going to Lori's parents for a week, then to Michael's parents for a week. Together."

The office was silent and dark. Whisint pulled the little chain on a green-shaded lamp. The top of the desk and Whisint's and Teecy's lap and hands, were lit.

"Are they getting married?" Whisint said.

"No," Teecy said quickly. "That's not the point. That's . . . I mean they wouldn't get *married.*" Her hands disappeared upward into the darkness and her voice was muffled and distorted as she spoke through them. "Now that they've done this to me they don't need to get married."

It was still snowing hard as they walked across the campus, leaning against each other and bending forward into the wind. "It's not much farther," Whisint called out. Teecy nodded exaggeratedly and trudged on. "Why aren't you wearing a real coat?"

"I gave mine to Lori," Teecy called.

They reached Whisint's car, the only one still on the lot, and got in. Whisint started it, then got out to knock snow off and scrape the windshield. She got in again and after concentrating on driving out of the deep snow on the lot, she said, "Are they staying in the apartment or renting a different one when they come back?"

"They aren't coming back," Teecy said low. Then louder— "I'm moving out."

"You don't want to hear this," Whisint said, "but this has probably worked out for the best. This might sound rather obvious, but it's true and it must be said, and you must hear it. You will eventually understand. The friendship that you and Lori and Michael had was . . ."

"I have wiped them out."

"Perhaps you see it as your fault that the friendship ended as it did, but . . . ."

She wasn't sure that was what Teecy meant. Perhaps she meant that she had already erased Lori and Michael from her memory, which of course was pitiful bravado. But Whisint went on with it, what she thought might ease the girl's pain. The friendship was good while it lasted, relationships constantly change—those that don't are artificial, false, sex is a wild card, and the only thing worse than suffering because of those we love is suffering because of those we used to love but now hate. It was a good lecture, calm and graceful—and sincere. And Whisint felt that Teecy actually listened.

Poor Teecy, poor brilliant, burning thing. So she wiped them out! Whisint loved that spirit, that fierceness. It was youth, of couse. But it was also integrity.

They were driving down the town's main street. The brightly decorated store windows and Christmas lights shone through the blowing snow with a stylized Christmas card, faraway softness. A few cars crept along the street, and some people hurried down the sidewalks, having done the last of their shopping, no doubt, and now on their way home to put the gifts under the tree and warm themselves by the fire.

They drove in silence through town and out a road where the snow was unrutted by the passing of cars. Whisint turned onto the narrow lane at the end of which she lived on the second floor of a large old house. As she raced the motor and spun the tires, lunging the car halfway up the driveway, the house seemed especially large because it was dark, for the old widow who lived downstairs had left to visit her children for Christmas.

Upstairs, Teecy stood in the middle of the large living room looking at the ceiling-high bookcases, the paintings and sculptures. Whisint was pleased, in spite of herself, that Teecy seemed impressed.

Whisint tossed two frozen dinners into the oven, then went down the hall to the rear bedroom and opened the door. The room was freezing cold and smelled stuffy. She opened the heat vent. From the bathroom she got some perfume. What are you doing? she almost said out loud. She stared at the bottle and didn't sprinkle any about the room. But she ran her hand along the bedside table, then got a towel and dusted the room. She wanted to draw back the bedspread and blankets to examine the sheets and pillowcases....

Are you actually *doing* this? She walked around the room. It was so cold. She yanked back the blankets. The sheets were clean. Of course they were. I hate you. I truly hate you.

And it expressed itself most strongly in matters of love. Why should that be? She went to the smaller bedroom, the one she normally used. She took off her suit and blouse, and washed her face and brushed her hair. She chose a pair of black slacks and a white turtleneck sweater that accented her brown eyes and the soft sheen of her face, like the mistiness that haloed the lights in town, after she smoothed on some moisturizer and gloss.

She stood in the bathroom looking at herself in the mirrors, hating herself because her heart was pounding hard and she felt so foolishly expectant and thrilled. The self-hatred rises all the way to the surface until it is on your face, you can actually see it, and in your eyes. In the arms of another person, in the face of another person, on the lips of another person it magically becomes love. Oh, if I could always be in love I would never hate myself, she told the intense, frowning women surrounding her.

Teecy was sitting on the leather couch with a book on her lap, the Stonehenge, a surprising choice, and she didn't look up until Whisint stood in the middle of the room. Teecy's mouth fell open. It literally fell open, went into a perfect O, her eyes full of amazement, and Whisint could feel her trying to think but being unable to, yet, until she could absorb the incredible, overwhelming fact of Whisint's beauty, of which she so self-centeredly, so stupidly, had been unaware up to this moment.

"I'm having a martini," Whisint said. "Would you like one?"

"Yes," Teecy said, her voice small. "Please."

Whisint went to the stereo. "Who do you like?" she said, not turning but feeling Teecy's eyes on her.

"Anything," Teecy said. "Whatever you like."

Something dull, for now, undistracting, then to the liquor cabinet. The music murmured and prattled the nice world, ordinary and unchanging, the never-never of everything out there. Ice from the kitchen. Martinis, dry, lovely, stern and true . . .

She took Teecy hers and sat, legs crossed, on the ottoman off the corner of the end of the sofa where Teecy sat. She lifted her glass and Teecy brought hers all the way to touch Whisint's. "To . . . what?"

Teecy shook her head. "I don't know."

"To us?"

"Okay." Their glasses tinged.

As Whisint lifted her glass to her lips, Teecy was amazed at how everything was shining, beautiful—the glass, the gin, Whisint's eyes, which Teecy realized she was seeing for the first time. And Teecy had a strange feeling, an amazing feeling, as she became completely aware of Whisint, became aware that she, Teecy, was here alone with the most . . . unusual woman she had ever actually met. Very unusual, and beautiful, and . . . powerful.

Teecy got drunk on one martini.

What a jerk. She hated herself. What do you do with yourself when you discover the full extent of what a jerk you are?

All right, she wasn't actually drunk but *somewhat* drunk. She and Whisint ate t.v. dinners there in the living room, listened to some new music which she put on when they started eating, peculiar music from India, sitar, which Teecy didn't like but which Whisint said she liked for very complicated reasons which she explained, but Teecy didn't listen.

Whisint talked in swoops with the music and she gestured a lot, and stopped eating to walk around, not pacing but gliding, almost dancing as she talked, with long pauses. Teecy liked watching her talk, it was so different from her lectures in class. This was a completely different person. And when Teecy tuned in to what she was actually saying, she was even using a different language. Yes, it was English, but it was so different from what Teecy would have expected. She said the sitar music was beautiful because it went all the way down into grief but then up again, for life doesn't stop even after the worst things imaginable have happened—and we go on, too, because life is so strong in us.

Then Whisint walked out of the room and was gone a long time. When she returned she was wearing a long, flowing, beautiful black negligee. Teecy knew that if she looked closely she could see through it, and she told herself, She's going to make love to me. And added with a giggle inside herself, So she's the one.

"You don't close your eyes," Whisint said.

"That's right."

Whisint leaned forward, this time not shutting her eyes, and stopped when their faces were almost touching, their breath quivering on each other's lips, their eyes whole worlds. "Teecy McTavish," Whisint whispered and closed her eyes slowly, her eyes rolling back, Teecy saw, as the eyelids came down. Whisint drew away and stood up.

She walked across the room to the large, uncurtained window, and Teecy saw Whisint staring at her in the black mirror of night on the window. She left the window, the negligee swaying gracefully, and she lit a cigarette. Without speaking—and only glancing at her—she offered Teecy the pack. Teecy shook her head and said, "No thanks," so low she couldn't hear it herself over the music. Whisint looked at her squarely, sternly. For a moment Teecy thought Whisint was going to strike her. Whisint sat down beside her and put her arm around Teecy's shoulders. She started to speak but stopped. She closed her eyes and lay her head back as if she had all at once decided to sleep. She slowly lifted the cigarette to her mouth, inhaled deeply without opening her eyes. She tapped the cigarette on an ashtray, finding it without opening her eyes. Then she ground out the cigarette and turned to Teecy.

She brought both hands up to Teecy's face and slowly drew her closer. She put her arms around Teecy and rubbed her cheek against Teecy's, and with her eyes closed she kissed Teecy softly and with her lips touching Teecy's she again said, "Teecy McTavish." Her eyes snapped open, she drew her face back and she stared at Teecy with her eyes wide open and clear and hard.

"Yes," Teecy whispered and shrugged her eyebrows and Teecy moved her face slowly forward, taking forever to travel the distance between them, until their parted lips touched lightly. She inhaled Whisint's breath and with the tip of her tongue touched Whisint's lips. With a little cry deep inside her, Whisint caved in.

Love belongs to women. Love is woman's. Or however you choose to say women know how to love because they know love is its own thing and not something on the way to something else. Which is how men do it. Men have the famous penis, which must erupt every so often or the testicles will burst internally or something unendurable like that.

But women are true lovers because for one thing they're not in a hurry, and every man Teecy has been involved with (there have been three) has been in a great rush, though it's unfair to say this about the actual men themselves for Teecy knows it is the penis that is in the great rush. The penis ruins love, turns it to a fuck. No man can be as completely into love as Whisint was that night with Teecy. Of course if a man could check his penis at the door that might make a difference. But if he did, he wouldn't even sit down and talk to a woman, he would go off on a hike with some other men. If it wasn't for their penises men would never go home, they would never get married so they wouldn't have homes to go to. They would work all the time and fall over dead at the age of 30.

All this was going through Teecy's mind as she lay in Whisint's arms letting her kiss her eyes and lips and throat a thousand, ten thousand, etc. slow careful patient kisses.

It was so nice. Teecy sighed. She felt better than she had in . . . months. This is what I've been waiting for—no, this is what I've been *living* for. It was the first time in months and months that she hadn't been worrying about her classes and Lori and Michael and her mother and father and a hundred other people who had changed from being people into grotesque monsters. Of course Lori and Michael were still *there.* But when she thought of them now, as Whisint kissed her, they were far away and small, little kids who were out playing in the yard.

She listened to the music and she and Whisint were inside it. It was wonderful. She breathed it out, "Wonderful," and Whisint responded by cupping Teecy's face and laying her own check against Teecy's mouth and slowly moving her head, with Teecy's parted lips moving over Whisint's face.

Teecy understood. Whisint wanted Teecy to kiss her. And Teecy would. Later. There was plenty of time.

Whisint leaned back from her. The music spun the world on and on. Whisint's lips were red, as if Teecy's fever (which Teecy suddenly realized she no longer had!) had passed to Whisint and was burning its way into her from her mouth. Whisint's eyes were half closed, her expression one of great patience and willingness, an expression which Teecy instinctively knew would under different circumstances convey boredom, endurance of sorrow, the fate of loneliness.

Teecy's face . . . . Oh lovely burning face, waif and woman, swollen with the strain of illness burning in the skin, the disease of germs and experience and ruinous wearing away of innocence until nothing is left but the sheer person hiding beneath a few pathetic and pathetically obvious defenses— "Personality" . . . . My God, Whisint thought, I actually *love* her. All Whisint's self was down. She was before the altar of the love that had gone along with her all these years, waiting, withdrawing farther into her as her life showed there was less and less reason and occasion for it to come forth. That Teecy was cruel, Whisint was fully aware. She was cruel and hard and she would get everything she wanted and she would break most of what she got and let it fall away as she went on, all this was clear on this girl's face. I'll stop now, Whisint told herself, meaning that from this night on she would love Teecy, but that she wouldn't let herself come even within touching distance of her, that the love she had for her was one thing, and it would exist forever in Whisint's heart, or until she died, but that she would not go on, now, and do more to put that love into words and touching and kissing and holding in her arms into sleep.

This could be Whisint's last love. This time here on the sofa could be the end of all that for her. She might spend the next 20 or 30 years in controlled, restrained movement through the routines of her work and formal social life. The awful thing was that Whisint could actually do it. She *could* stop now and hold herself together for 30 years without ever kissing or touching or in any way showing her love for this girl or any other person. She sat on the edge of the sofa looking down at Teecy, waiting for . . . .

She didn't know what she was waiting for. Perhaps for herself to "decide" if she would go on with the difficulties of involvement, the entanglements and the absurd complications and the heartbreaks and the nights of sleeping alone and lying awake all night alone even though there was someone who presumably loved her yet chose to be somewhere else while Whisint felt her loneliness ten times worse than the loneliness of that *other* Whisint who walked through her days with the clear understanding that life is a task, each day is a task, leading to that final task which can also be endured alone and lived through alone, if you just bring to bear all the intelligence, all the will, and all the courage you have—and never let yourself remember that you would rather be lying in the arms of someone who would make love to you all night.

Poor Whisint, she felt so alone, so old, so tired. Old Whisint—it was just a matter of time. And old Whisint sighed as she sat on the edge of the sofa looking at Teecy McTavish across a distance of years and years and . . . .

Teecy lay quite comfortably and contentedly looking up a column of light connecting her face with Whisint's. Everything outside that column softly faded off. Teecy's eyes moved from Whisint's face and she looked at the loose black gown, at Whisint's breasts.

Then Teecy believed she saw something in Whisint's face, in her eyes, a drawing back, though Whisint didn't move—it was more a withdrawing inward, a slow dimness that seemed to make Whisint recede into herself. It was just a moment. Perhaps a sigh. But Teecy was bothered by it, much in the same way she would be bothered by someone glancing away just when she was saying something important.

Now, Teecy heard inside herself. And though she wouldn't think about this moment for a long time and understand it in relation to other occasions when the same thing would happen with other people, her knowing that now was the moment came through clearly because she sensed that Whisint was going away.

But it wasn't Teecy's fear of being left or of being alone that caused her to lean up and slide her hand along Whisint's neck under her hair and draw Whisint slowly down to her, but because she wanted Whisint. She put her arms around her, kissing her, holding her and pulling her down until Whisint wasn't merely leaning over Teecy but lying against her. They kissed, then Teecy whispered, "I love you. Oh, I love you," and they kissed again, not taking their mouths from each other for so long Teecy believed the kiss would last all night. It was wonderful. She loved it. And she loved Whisint, she really did.

They ate gingerbread and whipped cream, and drank milk. When they finished, Whisint slid the tray off the bed and said, "I love you," as Teecy took her in her arms.

"I love you too," Teecy said.

They kissed, slowly closing their eyes.

"I can't believe this is happening," Whisint said. "I'm afraid it's a dream and I'll wake up and you'll be gone."

"I'll not leave," Teecy said. She abruptly turned her head away, pushed her face into the pillow, and started coughing.

"We've got to do something about that," Whisint said. "Tomorrow I'm taking you to a doctor."

"I'm okay. I actually feel fine," Teecy whispered, her

voice not recovered from coughing. "Anyway, tomorrow's Saturday."

"That's right. Then Monday I'll take you. We'll stay in all weekend and I'll take care of you. Maybe by Monday you'll be better and we won't have to go out. We could just stay here. Would you like that?"

"I would love it."

They talked, pausing again and again to kiss with luxurious slowness. Teecy fell asleep listening to Whisint. Without taking her arm from under Teecy's head, Whisint reached over and switched off the lamp. Light the color of peaches poured down the hall into the bedroom. Teecy breathed through her mouth, wheezing, coughing now and then in her sleep. Whisint kissed her cheek and lay staring at her lips.

But in the morning something was wrong. When Teecy woke, she blinked and looked around with a look which Whisint read as bovine alarm, as if she not only couldn't remember where she was but couldn't remember Whisint or why she was here or what they had done.

It didn't help that Whisint felt hungover, though she hadn't drunk that much, and she was exhausted from not having slept at all and from so much lovemaking.

And she resented the lovemaking, spitefully. Spiteful toward herself for feeling this way and toward her other self who last night had brought this person home. For this girl, this Teecy McTavish, was a crude little thing, a blunt , dull thing, crude and clumsy and even cruel in the way she had made love to Whisint. Whisint had started crying when the gray light of the winter dawn lit the bedroom like a dreary fake impressionistic painting. She cried because she wanted someone who would love her in the same beautiful, graceful way she loved. But she knew it was her fate to never find a lover as perfect as she. So she would wake, as she did this morning, exhausted but feeling cheated and wasted and spent, drained, seeing that last night each time she had poured herself out in coming she had given away, wasted, squandered more of herself, of the precious self that shouldn't have been given away to this blunt-faced, sick, inarticulate, unshaped, cruelly resilient and indomitable girl whose legs and stomach were hard as a frog's, and who had the hard, thick labia of a calf.

It isn't guilt, Whisint told herself several times. I have simply made a stupid blunder with a stupid person, and I pray to God it won't take all day to get out of this.

She went to the bathroom and took three Valium, three Lomotils, three aspirins, and three One-A-Days. Getting back into bed she deliberately scraped Teecy's leg with her toenails.

And it worked, Teecy woke, and Whisint didn't like the way she woke, didn't like the expression on her blunt little face, didn't like her eyes, her mouth. "Well. You seem surprised. Remember me?"

Teecy blinked. "Yes. Good morning."

"Did you have a good sleep?"

"Oh, yes. Wonderful"—and, turning, she put her arms across Whisint, surprise again showing on her face when she discovered Whisint had put on a robe. "Did you sleep well?"

"No. I didn't sleep at all. None."

"Oh. I'm sorry. I didn't know."

"How could you have known? You were sound asleep. You were snoring."

"That's because of my cold. It makes me . . . breathe hard."

"So I've noticed."

Whisint lay on her back looking up at the ceiling. Teecy lay on her side, her arm still across Whisint's stomach but her hand not touching her, or at least through the robe Whisint couldn't feel any pressure from the hand.

"What I have to say now must be said." Whisint's voice was steady but low. "We don't even know each other, but what we have done puts us in a very dangerous position. In different ways, but in equally dangerous positions. I could be

ruined," she said smoothly, her voice level, not faltering or
even quavering as the words leaped over that immense cre-
vice. "But you could be ruined too. I don't know who would
suffer more, you or me, but we could both be quite . . .
ruined. And the effects of that would last the rest of our
lives. That is what you probably don't realize, that it would
last the rest of your life." She glanced at Teecy.

She was listening with the same blank expression of
students in class: it was impossible to know how they felt
about what they were hearing, or if they were in fact listening.

"What I'm getting at," Whisint said, "is that you must
never talk about this to anyone. Not even to your best
friends. Not even to anyone who you think would understand. For no one understands. And not only must you never
talk about this to anyone, you must never let it show. You
must never come to my office or come here to my apartment
or do *anything* that would give anyone the least suspicion
that . . . ."

The voice shut off. The words were still there, she would
have gone on with it for five minutes, maybe longer. But the
throat, the voice, the tongue, the mouth shut off. *I hate
myself.* Would her mouth let her say that?

"You don't have to worry," Teecy said. "I won't cause
any trouble. I love you."

Whisint tried not to, but she turned her head away.

"You can trust me. Really you can. I'm not a fool. I'll
not do something outlandish."

Whisint stared at the corner of the ceiling while that
word spread over her.

"After all," Teecy said, and there was something in her
voice which Whisint hadn't heard before, a control and sure-
ness, confidence and canniness, which undoubtedly had been
there all along but hadn't an opportunity to show itself in
what Teecy had told about her life with those other clowns,
Lori and Michael, and which of course hadn't a chance to
show itself last night, "After all," Teecy said, "would a

girl who uses the word 'outlandish' ever do something outlandish?"

Never underestimate them, Whisint heard inside herself,
that begrudging respect the professor pays students, for
Teecy had of course known the word had struck a note in
Whisint, and moreover Teecy knew exactly what note it
had struck.

Whisint tried to speak and her mouth cooperated: "It is
very serious. All this is . . . very serious."

"I know it is. But *trust* me. All right?"

Whisint didn't like that, having to respond to a request
that was actually a command. It was like those interrogations
of the professor which a class sometimes launches into, usually after a tragic exam, when the professor finds herself/him-
self dodging and scrambling, all dignity torn to shreds.

That was the whole problem. This Teecy person had
caught Whisint at a moment when she was pitifully vulnerable, and the girl had ripped and torn through the fragile defenses which Whisint tried to put up, and she had stripped
Whisint of her dignity. Whisint couldn't stand to even look at
this girl's face, now, as she lay there with her arm across
Whisint's stomach. (The audacity of it!) Yet here she lay,
trapped, utterly robbed of dignity. And then to have this person lecturing her on trust!

Whisint wondered if it might all be a trap. How many
people were involved in it? Of course such suspicions were a
waste of time, for there is no way of tracing them down, unless one hires detectives, which is obviously out of the question. Whisint would never allow herself to become so paranoid as to do that. But she recognized as a definite possibility
that several girls, scheming late at night, could plan a series of
raids, so to speak, on certain professors, catch them at vulnerable moments and place them in compromising positions,
thereby giving the girls, the little devils, tremendous power
which they would use at the most strategic, most devastating
moment . . .

"What's your name?" Teecy said. "I don't even know your given name."

Whisint was silent. If she didn't tell her, she and the other schemers wouldn't have that, too, to use against her. Whisint saw herself before a committee of investigation formed by the administration of the college. Serving as her own defense, Whisint asks this Teecy McTavish, in cross examination, to tell the committee Professor Whisint's given name. "Ah ha," she says when Teecy can't answer. "So you don't even know my given name—yet you claim that we . . . *made love*?" —she says the words with such archness that the very idea of making love is absurd . . .

"Won't you tell me?" Teecy said.

Whisint stared at the corner of the ceiling.

"All right," Teecy said as she rose up beside Whisint— then swung over her, her hair hanging down around her face and her breasts hanging down. She looked like a wild woman. How quickly we become wild women, Whisint thought, her eyes filled with this creature who had violated all rules of civilized conduct and discreet behavior, who in breaking down Whisint's defenses and smashing all of Whisint's vulnerabilities now had her literally pinned down, hanging over her with her hair and breasts and arrogantly determined girl-face . . . .

"You're . . . you've changed your mind," Teecy said as they stared unblinking at each other. "That's all right. I guess I understand. What you want to do is your right. It's better for you to let me know now rather than waiting until it's worse for me, I guess. At least now I can . . . ." The words trailed off as if the face had forgotten what it was talking about, her face changing, though the expression, which was quite open and blank—just her, just Teecy—didn't change. But there was something in her eyes, they seemed to become larger, fuller. Then Teecy said softly, "But I just want you to know that I love you, no matter what. And I will always love you."

Close your eyes, a voice told Whisint. She closed her eyes. She took a deep breath and let it out slowly, more and more, all of it until there was nothing. "Martha," she whispered. She was so weak, her body so heavy with exhaustion and Librium and Lomotil and what in romance is called 'surrender," she could barely move except to turn slightly to the side and try, with great slow effort, to lift her hips as Teecy took the robe off her and then took off the bra and panties Whisint had put on, and as she sank away, feebling holding Teecy and letting her make love to her so sweetly, so earnestly and thoroughly, a detached part of Whisint wished she weren't so exhausted, wished she could hold her eyes open to watch, in the light of day, while Teecy made love to her, this detached part of Whisint becoming brighter by the moment until it was quite huge and yellow . . . . And Whisint is again walking in the museum of modern art in Amsterdam, stepping into the room where she sees Van Gogh's *Sunflowers.* "Oh God," Whisint says out loud. "I had no idea . . ." She would have said, "it was so large." But that wasn't all she felt, not even if she could have put into words the feeling she had for the brightness, the largeness, the boldness, the life—the *life.*

That brightness swelled Whisint into sleep, her arms extended straight out, flat on her back. It walked up and down, lecturing her, a lecture hall full of Whisints whose empty hands tried to take notes on their bodies.

"It's too late."

The house was burning. Not in the orderly and predictable way in which fire spreads when left to itself, but in rolling eruptions, the front room filling with fire, pouring out the windows, then the rear of the house bursting into flames as an explosion in the kitchen blew out all the rear windows and sent the back door sailing like a magic carpet. Then more explosions—one upstairs, one in the basement, another in the front room, the bathroom . . . .

Whisint had awakened burning and shaking. Teecy bounced out of bed and began doctoring her with aspirins, a hot water bottle, orange juice, the thermometer, and an ancient vaporizer which not only worked but worked with a vengeance, fogging over all the windows and turning the apartment into a hothouse.

How the subject of Lori and Michael came up was in itself infuriating—that they could be in danger, yet that Teecy would play cat and mouse with Whisint . . . .

After getting the vaporizer going, Teecy went to the kitchen. Whisint smelled burning toast and she closed her eyes and smiled. At last Teecy brought in a tray with a pot of tea, toast, and the little pewter keg, which Whisint used for paperclips, filled with honey. (She hoped Teecy had washed it.) She let Teecy fluff up the pillows. She asked Teecy to bring a mirror, then changed her mind, pushing back her hair with both hands and saying with a rather shaky laugh, "I'm afraid to see myself." She picked up the little pewter keg. "What a nice idea."

Teecy smiled a demure, plump-cat smile. She waited while Whisint ate the toast and drank the tea, then with their tongues and kisses they ate the honey. Teecy leaned forward and let Whisint unbotton her blouse and unbuckle her belt and unzip her jeans. When she was undressed and lying in Whisint's arms she said, "I'm afraid."

"Don't worry," Whisint crooned, drawing it out long and soft, "Don't worry. Don't worry."

"I mean about them. I left something for them. You might call it a surprise. And I wish I hadn't done it. It's terrible."

"You could go to the apartment and take it back or do whatever . . . . I don't even know what you're talking about."

"It's too late," Teecy whispered. "It will . . . kill them."

"What exactly do you mean? Do you mean that . . .?"

"It's too late," Teecy said, her voice shrinking as if to

hide, and Whisint saw the house where Lori and Michael lived bursting into flames as Teecy's timebomb went off.

Looking back, Whisint wasn't sure whether she believed Teecy McTavish set a timebomb (a crude gasoline timebomb) in Lori and Michael's apartment. These days, a girl certainly could build and set bombs. One part of Whisint was quite convinced, another part wasn't very sure of Whisint herself, for the thought floated up that she was vaguely delirious. And perhaps Teecy was slipping Valium into her orange juice. Obviously Teecy wanted to keep her here, doctoring her and loving her, bringing her aspirins and taking her temperature and, after giving her a sip of orange juice, leaning down and sliding her tongue into Whisint's mouth, all part of Doctor McTavish's treatment . . . .

While two young people were about to die.

Burn to death. Go blowing to pieces while Whisint lay in bed burning alive with fever and stupid passion and stupid love and confusion . . . languishing is the word, it occurred to Whisint.

"I don't know when they'll find it," Teecy said. "They might not find it until they come back."

Whisint opened her eyes and Teecy was calmly sitting on the edge of the bed looking at her. Whisint said, "I want you to do something."

"Yes?" Teecy reached down and stroked Whisint's hair.

"No. I mean . . . ." She sighed and let her eyes close, let herself sink backward down down down into the bed which was a deep cavern where she must spend the rest of her life. "Teecy," Whisint said with her eyes closed, "please tell me what you have done."

"Fallen in love." She came down and kissed Whisint's lips lightly. "I have fallen in love with Professor Martha Whisint."

"No." Frowning, her eyes still closed. "Please. What have

you done to Lori and Michael?"

"Forgotten them."

"But you said . . . ." But *had* she? "You said you put . . . something in the apartment and it will go off when they . . . . You must tell me when it will happen, because"—she opened her eyes, seeing it all very clearly now—"because we must stop it from happening."

Teecy stared blankly at Whisint as if she heard nothing she said. Or heard it but the words made no sense.

"Please tell me," Whisint whispered.

"Tell you what?"

"Tell me . . . ."

"It's too late," Teecy said without expression, her eyes loosening focus until Whisint felt she was gazing through her at something, someone, far beyond Whisint, perhaps she was watching the burning, exploding house, which Whisint watched again, too, marveling at how Teecy had placed the charges and/or fruit jars of gasoline to go off not all at once but in waves . . .

An actual *bomb*?

Whisint wouldn't know, of course, until it was too late. In which case, Whisint thought with cruel lucidity, her being here with Teecy would implicate her, Whisint, in the crime. Whisint wouldn't/couldn't be Teecy's alibi. (Do police actually talk that way? Whisint saw herself squatting on a short three-legged stool while cops leaned over, prodding her with questions about her and Teecy's lovemaking.) Whisint couldn't help Teecy by serving as her alibi. That is the grim beauty of bombs: you don't have to be there when they go off. While you're blowing up your ex-friends, you can be clear across town in bed with one of your professors . . . .

"I should go get it before they find it," Teecy said. "I can't do that to them, no matter what they did to me. But I can't go back there alone."

Whisint was already getting out of bed before Teecy finished, and her head was reeling, the room, the house, this end of town, tilting and gliding as she stood. "Where did you put it?" Whisint said as she went uphill then abruptly downhill to the dresser where the suit she wore yesterday, so many years ago, was wadded up.

"In Michael's room," Teecy said.

Ah ha. Under the bed. Whisint saw two, three—more!—jars of gasoline connected to a fuse fixed to the bedsprings and a flint that would scratch a spark . . . .

Teecy looked at the clock. "It's almost one." She shook her head. "Maybe they've already found it."

"And it's . . .?" But Whisint couldn't say it, couldn't waste the precious moments saying "It's timed to go off at one o'clock?!" as she saw Lori and Michael, absurdly as naked as she and Teecy were at this moment, walking around in Michael's bedroom, innocently wondering what that peculiar smell was or what's that funny ticking sound . . . . And one of them would sit on the chair or lie on the bed, or when their heads touch the pillow, or when the minute-hand on the clock wired to Teecy's bomb points straight up and it is one o'clock, the bomb will drive Lori and Michael up through the ceiling into the gray December sky.

Teecy was crying, slumping on the side of the bed as Whisint hurriedly, furiously got her own clothes on, saying, "Put your clothes on. Teecy. Put your clothes on." Then, when Whisint was at last dressed, without a bra or panties but at least with the suit and a pair of shoes, she grabbed up Teecy's blouse and started sticking the girl's arms in the sleeves, then her jeans, kneeling on the floor and sticking Teecy's blunt little feet with their blunt little toes into her tennies.

Everything took forever. She pulled Teecy down the hall toward the front door of the apartment. She put one of her own heavy coats on Teecy, threw a coat on herself, and sighed with relief when they were finally through the door and on their way down the stairs to the front door, then out into the incredibly cold afternoon, Whisint shivering deeply in herself and that part that never forgets itself or its mortality saying calmly, You'll probably get pneumonia out of this, while the other Whisint answered, Oh yes, that's all I need, that's all I need.

She got Teecy in the car, managed to start the car. "Now," she said. "Where is the apartment?"

Amazingly, Teecy gave the address. Whisint succeeded in backing the car out of the driveway and got it headed up the street and reached the corner without getting stuck in the snow and without skidding into the cars parked along the curbs or the few cars they met as she raced up the main street and through a red light, and when they reached the address the house was still standing.

She stopped the car, jumped out, yanked open the other door and pulled Teecy out. "Now," she said firmly in Teecy's face. "Where is it?"

"Inside," Teecy mumbled.

Of course, idiot child! "We can go through the door and . . . nothing will happen?"

Teecy looked up with an odd, quizzical expression. Then she giggled!

"We can go through the door and nothing will happen," Teecy said.

It passed through Whisint's mind that she was far from understanding all that was going on here. Why, Teecy might even be planning to share her suicide with Whisint . . .

Almost light-heartedly, Whisint put her arm around Teecy and marched her through the snow to the front porch, up the steps—and through the door.

"Upstairs," Teecy said.

When they reached the apartment door Teecy didn't hesitate but reached out, turned the knob. Whisint held her breath and squinted hard . . . . Teecy opened the door and walked in, but holding Whisint's hand and drawing her in after her.

A young man sat on an old sofa reading a book. His

face was round and had a soft grin, he wore black-rimmed glasses, and he looked like a panda. "Hi," he said. Then he called over his shoulder, "Lori, Teecy's here." Then to Whisint, "Hello."

She came in from the kitchen wearing red slacks and a dark brown turtleneck sweater which made her silver blonde hair shine. Her face was winter pale, smooth as milk, her eyes were calm blue, and she was smiling at Whisint. "Martha," she said, and Whisint's only thought was that she, herself, must look like holy hell, her hair wild, her face splotched with fever, her lips raw and cracked by fever and Teecy McTavish, and she was sorry she looked so badly, she actually thought, I'm sorry, apologizing not to herself but to Teecy and Michael's Lori as she said, "Hello, Lorine."

It lasted only ten minutes but seemed much longer to Whisint as she sat trapped in a canvas duck chair staring over her knees at Michael as he went bouncing around the room. He walked on his toes, perhaps because he was nervous, springing on the balls of his feet. Or perhaps he thought that walking that way made him appear catlike and lithe, though it only shook the floor and gave Whisint that nauseous feeling that she was on a trampoline. In the bedroom Teecy and Lorine/Lori were having a loud conversation. Michael tried carrying Whisint and himself through that with some conversation about the book he was reading, *Being and Nothingness.* He was an education major and claimed he wanted to broaden himself. He asked if Whisint had any suggestions for his Christmas vacation reading. She said, "No."

The bedroom door banged open and Teecy came in. Lorine/Lori followed her, both cheeks bright red. For a moment Whisint thought Teecy had struck her. But that wasn't it. Lorine was angry.

"Did you read this?" Teecy said loudly, holding out an unsealed envelope.

Michael, who in his bouncing about had roamed out to the kitchen for a handful of Graham crackers, gazed blankly at the envelope. He shook his head no. "Was I supposed to?"

Lorine/Lori said, "It was in the drawer with your underwear." She glared at Teecy, then at Whisint, the glare fading as she and Whisint looked at each other. Whisint couldn't tell what changes occurred exactly. It had been so long. . . .

"Teecy," Lorine said, "feels a good deal of resentment, it seems . . . ."

It seems . . . . Whisint couldn't place that, though this was the same person she had known. And of course Whisint's fever didn't help, this backward sinking feeling of not altogether being here.

". . . she was trying to hurt Michael and me as much as she could by . . . ."

Whisint chose not to listen. She wanted somehow to struggle up out of her duck chair and walk out of the apartment, down the stairs, and into the snow. But she couldn't rise and walk out. She couldn't even keep from hearing the conversation, though she toned out the particulars, concentrating hard and succeeding to the extent that Lorine and Teecy stopped looking at her as they argued and stomped back and forth between Whisint and Michael.

The drift of it was, naturally, that Teecy was finished with Lori and Michael, they could go to hell, they were phonies and definitely less than what she had trusted and believed they were, and they could never hope to be more than the weak, ineffectual, phony nonentities which they were too unaware to realize they were. "I would hate you, but it would be a waste of my time. I would pity you, but it would be wasted on you, for you don't even know how pitiful you are," Teecy said.

Whisint had plenty of time to look ahead to what this would mean to her. Though they had her trapped, sitting as judge, mother, professor, revered figure of esteem and authority to weigh their sides in this "hearing," she knew they were fully aware that they had brought her down, and it was very important to them that they had brought her down.

The cat's out of the bag, Whisint numbly told herself. For clearly Lorine had told Teecy about herself and Whisint.

Though there wasn't much to tell, actually. Certainly Teecy could now have told Lorine ten times more about herself and Whisint than Lorine had had to tell. Unless Lorine had done some embellishing—and the Lorine whom Whisint has known two . . . three?—years ago was capable of embellishing, not boastfully but because of a desire for more. Not necessarily a desire for more love itself, but a quality of specialness that was vague even in Lorine's own mind, and which could probably never be achieved. But it was, no doubt, Lorine's desire for more which had motivated the fat young man to read his absurd book, though he would never realize that, just as he would never realize he could never bounce high enough for his "Lori."

And if Lorine had told Teecy, whom else had she told? Whisint wondered about the random occasions in the past two years. She tried to recall anything that had been said, anything that had hinted at a connection with Lorine. Or to put it in the way in which Whisint punished herself, she tried to recall anyone who might have been a chicken Lorine had served up to her . . . .

No, that wasn't Lorine—she wouldn't do that. Whisint closed her eyes. She was going to cry. (The girls were crying, or a least Teecy was; Whisint didn't let herself look at Lorine.) Lorine was true. That is, Whisint could trust her, the actual person deep in Lorine. Whisint herself was not true, she told herself. She was under too many different kinds of pressure to be true. Her life was ragged, she simply didn't have the opportunity to be true, the time to concentrate on being true, and she hadn't the will, the energy, or especially the purpose to be true. How can a raw nerve be true?

She put her hand over her face as she sat there in the

stupid little living room crying—silently, she hoped. But when the girls stopped arguing, Whisint knew they had stopped because of her.

So this little bitch, Teecy McTavish, had gone through the elaborate performance of the last 24 hours just so she could parade Professor Whisint into Lori and Michael's apartment to show Lori what she could do?

Yes.

And had this little bitch, Teecy McTavish, also done it to hurt Lori because she knew that Lori's seeing Teecy dragging Whisint in would hurt Lori even more than the letter, which was the carbon copy of Teecy's "confession" to the Dean of Women, accusing Lori of being a "practicing and dedicated Lesbian who had corrupted countless innocent girls, including me"?

Yes.

It had been Teecy's plan—her "bomb"—that Michael would find the carbon copy, read between all the lines of the four months he, Lori, and Teecy had spent together as "friends," and then he would walk out, limping badly, with a crippled male ego. And the original of the letter to the Dean? Teecy threw it away as soon as she wrote it.

But when exactly did Teecy decide she was going to use Whisint?

Amazingly, Teecy didn't know that the prof Lori had told her about was Whisint, for Lori had withheld the name. Teecy hadn't known *definitely* that Whisint was the same professor until she saw the way Lori and Whisint looked at each other, though last night Teecy had begun to suspect Whisint was the one. "Last night when we were . . . you know, I . . . well, I guess it was then I started knowing it was you."

And it was then she had decided on her little trick?

Not really, though she had known that nothing on earth

would stop her from arranging for Lori to see Teecy and Whisint and know that they were in love.

And when Whisint became so worried about Lori and Michael, it occurred to Teecy that showing Whisint to Lori would wipe out Lori ten times worse than the letter. So the inevitable trap which Whisint had for so long dreaded and feared, had finally been set—and she had not only fallen into it, she had eagerly leaped in. How appropriate that when it actually happened it was such a clumsy, haphazard trap, made out of the strange inevitability of circumstances rather than cunning or viciousness. The trap had floated down onto Teecy's lap at just the right moment, and she had used it. ·

But though the trap worked, it didn't really.

"Because it merely surprised Lori. It hurt her some . . . but not really. I was hoping it would really wipe her out, because she told me she loves you more than she will ever love anyone ever again, and the time she had with you is more important to her than . . . anything else. She treasures it. It's her God."

So exhausted, sick unto death, wrung out, Whisint was completely awed by this revelation from this wretchedly dishonest, painfully honest little bitch, Teecy McTavish. As Whisint lay on her own sofa in her own blissfully silent apartment while snow fell from the black sky onto her roof, she closed her eyes as Teecy said, "That's why I did it." Teecy was crying. "But it didn't change anything. It hurt her, I know that—and I knew it would. But it didn't change the way she feels about you. Or not about *you*, I mean the way she will always feel for . . . well, for that time the two of you had together. I couldn't touch that. And I didn't want to. I just wanted her to see you with me so she would know that now I had you, and that we . . . well . . . ."

Whisint had not spoken since she said hello to Lorine. After all, what could she say? She had felt like a tool, a victim, a grotesque fool—the town fool, the campus fool—a pitiful middle-aged fool. Humiliation and self-hatred stood on Whisint's face and she wanted to close her eyes and never open them again. Teecy McTavish, the little bitch, had driven Whisint's car back to the big house at the end of the lane. And Whisint, too weak, too sick, too ruined to resist being led along, allowed the little bitch to take her upstairs, help her off with her coat, and lay her down on the sofa and cover her with a blanket.

And it all led up to this awe which Whisint still felt, a dull, golden awe. "Treasures," Whisint whispered.

"All right," she said surprising herself with how clear and actually firm it was. She sat up and looked at this little bitch, Teecy McTavish, whose face was so bright and intense, so determinedly *here*. "All right," she said, this time less certainly. "Now, about you and me."

Teecy nodded firmly, becoming even more intense, and said, "Yes," waiting for Whisint to go on.

FICTION COLLECTIVE

Books in Print

	Price List:	
	cloth	*paper*
The Second Story Man by Mimi Albert	*8.95*	*3.95*
Althea by J.M. Alonso	*11.95*	*4.95*
Searching for Survivors by Russell Banks	*7.95*	*3.95*
Babble by Jonathan Baumbach	*8.95*	*3.95*
Chez Charlotte and Emily by Jonathan Baumbach	*9.95*	*4.95*
My Father More or Less by Jonathan Baumbach	*11.95*	*5.95*
Reruns by Jonathan Baumbach	*7.95*	*3.95*
Plane Geometry . . . by R.M. Berry	*12.95*	*6.95*
Heroes and Villains by Jerry Bumpus	*13.95*	*6.95*
Things in Place by Jerry Bumpus	*8.95*	*3.95*
Ø Null Set by George Chambers	*8.95*	*3.95*
The Winnebago Mysteries by Moira Crone	*11.95*	*5.95*
Amateur People by Andree Connors	*8.95*	*3.95*
Take It or Leave It by Raymond Federman	*11.95*	*4.95*
Coming Close by B.H. Friedman	*11.95*	*5.95*
Museum by B.H. Friedman	*7.95*	*3.95*
Temporary Sanity by Thomas Glynn	*8.95*	*3.95*
Music for a Broken Piano by James Baker Hall	*11.95*	*5.95*
The Talking Room by Marianne Hauser	*10.95*	*5.95*
Holy Smoke by Fanny Howe	*8.95*	*3.95*
In the Middle of Nowhere by Fanny Howe	*12.95*	*6.95*
Mole's Pity by Harold Jaffe	*8.95*	*3.95*
Mourning Crazy Horse by Harold Jaffe	*11.95*	*5.95*
Moving Parts by Steve Katz	*8.95*	*3.95*
Stolen Stories by Steve Katz	*12.95*	*6.95*
Find Him! by Elaine Kraf	*9.95*	*4.95*
The Northwest Passage by Norman Lavers	*12.95*	*6.95*
I Smell Esther Williams by Mark Leyner	*11.95*	*5.95*
Emergency Exit by Clarence Major	*9.95*	*4.95*
Reflex and Bone Structure by Clarence Major	*8.95*	*3.95*
Four Roses in Three Acts by Franklin Mason	*9.95*	*4.95*
The Secret Table by Mark Mirsky	*7.95*	*3.95*
Encores for a Dilettante by Ursule Molinaro	*8.95*	*3.95*
Rope Dances by David Porush	*8.95*	*3.95*
The Broad Back of the Angel by Leon Rooke	*9.95*	*3.95*
The Common Wilderness by Michael Seide	*16.95*	*— —*
The Comatose Kids by Seymour Simckes	*8.95*	*3.95*
Fat People by Carol Sturm Smith	*8.95*	*3.95*
Crash-Landing by Peter Spielberg	*12.95*	*6.95*
The Hermetic Whore by Peter Spielberg	*8.95*	*3.95*
Twiddledum Twaddledum by Peter Spielberg	*7.95*	*3.95*
The Endless Short Story by Ronald Sukenick	*13.95*	*6.95*
Long Talking Bad Conditions Blues by Ronald Sukenick	*9.95*	*4.95*
98.6 by Ronald Sukenick	*7.95*	*3.95*
Meningitis by Yuriy Tarnawsky	*8.95*	*3.95*
Agnes & Sally by Lewis Warsh	*11.95*	*5.95*
Heretical Songs by Curtis White	*9.95*	*4.95*
Statements 1	*— —*	*3.95*
Statements 2	*8.95*	*2.95*

Fiction Collective, c/o Dept. of English, Brooklyn College, Brooklyn, N.Y. 11210